Then, slowly, her senses returned. Except what she now felt beneath her was hard, cold metal; she was lying down instead of sitting, and her hands were bound behind her back. Instinctively, she struggled against her bonds, but they did not yield.

She no longer heard alarms, but she did hear the constant thrum of a ship's systems. The ship, however, was not the *Euphrates*. A green-tinged miasma hovered in the very air, and it smelled like someone was burning plastiform. The gloom was palpable.

Then a huge figure stepped into view, walking purposefully toward her. The figure—whom Kira guessed was at least two-and-a-half meters tall, though her worm's-eye view gave her a skewed perspective—wore an imposing uniform of dark metallic armor. Most of its head was covered by a helmet with ridges that began close together at the forehead and spread out and around to the back of the head. The only displays of color beyond the blue-black of the armor were the alien's mottled brown face, the streak of white on either side of the helmet's middle ridge, and the streak of bright red under the left-most ridge.

The alien stopped, looked down on Kira, and spoke one word in a deep, resonant voice that carried the promise of a painful death.

"Prey."

STAR TREK
DEEP SPACE NINE®

GATEWAYS

BOOK FOUR OF SEVEN

DEMONS OF AIR
AND DARKNESS

Keith R.A. DeCandido

Based upon STAR TREK®
created by Gene Roddenberry,
and STAR TREK: DEEP SPACE NINE
created by Rick Berman & Michael Piller

POCKET BOOKS
New York   London   Toronto   Sydney   Singapore

An *Original* Publication of POCKET BOOKS

POCKET BOOKS, a division of Simon & Schuster, Inc.
1230 Avenue of the Americas, New York, NY 10020

This book is published by Pocket Books, a division of Simon & Schuster, Inc., under exclusive license from Paramount Pictures.

ISBN: 0-7434-1852-2

First Pocket Books printing September 2001

10   9   8   7   6   5   4   3   2   1

POCKET and colophon are registered trademarks of Simon & Schuster, Inc.

For information regarding special discounts for bulk purchases, please contact Simon & Schuster Special Sales at 1-800-456-6798 or business@simonandschuster.com

Printed in the U.S.A.

For David Henderson,
the world's most professional fan.

HISTORIAN'S NOTE

This novel takes place about two weeks after the events of the *Star Trek: Deep Space Nine* novel *Section 31: Abyss,* and also after the events of the *Star Trek: Voyager* episode "Pathfinder."

The doors of heaven and hell are adjacent and identical.

—Nikos Kazantzakis

DEMONS OF AIR
AND DARKNESS

I

THE DELTA QUADRANT

"SHIELDS ONE AND TWO are now down, shield three is buckling, and warp drive is down!"

Controller Marssi of the Malon supertanker *Apsac* snarled at Kron's report.

For years, she had heard stories of this ship and its strange alien crew. Some had called it the "ship of death." At least two other Malon export vessels had encountered it, and neither had come out of the experience intact.

Now it was attacking the *Apsac*. They'd already been forced to drop out of warp, dangerously close to a star system. Marssi had no idea what had prompted the attack, nor did she care. She just wanted it to stop.

"Return fire," she snapped, moving from her small

circular console in the center of the bridge to Kron's larger one against the starboard bulkhead.

"We *have* been," Kron said. "Our weapons have had no effect."

Marssi rubbed her nostrils. The smell of burning conduits was starting to fill the bridge. "I take it they aren't answering our hails?"

"Of *course* not. They don't want to talk, they want to destroy us, same as they do everyone else." Kron turned back to his console. "Shield three is now down. Our weapons banks are almost exhausted and we still haven't even put a dent in their hull. They're coming in for another pass." As he spoke, more weapons fire impacted on the *Apsac*'s hull.

Kron spit in anger. His saliva was tinged with green. He motioned as if to wipe hair off his face, which under other circumstances would have made Marssi smile. Kron had been making that gesture during times of stress in all the decades they'd served together, but the old man's gold-brown hair had long since thinned past the possibility of ever actually impeding his vision.

"Shield four just went down and shield five is at critical levels," he said. "They're on a parabolic course—they'll be back in weapons range in two minutes."

Marssi cursed. She had designed the *Apsac* herself, supervising its entire construction personally. The vessel was groundbreaking—it had seven separate shields in addition to the reinforced tanks. If that redundancy wasn't enough, the shields were strengthened by an enhancer of her own design. (In truth, designed by someone to whom she'd paid a considerable sum, but as far as she was concerned that made it hers.) Her ship had the lowest incidence of theta-radiation poisoning of any export vessel on Malon Prime and she'd set several records for hauling. Perhaps best of all, her core laborers had a survival rate of sixty percent—twice that of most other export vessels—and she was able to pay them well above the already-lucrative going rate.

Her profit margin was huge—the cost of constructing the ship and designing the shield enhancer had been recouped by her second run. With this latest trip, she would clear enough to finally buy that house in the mountains that she and Stvoran had had their sights on all these years.

And now, Marssi thought, *these be-damned aliens are going to ruin it.*

From the big console behind her, Gril said, "Controller, look at this." Gril was a new hire—this was his first run. *He's certainly getting more than he signed on for,* Marssi thought bitterly. *We all are.*

The controller walked over to the young man. "What is it?"

"We're getting an analysis of their hull—it's made of monotanium! Can you imagine that? No wonder our weapons have had no effect. If we could make our ships out of that—"

Rolling his eyes, Kron said, "Do you know how much it'd cost to mass-produce enough monotanium to build a tanker, Gril?"

"I know, I know, but think of it! We'd never have another tank rupture."

"We've never had one in the first place, you idiot," Kron muttered.

Defensively, Gril said, "You know what I mean."

Marssi looked more closely at the readouts as they

scrolled across Gril's black screen in clear green letters. In addition to the powerful hull, the small, squat ship had a very efficient dicyclic warp signature, decades ahead of anything the Malons had developed for faster-than-light travel.

"You're right, Gril," she said. "Those aliens do know how to build a ship."

An alarm sounded. Marssi heard the staccato rhythm of Kron's boots on the bulkhead as he ran to one of the other consoles. She turned to see that he seemed a bit blurry—a green haze was starting to descend upon the bridge. *One of those burning conduits must be leaking arvat. That's just what we need.*

Kron pushed a few buttons and then pounded the console with his fist. "Dammit! The warp core containment field is showing signs of collapse and the impulse drive is down." He turned to look at Marssi, his yellow eyes smoldering with anger, his golden skin tinged with sweat. "We can't even move now. And they'll be in range in one minute."

Wonderful, Marssi thought. *If the tanks don't rupture and the shields don't go down, we could still die from a containment breach.*

"Who *are* these people, anyhow?" Gril asked as he nervously scratched his left nostril. "What do they want with us?"

"The Hirogen are hunters," Marssi said grimly, walking back to her center console and running a check to see if she could get the propulsion systems back online. "No one knows where they come from, but they've shown up in every part of known space. Supposedly, they'll hunt anything and everything.

This particular ship has been reported in this sector at least twice."

"From what I hear," Kron said with a nasty look at Gril as he moved back across the bridge to his own console, "there's only one way to survive an encounter with them: don't be their prey."

"But—but we *are* their prey."

"Smart boy," Kron said with a grim smile, then glanced at a readout. "That's interesting, they've slowed down. They're still closing, but it'll be another minute or two before they're in range." He snorted. "They probably realize that we can't fight back, so they're going to take their time with us now."

Gril shook his head. "I don't get it. Why hunt *us?*"

"It's what they *do*," Kron snapped.

"Yeah, but whatever they do to us will kill them, too, if the tanks rupture or the core breaches. What's the good of being a hunter if you don't live to enjoy the fruits of the hunt?"

Marssi turned to Gril. "That's a good point. Maybe he just doesn't know." She looked at Kron. "Open a channel to them."

Kron snorted. "They haven't answered a single hail yet."

"They don't have to answer, they just have to listen. Open the channel."

Scowling, Kron pushed three buttons in sequence. "Fine, it's open."

Marssi took a deep breath—then regretted it, as the burning-conduit smell had gotten worse. "Attention Hirogen ship. If you continue with your present course of action, this ship will be destroyed and our cargo will be exposed to space. We are currently carrying over half a trillion isotons of antimatter waste. We have heard stories of how Hirogen hunters can weather anything, but I doubt that even you could survive being exposed to those levels of theta radiation. Over half our shields are down and a warp core containment breach is imminent. There's a danger of physical damage to the tankers as well. Any one of these can lead to this entire star system being irradiated and will result in the instant death of you, us, and anyone else in the immediate vicinity. Please, break off your attack—for your own sake, if not for ours."

Kron's eyes went wide. "They're replying."

"You sound surprised," Marssi said dryly.

"That's because I am," Kron said, shooting her a look. "On screen."

A face appeared on the console in front of Marssi. The creature fit the descriptions from the stories she'd heard of the Hirogen: a face of rough, mottled skin, with the rest of the body covered in metallic, faceted body armor. The helmet had four ridges that began close together at the forehead and spread out and around to the back of the head. This one also had a streak of white paint on either side of each middle ridge. As he spoke, he reached up to his forehead with a gloved hand. Red paint dripped from the index finger, and the Hirogen applied it to the section of the helmet under the leftmost ridge.

"Prey. You will surrender."

The screen went blank before Marssi could say anything in reply.

"Either they're immune to theta radiation, or they don't believe you," Kron said. "Or maybe they just don't care."

Again, Marssi cursed. "Any luck getting the propulsion systems back up?"

"No. The Hirogen ship's velocity is still pretty leisurely. Rumor has it they like to deal with their prey one on one. My guess is that they're going to try to board us."

Since the Hirogen ship was only a fraction of the size of the tanker, this seemed reasonable to Marssi. *There is no way I'm going to surrender to that monster. I've heard about what they do to people they capture—weird experiments, dissections, and worse.*

So, even if they surrendered, they were going to die.

If that's the way it's going to be, fine. They told me a woman could never be a controller. They told me the Apsac *would never work right. I didn't let that stop me then, and I damn well won't let it stop me now.*

She looked at the image of the Hirogen ship on her screen. *And if I don't, at least I'll have the satisfaction of knowing you'll die too, you waste-sucking toad.*

Kron announced, "They're firing again," and the *Apsac* lurched. "That did it. Shields five and six are both down and seven is buckling. One more shot, and we've got serious problems."

"Yes, Kron," Marssi muttered, shaking her head, "our problems until now have been quite droll."

"Controller, I'm picking up something!" Gril cried before Kron had a chance to reply. "Something just appeared a hundred and fifty *hentas* off the nose!"

"I'm picking it up, too," Kron said, much more calmly. "It's—a hole."

Marssi blinked. "I beg your pardon?"

"A hole."

7

"Can you be a *little* more specific, Kron?"

"No," Kron snapped. "That's the only way I can describe this. It's an opening of some kind, and based on the readings I'm getting—huh. There are stars and planets and such on the other side, but it's not matching anything on our star charts."

Another impact. Gril said, "Shield seven will go on the next shot!"

"So it's a wormhole," Marssi said to Kron.

Kron shook his head. "No, it's completely stable, and it doesn't have any of the properties of a wormhole. In fact, it doesn't have the properties of much of anything. I'm not picking up any particulate matter that wasn't there before, no changes in the chemical composition of the area around it. It's just—a hole." He looked over at Marssi, and the controller was amazed at the look of disbelief on her old comrade's face. "It's like it's some kind of—of gateway to another star system."

"What the *tuul* is it doing here?" Gril asked.

"Who the *tuul* cares?" Marssi said with a grim smile. *Maybe I will see Stvoran and Ella again.* "Kron, use maneuvering thrusters—I want the *Apsac* positioned so that the openings to the tanks are facing that hole."

Kron returned her smile, though his was less grim for a change. "Consider it done. Thrusters online."

Marssi nodded. She remembered one controller who had once been the most profligate of those who disposed of Malon's industrial waste. He had found, in essence, a hole to dump the waste into—a hole located in a starless region known simply as the Void. Unfortunately, another ship full of irritating aliens— the *Voyager*—had forced him to stop by cutting off his access to the Void. Marssi hadn't minded, as that opened the field a bit—his success was in danger of putting several controllers out of business—and it gave her the opportunity to secure the funds to build the *Apsac.*

Now she'd found her own version of that Void.

"Preparing to eject the tanks," Gril said.

"No," Marssi snapped, whirling on the young man. "We're just ejecting the contents into the hole."

Gril blinked. "But—but Controller, that'll expose the waste! The radiation—"

"We'll only be exposed for a short time, not enough to have any lasting effect. I'm not losing the tanks down that hole as well. Unless, of course, you want to replace them out of your earnings?"

"N-no," Grill said quietly, and turned back to his console.

"That may be academic," Kron said. "Shield seven just went down and the Hirogen is at four *hentas* and closing."

"Maybe. But even if we die, I want it to be just us who do. I won't let Stvoran and Ella live with the disgrace of being the husband and daughter of the woman who destroyed a star system."

"Very considerate," Kron said dryly. "We're in position now."

"Begin ejecting the waste."

Marssi stood at her console and saw the external camera's image of the green-tinged toxic material start to jet its way into the vacuum of space.

Soon enough it'll be in the hole and someone else's problem. My problem is the Hirogen. Once we no longer have to worry about the tanks rupturing, maybe we'll have a better chance against them.

Right on cue, the Hirogen ship came into view.

An errant cluster of waste material tumbled right toward it. It collided with the hunter's small vessel with sufficient impact that even a monotanium hull couldn't save it.

Like all explosions in space, it was brief, but no less spectacular for all that. It blossomed evenly, then contracted into nothingness—aside from the green mass that had caused the explosion, which continued to tumble toward the hole.

To Controller Marssi, it was the most beautiful sight she'd seen since the completed *Apsac* was first unveiled on Malon Prime.

She still had no idea what that hole was or where it came from, and right now she didn't care. All she knew was that if it hadn't shown up when it did, she never would have ejected her payload, and the Hirogen ship would still be in one piece.

"Looks like you beat the odds again, Controller," Kron said with a smile, his words mirroring Marssi's own thoughts.

Laughing, Marssi said, "Did you ever doubt it?"

"Yes, every second. But, like all the other times you've proved me wrong, I'm glad you've done so."

"Controller," Gril said, his voice shaking, "I must protest this! We don't know what's on the other side of that hole! What if—"

Marssi knew exactly what Gril was going to say, and so was happy to interrupt him. "Gril, what is the mission statement of this vessel?"

"To—to dispose of the waste that accrues from our use of antimatter in a manner that will not be harmful to the Malon community as a whole," he said as if

10

reciting from a textbook—*probably*, Marssi thought, recalling Gril's age, *read recently*.

"Exactly," she said, advancing slowly on the young man who, for his part, started to cower as she moved closer. "And we have done that, and also kept this star system from being contaminated. We've saved millions of lives today—most notably our own—eliminated one of the scourges of this sector, *and* we've done our job. Not to mention the fact that we've made an astonishing discovery that could very well spell even more profit for us down the road. So what, precisely, are you protesting, Gril?"

Gril swallowed, and once again scratched his left nostril. "Well, when you put it that way, Controller, I guess—nothing."

"Good. Keep an eye on the waste, and tell the core laborers to keep on their toes." Blinking a few times, she added, "And get someone to fix that damn *arvat* conduit—I don't know what's worse, the haze or the smell."

"Yes, Controller." Gril returned to his console.

Kron shook his head and chuckled. "Were we ever that young?"

"I was," Marssi said. "But not you. When you were born, you were already a cranky old man." Placing an encouraging hand on her old friend's shoulder, she said, "We need to get the warp drive fixed. As soon as the last of the waste has gone through that hole, I want to get back home and file a claim on this little discovery of ours."

"The drive'll take at least a day or two to fix."

Marssi shrugged. "It'll be at least that long before all the the tanks are emptied."

"Good point," Kron said, and with a nod to Gril,

sent the younger Malon down to engineering to surpervise the repairs.

Marssi turned back to her console, and watched as the first bit of waste material approached the event horizon of the hole and then disappeared from sight. Even if she wanted to know what was on the other side, she'd have a difficult time getting a proper sensor reading now, with all the radiation in the way.

Besides, she didn't want to know. She didn't care. She'd done her job. *I can't wait to tell Ella about this,* she thought with a smile. Her ten-year-old daughter always loved to hear stories about her mother's trips. Marssi predicted that this one—where she defeated one of the most brutal foes imaginable and also made an astounding new discovery—would quickly become Ella's favorite.

2

THE GAMMA QUADRANT

"THE COMMUNICATIONS ARRAY is now online, sir."

Commander Elias Vaughn didn't smile at Nog's report, but the lieutenant hadn't really expected him to. In the month since Vaughn had been assigned as the first officer of Deep Space 9 and commanding officer of the *U.S.S. Defiant,* Nog had seldom seen the human smile while on duty.

But when the young Ferengi turned to look at Vaughn in the *Defiant*'s command chair, he did notice a slight curling of Vaughn's lips under his gray-and-silver beard.

Vaughn turned toward the bridge's port side. "Excellent work, gentlemen," he said to Nog and the Andorian sitting at the console to Nog's right.

Ensign Thirishar ch'Thane didn't smile, either, but

13

Nog had learned to read the young science officer's facial features well enough to see that he, too, was pleased with himself. Nog and Shar had spent the last week going over every square millimeter of the communications array, and they were quite proud of the work they'd done.

Now, at last, everything appeared to be ready to go.

"Address intership, please, Lieutenant," Vaughn said to Nog.

Nog couldn't resist smiling as he complied. "Yes, sir. Intership open."

"Attention all hands, this is Commander Vaughn. Starfleet's primary mission has always been one of exploration. Over seven years ago, Benjamin Sisko and Jadzia Dax discovered a stable wormhole in the Denorios Belt, one which opened the door to an entire quadrant of new worlds for us to seek out. Five years ago, Starfleet, Bajoran, and Cardassian personnel worked together to install a subspace array on the Gamma Quadrant side of the wormhole to provide communication between the quadrants. Unfortunately, that array did not survive the hostilities of the Dominion War—a war that, sadly, also closed the door that Benjamin Sisko opened.

"But the war's over now. And thanks to efforts by the crew of the *Defiant* and Deep Space 9, a new communications array has been successfully deployed and is now online. As of this moment . . . we're back in the Gamma Quadrant."

Nog's smile broadened, and he drummed his hands against the edge of his console in applause. At conn, Ensign Prynn Tenmei clapped, and Lieutenant Sam Bowers at tactical let out a celebratory whoop. Over the com system, Nog could hear other expressions of jubilation from all over the ship.

Looks like we're finally putting the war behind us, Nog thought with satisfaction. The repairs and upgrades to the station and the *Defiant* had been completed, and now the communications array was up and running—the prelude to the *Defiant*'s upcoming mission of exploration to the Gamma Quadrant. Things were finally starting to get back to normal.

Shar, meanwhile, had turned back to his console. "All systems are functional, and the silithium receptors are aligned. We're ready to send our first message to DS9, Commander."

"Very well," Vaughn said, standing and walking toward the viewscreen. "Open a channel and transmit the following: 'Watson, I need you.' "

Shar's antennae lowered slightly. "Sir?"

Vaughn's lips curled again. "Old joke. A human one, so Colonel Kira won't get it, either. Send the message please, Ensign."

Shar nodded. "Yes, sir."

After a moment, Colonel Kira Nerys's sharp voice sounded crisply through the speakers. *"Who the hell is Watson?"*

"Excellent," Shar said, letting out a breath. Then he muttered some kind of supplication to the Andorian deity.

I guess he wasn't sure it was going to work, Nog thought with a smile. Nog, on the other hand, had known in his lobes that the array would function just fine.

"Old joke," Vaughn repeated. "Just a little test, Colonel. The new array seems to have passed it."

"Glad to hear it. Your timing is perfect. Get back over here right away, Commander. We have a meeting with Admiral Ross in half an hour."

Nog's lobes pricked up at that, and he felt a phantom twinge in the biosynthetic that had replaced his left leg, lost in the war. Ross had been the commander of Starfleet's forces against the Dominion. They'd already had one near-miss with renegade Jem'Hadar trying to start hostilities again.

The war's supposed to be behind us, dammit.

"Starfleet's declared a state of emergency," Kira went on to say, *"we've received a distress call from Europa Nova, and both the* Tcha'voth *and the* Makluan *have been recalled."*

Nog frowned at that. Those two ships had been posted to Deep Space 9 by the Klingons and Romulans, respectively, to bolster the station's defense, along with the *Defiant.*

"I want you to go to yellow alert. We're doing the same on the station."

"Acknowledged," Vaughn said, calmly sitting back down in the command chair. "We'll be back at the station in ten minutes. *Defiant* out." He turned to tactical. "Signal yellow alert please, Lieutenant Bowers. All hands to general quarters." Looking forward, he said, "Ensign Tenmei, set course for the wormhole, full impulse."

"Yes, sir," Tenmei said, and Nog noticed, not for the first time, the change to the ensign's voice that occurred every time she had to address Vaughn. It was subtle—a slight alteration in timbre that only a Ferengi would notice, but it happened only with the commander.

Although it had become common knowledge among the crew that Prynn was Vaughn's (apparently) estranged daughter—Uncle Quark had hardly been been able to contain the information once he'd found out—Nog wondered what the source of that estrangement was. Generally, Tenmei was friendly and outgoing off duty—Nog had even talked her into trying a tube grub in the mess hall yesterday. (Like most humans, she didn't have the stomach for it and spat it back out.) On duty she was an exceptional pilot and a consummate professional, and apart from that slight shift in her voice that no one else seemed to notice, there was no obvious indication that she had any issues with Vaughn at all. And yet . . . Nog was certain there was something there, something that made him wonder if the *Defiant* bridge didn't have a serious problem on the horizon.

As the *Defiant* came about, Nog's thoughts changed course as well and he turned to Shar. "I told you we could do it."

Shar was hunched over his console, making sure that the automatic settings on the array were running properly so that it would continue to function after the *Defiant* was out of range. "I never doubted it."

"Oh really? Who was the one who thought the alignment of the subspace antenna was wrong?"

"That was me," Shar admitted.

"Who was the one who said that we'd need twice as many flux capacitors as we actually did need?"

"That was me, too."

"Who was the one—"

Shar finally looked up, brushing a lock of his coarse white hair off his face. "Nog, just because I

17

was critical of some details doesn't mean I doubted that we'd get the array online."

"Hah. You say that now."

"Yes, and I would've said it then if someone had asked."

The young Ferengi chuckled and relaxed for the first time in a week. While no words to the effect had been spoken, Nog knew that no one was entirely sure about whether or not he and Shar could get the job done. After all, from the time the station was turned over to Bajoran and Starfleet control by the Cardassians, over seven years earlier, the responsibilities of science officer and chief of operations had belonged, respectively, to Jadzia Dax—a Trill scientist with three centuries' and eight lifetimes' worth of experience—and Miles O'Brien—a Starfleet veteran of over twenty years. They'd now been replaced by a recent—albeit brilliant—graduate of Starfleet Academy and a junior-grade lieutenant who owed his rank to battlefield commissions rather than full Academy experience. Nobody had forgotten that, when Chief O'Brien first took over, Nog was a child being arrested by Odo for stealing from the assay office.

From the conn position, Tenmei said, "Entering the wormhole."

Nog looked down and made sure that all the ship's systems were within expected parameters for a trip through the wormhole. Most of the time, they were, but more than one such trip had been fraught with danger, from Kira and Dr. Bashir's unexpected jaunt to a parallel universe to the aliens who resided in the wormhole causing an entire Jem'Hadar fleet to vanish. Nog didn't want something like that to happen to them now because he was too busy ribbing Shar to notice an anomalous reading.

However, everything seemed to be fine. Nog set the viewscreen on his console to show the wormhole as they passed through it.

For a long time, Nog had thought of the wormhole solely as the thing that brought Uncle Quark all the new business. Then it was something they talked about in school occasionally. But he'd never really looked at it until Jake Sisko dragged him to the catwalk over the Promenade to watch the wormhole open and close one afternoon. It was then that he truly started to appreciate it. He hadn't admitted it to Jake—nor to anyone else—at the time, but it was the most glorious sight he'd ever seen, and he wanted to know more about it. Nog often suspected that that moment, when he found his mind flooded with questions about the wormhole, was probably the first step on his journey to the Academy and Starfleet.

Studying the wormhole in school didn't prepare him for seeing it, and seeing it didn't remotely prepare him for what it was like to go through it.

His studies told him that the streams of white and silver light were verteron particles and silithium streams and various other bits of particulate matter, but that only mattered to Nog when duty required it of him. Times like this, he liked to just sit back and watch the dance of lights as the ship shot through seventy thousand light-years in a matter of minutes.

As they emerged from the Alpha Quadrant mouth of the wormhole into Bajoran space, Shar spoke up, apparently not willing to let the subject die just yet. "It's actually quite intriguing the way you keep doing things that don't match the specifications. Especially since you're always right."

Nog chuckled. "Well, not *always*. But when I'm wrong, I've gotten very good at making it seem like it was what I meant to do all along. I met Captain Montgomery Scott recently, and he said something great." Shar didn't seem impressed by the name-dropping, so Nog added, "You've heard of him, right?"

"Oh, sure, I know Scotty," Shar said.

Nog felt his jaw drop open. "You call him 'Scotty'? I don't think I'd ever have the lobes to do that."

"My *zhavey* introduced us, and he insisted I use the nickname."

Nog shook his head. He kept forgetting that the unassuming young Andorian had a parent on the Federation Council. "Anyway, he said, 'The established norms are just guidelines, and your job as an engineer is to find a better way around them.' "

"That certainly sounds like Scotty."

From behind him, Nog heard Vaughn's rock-steady voice say, "Deep Space 9, this is the *Defiant* requesting permission to dock."

"Granted," came the reply from Selzner in ops.

Something caught Shar's attention on his console. "Commander, we're getting a message from the array. It's relaying something on a Federation civilian frequency from the Kar-telos system, just a few light-years into the Gamma Quadrant."

"Put it on screen, please."

"It's audio only, sir," Shar said quickly.

Vaughn looked over at Shar and fixed him with an intense, calm gaze that was as scary as anything Nog had ever seen. "Then put it on speakers, Ensign ch'Thane."

"Yes, sir."

"This is Captain Monaghan of the Mars freighter Halloran. *I need some help here. I was doing the Jovian run, and now—well, I think I'm in the Gamma Quadrant. I haven't the first clue as to how I got here. Someone please help me!"*

"You said it was a civilian frequency, Ensign?" Vaughn asked Shar.

Shar nodded.

"That explains it, then. Open a channel."

Manipulating his console, Shar said, "Channel open."

"Freighter *Halloran,* this is Commander Elias Vaughn, first officer of Deep Space 9. You are, in fact, in the Gamma Quadrant."

"How the hell did I wind up here?"

"That's a very fair question, Captain. I wish I had an answer for that. What I can tell you is that we will dispatch a runabout to your position right away and lead you back to DS9 through the Bajoran wormhole. Is that acceptable?"

Captain Monaghan started to sound panicky. Nog's sensitive ears noticed the change in the timbre of her voice, even over the communications system. *"I guess so. Isn't this where the Dominion came from?"*

"Yes, ma'am, it is."

"Should I be worried about the Jem'Hadar?"

"No," Vaughn said with calm confidence that Nog—remembering the recent attack on the station—didn't share. "You're quite safe, I can assure you. Nonetheless, we'll dispatch the runabout immediately."

"Thanks, Commander." Nog noticed that the timbre of her voice had changed again. Vaughn's words had obviously reassured her. "Halloran *out.*"

Vaughn turned to Bowers. "Lieutenant, when we dock, prepare the *Sungari* for departure and take it to the Kar-telos system."

Bowers nodded.

Shar was staring at his panel. "How is it possible that a ship in the Terran system suddenly found itself in the Gamma Quadrant?"

"Let's hope, Ensign, that it relates to why we're at yellow alert right now."

Nog frowned. "Why would we hope that, Commander?"

This time, Vaughn's hard stare was turned on Nog. "Because, Lieutenant, I've been through more Starfleet states of emergency than I care to count. And the last thing you want to have to do during one is split your focus."

3

DEEP SPACE 9

ELIAS VAUGHN HATED MEETINGS.

Oh, he understood the need for them. There were times when such things were vital, and it was good for groups of people who worked together to gather regularly and keep each other abreast of their duties, lives, or anything else of import.

But the ideal meeting was short and to the point. Vaughn's long years of experience had shown him that most meetings were neither, and were primarily an impediment to actually getting anything accomplished. One of the many—although lesser—reasons Vaughn had declined so many promotions over the years was the surety that a higher rank would result in more meetings.

As he and Kira approached Quark's bar, Ensign ch'Thane's voice sounded through Kira's combadge. *"Ops to Colonel Kira."*

Tapping her combadge, Kira said, "Go ahead, Shar."

"Colonel, we're receiving detailed information from Europa Nova. It isn't good, sir."

They entered the bar, occupied solely by a few civilians—including Morn in his usual seat toward one end of the bar. With the station at yellow alert, the Starfleet and Bajoran Militia personnel were either at their duty stations or on standby, and most of the rest of the station's population probably felt safer on their ships or in their quarters.

"Anything new I should know?" Kira asked as she walked up the tightly winding staircase to the second level.

"They are primarily confirming the original distress call—theta radiation is appearing in orbit from an unknown point of origin and will reach lethal levels within fifty-two hours. The only new data is that the source of the radiation appears to be some kind of antimatter industrial waste."

Kira frowned. "That's odd."

Vaughn searched his memory for anyone in the quadrant who still generated waste from their matter-antimatter power sources, and couldn't find any. Every warp-capable species he knew of that used such reactors had conquered the waste problem in fairly short order.

"Lieutenant Bowers has rendezvoused with the Halloran. He reports no problems, and should be back within the hour. We've also received several odd reports in the usual dispatches."

"Odd in what way?" Kira asked.

"Apparently, Orions have been sighted on Ferenginar, near the Grand Nagus's home, the Deltans and Carreon have mutually broken their treaty in a manner that defies logic, there's a medical crisis on Armus IX thanks to an unauthorized alien presence—the list is quite extensive, and has a common element of people not being where they should be."

"Keep a log of the odd reports, Shar," Kira said. She and Vaughn arrived at the door to one of Quark's holosuites on the bar's third level. Nog was already there, making some adjustments to an outer panel. "We're about to go into the meeting—maybe we'll find out what this is all about. Kira out." She looked at Nog and said, "Report."

"Just a second, sir." Several seconds later, Nog stood up and turned off the polarizer he had been using. "It's ready, Colonel. The connection to Starfleet Headquarters is functional. We just need them to activate it on their end."

"Any problems?"

Nog gave a lopsided smile. "None, sir. My uncle's off-station, after all."

Kira gave an equally lopsided smile in return.

"I take it Quark would have been something of an impediment to using the holosuite this way," Vaughn said dryly as he followed Kira through to the presently inactive holosuite.

"A small one. He would've complained and asked for compensation and generally made a nuisance of himself—the usual. But, whatever Quark's failings," she said in a tone of voice that implied that she found those failings to be legion, "he's a good Ferengi. His underlings are usually competent enough to keep the business from going under while he's away, but not good enough to be a danger to his position as the boss."

"So they're easy to intimidate."

Nodding, Kira said, "Especially by the son of the new Grand Nagus."

Nog's voice came from over the intercom. *"Signal coming in from Starfleet now, Colonel."*

The holosuite environment didn't change, but Vaughn suddenly found himself in a room full of red-trimmed uniforms, his ears assaulted by several simultaneous conversations all being piped in at once. It was as if a cocktail party had suddenly been beamed aboard the station. However, the noise almost immediately dropped to near-silence as people realized that they were "on."

In recent years, holographic technology had been refined to the point where it could be combined with subspace communication, allowing two people to converse while each appeared to be in the same room with the other, even though they were in fact separated by light-years. What Starfleet had done here was take that to the next step by linking the holocoms of various ships and starbases to the one at Starfleet HQ on Earth so that dozens of people from all across the quadrant could meet. Just as it appeared to him that these men and women were standing in the holosuite, Vaughn knew it appeared that they were all standing on the holodecks of each officer in attendance.

All of those present were of command rank, but only one—William Ross—was from the admiralty. *These are some of Starfleet's most prominent leaders,* he thought, *but not the ones who run it. This is a room full of "doers." Interesting.*

Just as interesting was Kira's distinction within the

gathering as the only non-Starfleet command officer present, her Bajoran Militia uniform standing out in stark contrast to the others. Vaughn knew there were those at Starfleet Command who were less than pleased with the idea of a non-Federation officer commanding Starfleet personnel and a facility as important as DS9 was strategically. As far as Vaughn was concerned, the naysayers were simply ignorant.

Not this group, though. Kira had worn the Federation's uniform once, he knew, during the final weeks of the Dominion War and under extraordinary circumstances. But Vaughn wondered how many in the meeting actually knew that, or if their clear and unflinching acceptance of Kira as part of this very special circle of officers stemmed rather from the strength of her reputation and her record. She stood next to him, her arms folded expectantly as she studied the faces of the other officers, exchanging nods with the few that she knew, secure in her own authority and ready to get down to business. Not for the first time, Vaughn found himself uncharacteristically impressed with his commanding officer.

For his part, Vaughn knew most of the people in the room personally, including Captain Solok of the *T'Kumbra* (not a bad ship commander, as Vaughn recalled, but something of a jerk personally); Commander Ju'les L'ullho of Starbase 96; and Captain Walter Emick of the *Intrepid.* A few—Captain Elizabeth Shelby of the *Trident;* Captain Elaine Mello of the *Gryphon;* and Captain Mackenzie Calhoun of the *Excalibur*—he knew only by reputation. Some, of course, had more of a reputation than others, and Calhoun's was fairly bizarre. He had, Vaughn knew, done quite a bit of work for Admiral Nechayev's little corner of Starfleet Intelligence. Vaughn had thought that Calhoun was a bit too much of a loose cannon for that kind of work, but Alynna seemed to find him useful. Calhoun was also supported by Jean-Luc Picard and intensely disliked by Edward Jellico, both points in his favor.

Speaking of Jean-Luc, the *Enterprise* captain stood in the center of the room next to Bill Ross. Picard seemed strangely unreadable as he surveyed the gathering, but Ross had a hangdog look that spoke more than anything to the gravity of the situation. The admiral hadn't looked this bad since the worst days of the Dominion War.

"Good afternoon," Ross said. Gestures and muttered returned greetings filled the room momentarily before he went on. *"It's nice to know our relay systems are fine-tuned enough to allow holoconferences like this to occur. It certainly beats trying to find parking orbits for all of you."* Ross attempted a smile, but the joke fell flat. *"I'm placing you all on yellow alert until further notice."*

Next to him, Kira's eyes smoldered. Vaughn immediately recognized her "gee-how-brilliant-of-Starfleet-to-do-something-I-already-thought-of" expression.

Ross continued. *"As for why we're doing this, we have a new problem. A few days ago, the Federation Council was approached by a group of beings who identified themselves as the Iconians."*

Vaughn watched the reactions of the others around the holosuite. Some nodded in understanding—ones probably familiar with the two on-record Iconian encounters and/or the legends that had surrounded that ancient, and supposedly extinct, species—others looked confused, still others asked people off-circuit to check up on the name.

Once the brief commotion settled down, Ross turned to the *Enterprise* captain. Vaughn remembered that Jean-Luc had always had a fascination for Iconian legend. *"Captain Picard, would you please detail what we know of the Iconians?"*

"Of course, Admiral. The Iconians were known to exist in this quadrant of space some two hundred millennia ago. Their culture and technology were unparalleled in that time period but records about them are scant. About a decade ago, Captain Donald Varley of the U.S.S. Yamato *determined the location of their homeworld in the Romulan Neutral Zone, but was lost along with his ship when a destructive Iconian computer program inserted itself into the* Yamato's *mainframe. Even after all that time, the technology on the homeworld remained functional—including the gateways.*

"These gateways provide instantaneous transport between two points that could be meters or light-years apart. Two functional gateways have been found over the last few years: one on the homeworld, which I myself destroyed rather than allow gateway technology to fall into Romulan hands; and one discovered by the Dominion in the Gamma Quadrant, which was destroyed by a joint Starfleet/Jem'Hadar team from the U.S.S. Defiant."

Ross nodded. *"Thank you, Captain. The Iconians who have come forward now have offered us the gateway technology for a price. The Council is considering the offer, but it's a bit more complicated than that.*

First, they are offering the technology to the highest bidder. Similar offers have been made to governments throughout the quadrant. Clearly, this could have a devastating impact should any antagonistic or ambitious government obtain the technology exclusively.

"Second, and most immediate: the Iconians have chosen to demonstrate how useful the gateways can be by activating the entire network. Gateways have opened up all over the quadrant and beyond. The Iconians have seen fit to withhold how to control them and have chosen not to provide us with any form of useful map."

Once again a brief commotion broke out, as the officers present reacted to the news. Vaughn scratched his salt-and-pepper beard thoughtfully. *That,* he thought, *would explain the* Halloran *and all those odd reports of Shar's. And, quite probably, what's happening to Europa Nova.*

"As the gateways came online," Ross continued, silencing the group, *"we immediately began studying their output, trying to get a handle on how they work."*

As Ross spoke, another figure came in. Vaughn almost smiled. This was another captain, and probably the only human in the room older than Vaughn himself.

"We became rather alarmed at some of the readings, and so turned the study over to the Starfleet Corps of Engineers. We now have a preliminary report." Turning to the new arrival, he said, *"Captain Scott, thank you for joining us."*

"It's not a problem," Montgomery Scott said, after giving a quick, affectionate glance to Picard. Vaughn remembered that the *Enterprise* rescued Captain Scott from the *U.S.S. Jenolen,* where he'd been trapped in a sort of suspended animation for over seven decades as

a transporter pattern. In the years since, the man out of time had traveled far and wide and performed a variety of tasks; most recently, however, he'd been assigned to serve as the liaison between the Starfleet Corps of Engineers and the admiralty.

Scott continued. *"Those gateways, to be blunt, are behavin' in ways we never imagined. It seems that when they exhaust their power, they tap into any other power supply that's available. Like pussy willows here on Earth, that seek water and break into pipes to find it. These gateways are so beyond our ken tha' figuring out how they tick and stoppin' them will be almost impossible."*

"Do you mean, they could tap an entire planet's resources and drain them dry?" Ross asked.

Scott took a deep breath. *"Aye. Worse, for those worlds using predominantly geothermal or hydraulic power. Their ecosystem could be compromised. We don't have all the figures in yet, but one o' my ships is measuring solar consumption. My fear is some stars might be destabilized by additional power demands. It's a very nasty bit o' business."*

Turning back to the assembled commanders, Ross said, *"All the more reason for us to mobilize the fleet. Duty packets are going out now with specific sector assignments. We'll need to maintain the peace. Some of our scientific vessels will be working with the S.C.E. to determine just how severe the problems might become. Captain Solok, I will want you and your crew to begin monitoring all incident reports from gateway activity. If the Iconians won't give us a map, I want us to make one."*

Speaking gravely, the Vulcan captain said, *"Under-*

stood. I should point out that it will not be complete and therefore not entirely accurate."

"Noted," Ross said. "I'll take whatever we can get since it's better than the nothing we have right now."

Ross then looked directly at Vaughn and Kira. *"Colonel, Commander, our scientists have done some preliminary mapping based on the gateway power signatures and we've discovered something very interesting out your way. We're estimating no gateway activity within ten light-years in any direction of Bajor."*

Interesting, Vaughn thought. *Europa Nova's ten light-years from here.* Aloud, he said, "The wormhole."

"We think so, yes."

Kira said, "It could be the Prophets protecting this region."

"That's certainly a possibility. Vaughn, given your experience with the gateways, I want you out there, finding out why there aren't any gateways near Bajor. Is it something natural? Is it the doing of the aliens—that is to say, the Prophets?" he amended with a conciliatory glance at Kira. *"What properties are being displayed, and can they be harnessed beyond your sector?"*

"You're hoping we can turn it into a practical countermeasure."

"Exactly."

Picard then said the words that Vaughn had been half-expecting from the moment the Iconians were mentioned. *"I was unaware, Admiral, of any encounters with gateways beyond those by the* Enterprise *and the* Defiant."

Next to him, Kira was giving Vaughn a rather penetrating gaze. "Neither was I."

"It was a few years ago," Vaughn said neutrally.

The mission to Alexandra's Planet had been classified, and Vaughn had yet to be given any reason to disregard that.

Ross gave Picard a reassuring look. *"The relevant portions of Commander Vaughn's mission will be declassified in light of the present emergency."*

Picard nodded. *"Good."*

Vaughn gave Kira a quick nod that he hoped matched Ross for reassurance. Kira seemed dubious, but willing to table any further discussion.

Particularly since there were more pressing matters. "Admiral," she said, "we have another problem. Europa Nova is suffering a planetwide catastrophe, possibly a result of this gateway problem. Some kind of antimatter waste field is appearing in orbit, seemingly out of nowhere. We need to evacuate the settlement immediately, and we're going to need the *Defiant* and as many more ships as possible to assist. The *Tcha'voth* and the *Makluan* were recalled suddenly, so we're even more shorthanded. Lieutenant Dax is assembling a task force of Bajoran and civilian ships, but—"

"Say no more, Colonel. We're aware of the situation on Europa Nova. There's a Federation Councillor there right now negotiating with their parliament, and we received the same distress call you did. Since the Klingons and Romulans have recalled their ships, I've assigned the Gryphon *and the* Intrepid *to be at your disposal."* Turning to Captains Mello and Emick, he asked, *"Captains, your ETAs?"*

"Two and a half hours, Admiral," said Captain Mello, a short, robust woman with a round face and curly brown hair. The *Gryphon* had delivered the *Defiant*'s replacement warhead module over a week ear-

lier, but Vaughn hadn't had the chance to meet her captain then.

Captain Emick—a man who came from a long line of Starfleet officers dating back to the founding of the organization—turned to Kira and said, *"DS9 is actually on our way there, so with your permission, Colonel?"* Kira nodded. *"The* Intrepid *will rendezvous with the* Defiant *in two hours."*

"Good," Ross said. *"I only ask that you hold back one runabout to investigate the wormhole, Colonel."*

Kira inclined her head. "Of course, Admiral. The *Sungari* will handle it as soon as it returns from the Gamma Quadrant."

At Ross's frown—at present, only the *Defiant* had authorization to go through the wormhole—Vaughn quickly explained the situation with the *Halloran.*

"Understood. Keep us posted on Europa Nova." Ross then turned to Captain Calhoun and started to detail the *Excalibur*'s assignment.

Vaughn looked at Kira with a raised eyebrow; she inclined her head, and the commander then stepped aside so he wouldn't disturb the rest of the meeting. Kira would keep track of what was going on while her first officer started getting all the balls that needed rolling into motion. Possibly Ross might have preferred that the highest-ranking Starfleet officer on Deep Space 9 be the one to participate in all aspects of the meeting, but, Bajoran Militia or not, Kira was in charge.

Besides, Vaughn *really* hated meetings.

"Vaughn to Dax."

"Go ahead."

"Lieutenant, add the *Intrepid* and the *Gryphon* to our list and take the *Sungari* off it. As soon as Lieutenant Bowers returns with the *Halloran*, have the runabout prepped for Lieutenant Nog and Ensign ch'Thane to take it back to the wormhole. And assemble the senior staff in ops. The colonel and I will meet you there shortly."

"Yes, sir. Uhm—Starfleet's only sending two ships?"

"That's correct, Lieutenant."

"I take it there's more going on than just Europa Nova's crisis?"

Vaughn turned and looked back at the meeting. Calhoun had apparently just cracked a joke, and several of the assembled officers guffawed—pointedly, Bill Ross was not among those laughing. "Quite a bit more, yes."

"Well, it's been almost an hour since the galaxy was last in danger of destruction." Vaughn could almost see Ezri's wry grin. *"By the way, the Bajoran Militia has detached the Lamnak fleet to us for the crisis—that's their ten biggest ships under the command of Colonel Lenaris Holem. I've also signed up the* East Winds."

"The *East Winds?*"

"It's a ship out of Risa. Cassandra—she's the captain—had some kind of deal going with Quark, but since he's not here, she's at loose ends."

"So she's agreed to help?"

"Yup. She's, ah, an old friend of Curzon's."

Vaughn decided that he didn't want to know. "Very well. Carry on, Lieutenant."

"Dax out."

As Vaughn turned back to the meeting, Ross was saying, *"These will be some trying days ahead of us all. I want to keep in constant contact and I'll be reachable any time you need me. Good luck."*

Then the room turned back to the default holosuite setting, leaving Vaughn and Kira alone.

"I've called a briefing in ops," Vaughn said as he followed Kira out of the holosuite.

"Good."

"I love you, too."

Both Vaughn and Kira looked up at that.

Nog, still standing by at the holosuite control panel in the hallway and now holding a isolinear rod, had heard it, too, through the open door. At the two officers' questioning glances, he shrugged. "The connections didn't all break at once. It's impossible for them to coordinate that perfectly. That was probably a stray transmission."

"That sounded like Calhoun's voice," Kira said.

"Well, my understanding is that he and Captain Shelby recently married," Vaughn said.

Kira snorted. "Let's hope she got the message." Shaking her head, she moved toward the staircase, Vaughn and Nog following. "Two ships. It's a good thing we heard the entire briefing, otherwise I'd accuse Starfleet of shortchanging us again. Now, though, I'm wondering if they can even spare those two."

Vaughn nodded as they went downstairs. As the trio exited Quark's, Captain Kasidy Yates approached them. The skipper of the civilian cargo vessel *Xhosa* quickly fell into step with them as they moved across the Promenade.

Yates, now five months pregnant, was living on Bajor, in the house that had been begun by her husband, Benjamin Sisko, before his disappearance. Vaughn was surprised to see her on the station.

"How're you doing, Kas?" Kira asked.

"Fine. I was up for my monthly prenatal with Dr. Bashir—you'll be happy to know that everything's fine—when I heard about Europa Nova. The *Xhosa*'s ready to volunteer for evac duty."

Nog winced, and looked down at the captain's belly. "Captain Yates, with all due respect—is that really a good idea in your condition?"

Yates fixed the young Ferengi with a reproachful glare. "Nog, you say one more condescending word about my 'condition,' I swear you will *not* live to regret it. I'm pregnant. I'm not dying. And I'm still perfectly capable of doing my job."

Nog's eyes went wide and he stammered, "Of—of course, Captain, I didn't—I didn't mean—"

Kira, who had a huge grin on her face, said, "Thanks, Kas. Coordinate with Dax; she'll fill you in on the details." Nog looked relieved at the interruption.

"I'll be ready, Nerys," Yates said. Nodding cordially to Vaughn, she said, "Commander," then gave Nog another withering look before she turned and walked off.

As they entered the lift, Kira said, "Ops," then turned to Nog. "Safety tip, Lieutenant: don't treat pregnant women like they're made out of glass. I know whereof I speak."

"Yes, sir," Nog said crisply.

"Besides," she said more gravely, "we can use all the help we can get."

"Of course, sir."

The lift arrived at ops, which marked the first time in days that Vaughn had set foot in Deep Space 9's nerve center. The arrangement of personnel was somewhat different—and more chaotic—than it had been when he was last here. One thing, however, remained constant: Taran'atar. He stood in the exact same spot in the exact same position on the upper level of ops with the exact same expression on his face. The Jem'Hadar had been sent to the Alpha Quadrant by the Founders of the Dominion as a cultural observer, and it was in precisely that capacity that he maintained his frequent presence in ops. By now, the crew had gotten used to his almost statue-like presence. Sergeant Gan Morr, whose sensor maintenance station was right next to where Taran'atar stood, had been most distressed at first, but now he seemed completely oblivious to the Jem'Hadar's presence.

As Kira, Vaughn, and Nog proceeded to the table on the lower level, Dax, Bowers, and ch'Thane did likewise from their stations. Bashir was already sitting on the edge of one of the chairs, portable medikit over his shoulder, poised as if ready to leave at a moment's notice.

"As you know," Kira said once everyone had settled, "the planet of Europa Nova is suffering a global catastrophe. What appears to be antimatter industrial waste is appearing in increasing quantities in orbit around the planet and the level of theta radiation is rising steadily. We don't know where it's coming from, and right now that's a secondary concern to evacuating the planet. There are three million people on Europa Nova, and they're all in danger of lethal exposure to the radiation within fifty-two hours." She turned to Dax. "Lieutenant, what's the status of our convoy?"

Dax consulted a padd. "We've got the *Defiant,* the *Intrepid,* the *Euphrates,* and the *Rio Grande* from

Starfleet, with the *Gryphon* meeting us at Europa Nova. We've also got four civilian ships: the *East Winds*—"

"Cassandra's ship?" Kira asked, and Vaughn noted the distaste in Kira's tone.

Grinning, Dax said, "Yup."

"You did say we can use all the help we can get," Vaughn deadpanned, which earned him a glare from Kira.

"Fine," she said with a nod to Dax, "go on."

"The other civilian ships are the *Ng,* the *Goldblatt's Folly,* and the *Halloran.*" She looked up and smiled. "I convinced Captain Monaghan that it was the least she could do after we rescued her."

"Add the *Xhosa,*" Kira said. "We bumped into Kasidy on the Promenade."

"Okay," Dax said, making notes on her padd. "We can leave here as soon as the *Intrepid* arrives in two hours. The Lamnak fleet—that's ten Bajoran Militia ships—will rendezvous with us at Bajor on the way."

"So that leaves us with twenty ships?" Kira asked.

Dax nodded. "A lot of them are cargo ships, or at least ones with plenty of space. I also talked with Minister Lipin and Vedek Eran about arranging for emergency housing for the majority of the refugees on Bajor, and Ensign Ling has started working with Ro's people to get temporary accomodations set up here."

"Good work." Kira said. "Let's hope it's enough ships to get three million people off within fifty-two hours."

Bashir leaned forward. "It might well be. Assuming the reports we have on the number of ships available on Europa Nova itself are accurate, and based on the capacity of each of the ships in the convoy, and assuming the current rate of radiation increase, it's mathematically possible for us to complete the evacuation before we reach fatal exposure."

From anyone else, the statement would have been arrogant and presumptuous, but Vaughn was sure that Bashir's genetically enhanced brain was more than capable of making all the calculations necessary to back the claim up. Turning his gaze on the doctor, Vaughn said, "The problem with mathematical predictions is that they involve variables. And this particular equation is littered with them." Before Bashir could reply to that, Vaughn added, "Speaking of fatal exposure, Doctor, what's our medical status?"

Taking only an instant to switch mental tracks, Bashir said, "I've had the lab replicating arithrazine nonstop since we first received the distress call. The *Defiant*'s dispensary is already full, and I should have enough for the *Intrepid* by the time they arrive."

Bowers frowned. "I thought hyronalin was the standard for radiation."

"Usually, yes, but arithrazine specifically deals with the peculiar side effects of theta radiation. Hyronalin will do in a crunch, but in a case like this, arithrazine is preferred."

"Colonel," ch'Thane said, "I'm not familiar with Europa Nova. They're not a Federation world?"

Shaking her head, Kira said, "No, but it's a human colony. They settled there about a hundred years ago, but never joined the Federation. They actually managed to repel a Breen attack during the war."

Several eyes widened at that bit of information.

"I'm surprised," Vaughn said, "that you're not familiar with the world, Ensign. Andor has several trade agreements with Europa Nova."

"I haven't been home for some time, Commander," ch'Thane said quietly.

Vaughn filed the fact away for future reference. Now wasn't the time or place to pursue this, but there was significant weight to the ensign's statement, especially given who his mother was.

"What about the *Sungari?*" Bowers asked. "I mean, I realize that runabouts won't be all that helpful in evacuation compared to the others . . ."

"No, they won't," Kira said. "In fact, the main purpose of the runabouts will be to try to figure out where the radiation is coming from."

"And," Vaughn added, "how it might relate to the gateways."

"Gateways?" Bashir and Dax both asked simultaneously.

Vaughn very quickly summarized the salient portions of the meeting with Admiral Ross, concluding with: "Lieutenant Nog, you and Ensign ch'Thane are to take the *Sungari* to the wormhole and investigate this phenomenon. There are two encounters with gateways on record: the *Enterprise* and the *Yamato* in the Romulan Neutral Zone on Stardate 42609; and the *Defiant*'s mission to Vandros IV on Stardate 49904. A third, on Alexandra's Planet on Stardate 44765, has been partially declassified for this mission. There are also extensive research notes taken by a Professor Chi Namthot at Memory Alpha. You should both become as familiar with those records as time will allow. Your task is to try to figure out why there are no gateways within ten light-years of Bajor and determine if that reason is something we can harness for practical use. At the moment, we have no control over the gateways, and it's resulted in no small amount of chaos throughout known space."

"Those odd reports," Shar said, nodding. "The presence of Iconian-type gateways would explain most of them—if not all of them, including Europa Nova."

"Exactly. If your mission succeeds, we may be able to get some control of our own."

"Uh, Colonel?" Nog said tentatively.

"Yes, Nog?" Kira said.

Nog held up an isolinear rod he'd been carrying. Vaughn peered at the markings, and saw that it contained a replicator pattern. "I, ah, have something that might help. It's a shield modulator that I—acquired from the Shelliak."

Everyone whirled and stared at Nog. Dax's mouth was hanging open.

Bashir asked, "Aren't the Shelliak among the most xenophobic species in the galaxy?"

"Xenophobic's the wrong word," Dax said. "More like xeno-disdainful. They don't really fear other species, they just don't think all that much of them."

"How the hell did you manage to make a deal with them?" Bowers asked.

Nog smiled. "A good Ferengi never reveals his methods."

"What does this modulator do?" Kira asked, yanking the discussion back on track.

"It strengthens shields against the effects of radiation."

"That's handy," Dax said.

Nog continued, "The problem with it—and it's one

of the reasons why it isn't used much—is that it weakens shields' effectiveness against weapons fire."

Bashir said, "That's *not* so handy."

"Still, in this case," Kira said, "we need protection from radiation a lot more than we need protection from phasers. Good work, Nog."

Beaming, the young Ferengi said, "Thank you, Colonel. We were lucky. I've been working on this deal for four months now. I figured this type of modulation might be useful for navigation in the Badlands. It finally arrived while we were in the Gamma Quadrant."

A pity Dr. Bashir didn't have use of it on his mission to Sindorin, Vaughn thought, and he could see by the pensive look on the doctor's face that he was thinking much the same thing.

Nog continued. "I can have the modulators replicated and installed on the *Defiant* and its shuttles, the *Euphrates,* and the *Rio Grande* by the time the *Intrepid* gets here, and their chief engineer should also be able to install one with no problem."

"All right, get to work on that, then report to the *Sungari.*"

"Yes, sir," Nog said, and he moved toward the lift. Then he stopped and turned back to Kira. Vaughn noticed that the young Ferengi now had a rather pained expression on his face. "Colonel? If we're committing all these ships—does this mean we've given up searching for Jake?"

That pained expression flew around the table, particularly to Dax and Bashir. Kira looked like she'd been gut-punched. Where the room previously had the crackling tension of a group of trained professionals about to embark on a complex mission, now ops felt almost like a mausoleum.

For the past two weeks, Deep Space 9 had been co-ordinating a sector-wide search for Jake Sisko, the son of the former station commander and also, Vaughn knew, a close friend of Nog. Young Mr. Sisko had last been known to be on his way to Earth to visit his grandfather. But when Captain Yates had contacted Earth, Joseph Sisko had professed no knowledge of any visit from his grandson.

However, as continued searches had turned up negative, the efforts, of necessity, had diminished. The *Defiant* was needed to set up the communications array, and Nog—who had been at the forefront of the rescue attempts—was needed to assist Shar in the engineering thereof.

"We haven't given up anything, Nog. But we've done everything that we can do to look for him. We still have an open call to all ships to look out for him, and Ro's people have been questioning everyone who comes on-station. The authorities on Earth are looking, too. We'll find him. But right now, we have to give priority to the three million people on Europa Nova." As she spoke, Kira's face hardened up again, and by the time she reached the words "Europa Nova" she was back to her firm, commanding self.

Kira's words—and, more important, her tone—had an effect. Nog, Dax, Bowers, and Bashir still looked concerned, but the crackling tension of the immediate crisis had returned.

Turning to Dax, the colonel said, "Lieutenant, you'll be in charge of the station while we're gone. Keep coordinating with Lipin and Eran—we'll need housing set up for the refugees within the next twelve hours or so."

Dax nodded.

"Commander Vaughn, you'll take the *Defiant*. I'll take Ling and the *Euphrates*. Bowers, you'll go in the *Rio Grande* with Roness." She looked around the table. "Let's get to work, people. Dismissed."

Good thing we haven't reopened the wormhole for business yet, Vaughn thought. If that had been the case, the station would probably be full to bursting with ships bound for the Gamma Quadrant. Not that they weren't dealing with considerable traffic as it was, especially with all the relief ships going to and from Cardassia, but all things considered, their position could be much more difficult.

As the meeting broke, everyone headed for their stations or the lifts. Vaughn followed Kira up the stairs toward her office. They were intercepted by Taran'atar. "Colonel, request permission to join the mission."

Kira seemed to size up the Jem'Hadar. "Any particular reason?"

"I may be of some use."

"How?"

"I don't know. Nor did I know how I might be of use on Dr. Bashir's mission to Sindorin, yet you yourself said that the mission would have failed without me. For that matter, I've yet to comprehend how I may be of use on this station at all, yet Odo said that I would be. It seems reasonable that I continue seeking ways to make myself useful. Your mission to Europa Nova seems like such an opportunity."

I guess he's getting bored standing around ops,

Vaughn though bemusedly. *But he makes an interesting point. And it might do him some good to see a Federation rescue mission.*

Kira turned to Vaughn with a questioning glance. Vaughn looked in the colonel's eyes, and saw that Kira had already made up her mind. She wasn't looking for his approval, just wanting to know if he had any objection. He shook his head slightly.

"Fine, you'll come with me on the *Euphrates*. Commander, see to it that Lieutenant Bowers knows that Ensign Ling is to remain on the station."

Vaughn nodded. "Yes, sir."

Taran'atar inclined his head. "With your permission, then, Colonel, I will report to runabout pad A and prepare the *Euphrates* for our journey."

4

FARIUS PRIME

"THIS IS *SO* EXCITING!"

Quark tried to ignore the bleating of the blond,
scantily-clad Bajoran woman walking alongside him
down the corridor of the Orion starship. *Why did I
ever think taking a dabo girl along for show would be
a good idea?*

Then he looked at their two escorts, a pair of tall,
burly, green-skinned Orion men who kept their eyes
primarily focused on the outfit his companion wasn't
wearing, so to speak, and thought, *Oh, right—that's
why.* The next time he saw Garak he had to once again
thank the Promenade's erstwhile tailor for his amazing work on the dabo girl outfits—every one a master-
piece of textile engineering, they managed to show
everything yet reveal nothing.

Especially useful when you're dealing with Orions—after all, they appreciate sexy women.

The only parts of the outfit he thought were a little much were the four large, round tassels that dangled from the waistband of the pants—two on either hip. Those pants had slits on both sides of each leg, showing a generous display of flesh, with the waistband just below the pelvic bone. To Quark's mind, the tassels detracted from the effect. *Still, I suppose they serve a purpose.*

They had just disembarked from an Orion transport that had taken them from Deep Space 9 to the Clarus system. It had taken no time at all to get from there to Farius Prime. Quark had, in fact, been stunned at how fast the trip had been—it should've taken several hours at warp six, but was over in less than five minutes.

Now they traversed the corridors of a large vessel that appeared to be based on Vulcan designs, albeit with some modifications. Besides, Quark knew the sound of a Vulcan impulse engine—their Cochrane distortion spiked much higher than on any other vessel. *That's the Orions for you,* he thought with admiration, *always stealing from the best.*

To one of the Orions, he asked, "So how'd we get here so fast, exactly?"

"You'll find out soon enough, Ferengi." The Orion did not take his eyes off the generous display of cleavage that they'd been fixed on since they'd left Deep Space 9 a day earlier. The dabo girl wore a necklace with a Spican flame gem at its center—the necklace acted as an arrow that pointed to her chest, and the flame gem did a marvelous job as that arrow's rather prominent point.

The dabo girl grinned widely and said, "I can't *wait* to find out. This is so unbelievably amazing!"

They arrived at a meeting room that was much more lavishly decorated than one would expect on a Vulcan-designed ship. Most of it consisted of low-quality (in Quark's informed opinion) erotic artwork, ranging from paintings to holosculptures. There was also an impressive display of jewels—including a remarkably good fake of the Zateri emerald—under directed floodlights that cast odd shadows about the room. At the center of the room was a table made of what appeared to be real oak, which couldn't have been cheap.

A small, sour-faced, stoop-shouldered, elderly Orion man whom Quark had last seen on the station sat at one end of that table. His name was Malic, and he had been the one to recruit Quark for this particular endeavor.

His gnarled green fingers moved furiously about the controls of a padd. Said speed was astonishing, given that he wore a ring with a heavy precious stone on each of those fingers. The padd itself was quite impressive, too—its border had an ornate pattern of fighting Aldebaran serpents, and the back had a relief representation of a nude Orion female carved into it. Several more ordinary-looking padds sat on the table in front of him.

"Ah, Quark," Malic said without looking up from the padd. "Glad to see you've arrived in one piece. We're almost ready to begin." Finally, he looked up, and, typically, his eyes went straight to Quark's companion. "And I see you brought company."

Indicating the blond Bajoran with an exaggerated flourish, Quark said, "This is Tamra, one of my finest dabo girls."

"You expect to be playing dabo, Quark?" one of the huge Orions said with a laugh.

"No, but Malic indicated that this might be a protracted negotiation. If I'm going to be away from home this long, I'd like to have some—companionship." On that last word, his hand brushed across his right lobe.

The Orions chortled knowingly.

"Of course," Quark continued as he walked to the other end of the table, "it would help if I knew just what it is I'm supposed to be negotiating. It's hard to prepare to do business when I don't know what the business is."

He sat down on the seat opposite Malic. Malic frowned—or, rather, his perpetual frown deepened—at that action. A chair had been set out at the table to Malic's left, which Quark knew was intended for him. However, he preferred to be on an equal footing—or, in this case, seating—to Malic, so he sat at an equivalent spot rather than the inherently subordinate position that had been set aside. Tamra moved into place behind Quark.

Perhaps in response to Quark's symbolic gesture, perhaps just to generally reassert his superior position here, Malic remained hunched over his padd for a full minute. Quark waited patiently, though Tamra shifted her weight from foot to foot. *I've been stalled by the best,* Quark thought with pride at the Orion. *I can wait as long as you want.*

Finally, Malic placed the padd in the inner pocket of the lavishly patterned dark green jacket he wore.

"Have you ever heard of the Iconians, Quark?"

"Sure. Ancient species, conquered most of this part of the galaxy some two hundred thousand years ago. I've auctioned some artifacts and relics of theirs over the years." *Some of them might have even been authentic.* "They're extinct, though."

Malic's wrinkled lips pulled back into a rictus that one could charitably call a smile. The jewel in one of his rear molars twinkled in the glow of one of the floodlights. "Not so extinct, it would seem. The Iconians have returned, Quark, and they want to deal. And they've activated all their gateways."

"Gateways?" Quark asked.

"Portals that provide instantaneous transportation from one point in space to another. It's how the Iconians created and maintained their empire. There are thousands of them throughout the galaxy."

Nodding, Quark said, "That's how we got here from Clarus so fast."

"Exactly. There are two types of gateways—the older ones that can move ships across great distances and are usually located in planetary orbits; and the later, smaller ones on planets that can take people from one place to another in the time it takes to step through them."

"So they're like wormholes?"

"The orbital ones are similar, but they're completely stable—and I don't just mean stable the way your wormhole is stable," Malic said with another of his pseudosmiles. "I mean stable in every sense. And you arrive at your destination with much greater dispatch and less risk."

Several possibilities danced through Quark's head. He thought about the economic boom that had resulted from the opening of the Bajoran wormhole—increased traffic to Deep Space 9 and his bar; new resources to exploit and riches to obtain; more profit for Bajor, which meant more wealthy Bajorans who liked to spend money at his bar; trade with the Dominion, which increased his profit margin, since he was the first to open relations with the Dominion; and so much more. True the war had upset much of that, but one needed only to remember the Thirty-Fourth Rule of Acquisition: "War is good for business."

From what Malic was saying, this was like the opening of the wormhole, but increased by a factor of thousands.

"Where do I come in?"

"The Iconians are auctioning off the rights to the gateways to the highest bidder. We've been able to secure private negotiations on this ship with one of their mediators."

"What are the terms?"

Malic looked up at one of the two big Orions, who walked to the table, picked up one of the padds, and handed it to Quark.

Quark took it and thumbed it. It contained three lists.

"The first list is the initial offer," Malic said, "followed by the secondary offer—"

Putting the padd down, Quark finished, "And the third is the last-resort add-ons when the bidding gets fierce, I know. This isn't my first negotiation, Malic. If it was, you wouldn't have gone to the trouble of asking for me." He picked up the padd again and held it screen-out toward Malic. "And this list needs work."

Again, Malic's frown deepened. He removed his fancy padd from his jacket pocket and looked at the screen—presumably he had called the same list onto it that Quark was speaking of. "What do you mean?"

Looking back down at the list, Quark said, "You've got rights to the dilithium mines on Dozaria in the second list. The Iconians are *getting rid* of a method of instantaneous transportation. Do you really think that dilithium mines are going to be a sweetener for them? It's just a source of extra profit, but not a compelling offer in and of itself."

"It was extremely—difficult to obtain those rights from the Breen," Malic said. "We're reluctant to part with them so easily."

"Then don't part with them at all. They're a minor component of this deal, and if they're that precious to you, save them for some time when you'll really need them. On the other hand, the acribyte futures should move to the second list—maybe the third. Acribyte wasn't discovered until long after the Iconians were last seen in this quadrant, and it only exists in one star system. It's something brand new to them, and also something immensely profitable. That's much more compelling to this type of client."

Quark suggested other rearrangements of the list before Malic finally said, "Have a care, Ferengi. Don't presume to—overstep yourself."

"I'm just trying to complete my task, Malic," Quark said, opening his arms wide.

"Your task is to negotiate with the Iconians."

"On your behalf," Quark added, "and in order to do that, I need to negotiate from the best possible position. Now if you don't want my advice, why bring me here?"

Malic said nothing.

"Fine, I'll answer my own question, then. You need me."

"The Orion Syndicate needs no one."

Quark made a "tchah" noise. "Posturing now?

C'mon, Malic, I expected better from you than that."
He leaned back in his chair. *Have to play this carefully.* The fact of the matter was, the syndicate could
crush him like a tube grub, and Quark knew it. The
Orions had their grubby green fingers in most of the
illegal activity across half the quadrant—and a decent
amount of the legal activity, too. They'd stayed one
step ahead of Starfleet Intelligence, the Tal Shiar, the
Obsidian Order, Klingon Imperial Intelligence, and
the Ferengi Commerce Authority for decades.

Taking a breath, Quark continued. "Look, I freely
admit that I owe you for not exposing my little scheme
back on the station. It's true, you've done me a
favor—but you're not doing me any favors, if you
know what I mean. I can turn right around and walk
out of here and take my chances back on Deep Space
9." The two guards moved forward menacingly.
"Metaphorically speaking, of course," Quark added
hastily. "The point is, I can handle Starfleet, and I can
handle the Cardassians. Been doing it for years."

"Really? Shall we test that theory?" Malic asked
nastily. "All it will take is a simple command on this
padd, and all the details will be transferred to a Commander Ju'les L'ullho on Starbase 96 and to certain
individuals on Cardassia Prime."

"That won't be necessary," Quark said quickly.
"What I'm trying to say here is that—well, no offense, but, you're pirates. You're used to taking what
you want, not asking for it. That's why you need
me—I know how to get you a bargain. So are you
going to take advantage of my skills—which were the
whole reason why you talked me into coming here in
the first place—or are you going to guarantee that

you'll lose the gateways before I ever even walk into the negotiating room?"

Malic glowered at Quark for several seconds. Quark didn't move, didn't even blink. *I've sat through Odo's interrogations, I can sit through this old slug's stare.*

Finally, Malic looked down at his padd and said, "What other changes would you like to make?"

Smiling, Quark proceeded to continue with his suggested changes to the list.

Once they'd gotten everything to a satisfactory level, Malic said, without looking up, "Bring some tube grubs for our negotiator—and see if there are any Bajoran hors d'oeuvres left for his companion." One of the two Orion landmasses moved toward the door.

Quark inclined his head toward Malic. "I admire a man who knows how to treat the hired help."

Another Orion entered the room. "The Iconians have arrived, along with their mediator. I've installed them in the conference room."

"Good." Malic looked up at Quark. "Do well for us, Quark. The syndicate does not tolerate failure."

The implication came through quite clearly: if the Orions did not wind up with control of the gateways, Quark would be held responsible. Never mind exposing his scam on Cardassia—Quark suspected that the syndicate's ideas of retribution would get a good deal more unpleasant.

The oversized Orions stood on either side of Quark. "Let's go," one of them said.

"Don't I get my tube grubs?" Quark asked, looking up at one of the Orions—who was actually staring at Tamra as he spoke.

"We'll bring 'em to the table. Move."

"Fine."

Quark got up, and he and Tamra followed the Orion out the door, then down a corridor to another conference room.

This one was somewhat larger than the previous room, and much more tastefully decorated. No erotica here, but an impressive array of paintings lined the walls, including the best fake of T'Nare of Vulcan's *ShiKahr Sunrise* Quark had ever seen. *If I'd had fakes that good when I was selling that alleged lot of T'Nare's work, I wouldn't have had to pay that fine.* This table also appeared to be made of oak, but Quark's practiced eye recognized it as an Ordek transformer table, which could take on different appearances. At its center was a pair of opaque pitchers and two mugs.

Personally, Quark thought, *I'd have chosen something a bit more friendly. There's something foreboding about oak.*

Then Quark looked at the people in the room, and tried to keep his jaw from dropping.

Standing around the table were two tall, skinny bipeds with yellowish skin. Their features seemed unfinished, almost like Odo's. They wore outfits of green satin similar to the type favored by the more well-to-do members of the Orion Syndicate—light green cape with dark green brocade, a loose-fitting tunic and tight pants the same color as the brocade.

All of that registered in Quark's mind peripherally. Most of his attention was focused on the person sitting at the head of the table. It was a Ferengi with small beady eyes and sporting a huge sneer. He was dressed in a suit of the finest Tholian silk. The Forty-

Seventh Rule of Acquisition came to mind: "Never trust a man wearing a better suit than your own."

And this Ferengi was definitely not one to be trusted, regardless of his suit.

"Gaila." Quark said the name in a dull monotone.

"Pleasure to see you, cousin," Gaila said. His sneer widened.

Gaila, to whom Quark had made a loan years ago to help him start his business. Gaila, whose subsequent success as an arms dealer was profitable enough to allow him to buy his own moon. Gaila, who gave Quark a ship in order to repay that loan, but sabotaged it, an incident from which Quark, his brother, and his nephew barely survived. Gaila, who brought Quark into the weapons business to help alleviate Quark's near-destitute state after he'd been banned by the Ferengi Commerce Authority.

Gaila, whom Quark had betrayed to General Nassuc of Palamar, which had resulted in Gaila becoming a target of the general's "purification squad." Gaila, whom Quark had last seen on Deep Space 9 as a wreck, a shadow of his former self, aiding Quark on a lunatic mission to rescue Quark's mother, Ishka, from Dominion forces.

"I was wondering where you've been keeping yourself," Quark said.

"I've been busy. But we're not here to talk about old times, cousin. Please, have a seat. Let's get started." Gaila smiled. "We have a *lot* of work to do, if we're to hammer out any kind of deal here."

"Of course," Quark said agreeably, and sat at the place opposite Gaila.

He could feel in his lobes that Gaila was going to

make sure that this deal would, in fact, be as much work as possible.

The preliminary negotiations were just that—nothing ever got accomplished during an initial session. Generally, it was just an opportunity for the negotiators to get a feel for each other, and for the precise nature of the deal to be spelled out. The Iconians were offering exclusive rights to, and complete instructions on how to operate, all the gateways in the galaxy. Not just the Alpha Quadrant, but the entire galaxy.

Mentally, Quark had had to rearrange the order of the list. He had not realized quite how far-flung these gateways were, and certain items would need to be moved further up the list if they were even going to have a hope of negotiating with these aliens.

Of course, the negotiator wasn't alien at all. Quark and Gaila had known each other since they were boys cheating the younger kids out of their lunch money so they could buy the latest Marauder Mo action figures.

The question is, will Gaila take advantage of this negotiation to get some of his own back? After all, the last two times he and Quark had been together, Gaila had almost gotten himself killed, and Quark had also been more or less directly responsible for Gaila hitting absolute bottom. Ferengi generally didn't let personal grudges get in the way of business, but Quark couldn't really count on that.

Now they were taking a half-hour break—ostensibly for a meal, but truthfully so each side could figure out what their offer was really going to be. As soon as

Quark, Tamra, and the two giants entered Malic's private conference room, the elderly Orion said, "So he's your cousin, is he?"

"Yes, Gaila's my cousin. We've known each other since we were kids. He and I have even done a few business deals together."

"Is that going to be a problem?"

Quark shrugged, and lied. "I don't see why it should be. Gaila's a businessman. I'm a businessman. We're both going to do the best we can for our clients. And, before you ask, I won't be able to prevail upon him to give me a break because I'm family."

"I wasn't going to ask that," Malic said sourly. "I've done my research on you, Quark. The last person I would expect to give you a break is someone who's known you since you were a child."

Nodding, Quark said, "It's possible that Gaila's presence will slow the negotiations down a bit. After all, Gaila and I know each other's tricks—it just means we'll each have to come up with new tricks, so I wouldn't be *too* concerned. As a matter of fact—"

"Quark, the more you try to convince me that there won't be any problems, the more convinced I am that there will be. So kindly shut up, and take a look at this." He indicated a padd on the table, and one of the Orions picked it up and handed it to Quark.

The display showed a report from a Starfleet vessel called the *T'Kumbra*. Quark remembered that as Captain Solok's ship—*the ones who defeated us in that silly human bays-ball game of Captain Sisko's*. The report was incomplete, but one of the items in it was that there were no gateways at all in the Bajoran system—a twenty-light-year-diameter hole in the gateway lattice, in fact.

Smiling, Quark said, "Interesting that the Iconians didn't mention this when they were carrying on about how there were gateways *all* over the galaxy."

"Very interesting. I think it's worth mentioning at the next session, don't you?"

Quark nodded.

A half an hour later, Quark didn't even sit down before he said, "You told us that these gateways were in every sector of the galaxy."

Frowning, Gaila said, "They are."

"Really?" Quark stood next to his chair and looked down at Gaila on the other side. "Then why is it that there isn't a single gateway within ten light-years of Bajor?"

Gaila, to his credit, barely missed a beat. "What need is there for one? You have the wormhole, after all."

"Which was discovered less than a decade ago." Quark finally sat down. "Whereas the Iconian gateways were—apparently—built around it long before anyone knew it was there. Seems to me that this should have been mentioned at some point."

Gaila leaned back. "We're under no obligation to explain ourselves to you, Quark."

"No, but it does make me wonder what other little facts you've managed to leave out."

"We've left nothing out, Quark."

Quark regarded his cousin with what he hoped was a penetrating gaze. "You've said that before."

"It should be pointed out," Gaila said, "that the Breen, the Romulan Empire, and the Klingon Empire don't much care if there aren't any gateways around Bajor. After all, with the gateways reactivated, the strategic value of the wormhole will plunge to nothing. And they've all made very competitive offers."

"You forget, cousin, that I'm not here on my behalf, but as a representative of the Orions. They don't care about Bajor, either—they do care about being lied to in a good-faith negotiation."

Smiling, Gaila said, "Quark, you're always working on your own behalf—one way or the other."

Quark swallowed, but said nothing.

"Hig."

"Hig here. What is it, Kam?"

"There's a problem."

"Another one?"

"This is serious, Hig."

"I'm always serious. What's the problem?"

"There's apparently some kind of flaw in the gateway network. There aren't any gateways within ten light-years of System 418—the natives call it Bajor."

"That's where that stable wormhole is, yes?"

"Yes. I want you to head over there right away."

"Why?"

"Two reasons. One, see if you can figure out why there aren't any gateways there. Two, see if the Bajorans or Starfleet or anyone else is trying to figure out why there aren't any gateways there."

"What if they do find out?"

"Do whatever's necessary to stop them. We can't let anything slow these negotiations down. We're going to have enough problems as it is—the Orions have already complicated things by bringing a Ferengi of their own in. Those two will likely go at it for days. The longer this takes, the harder it will be to maintain the illusion."

"Fine. I'll take the gateway to System 429 and head to System 418 from there. I'll let you know what I find out."

"Good."

5

THE WORMHOLE

"Nog, can I ask you a question?"

At Shar's words, Nog turned to look at the Andorian sitting in the *Sungari*'s copilot seat. Shar had waited until they had come to a relative stop near the mouth of the wormhole before posing his query.

"Sure."

Shar was still working his console as he spoke. "Why haven't you asked me about my *zhavey?*"

Nog broke into a smile. Shar's *zhavey*—apparently, the Andorian equivalent of a *moogie*—was a Federation Councillor, a fact that had come to light around the same time as that mess with the Jem'Hadar.

"To be honest, I've gotten so sick of people asking

me what my father is like, I didn't think you'd appreciate being pestered with the same question."

"Sensors are calibrated—beginning sweep." Once that was done, Shar finally looked up at Nog. "Interesting. So people ask you about your father?"

"All the time. Well, mostly asking how he's changed. See, that's the thing, Father lived on the station for ten years before he became Grand Nagus, so everyone knew him."

"Interesting," Shar repeated. Then he looked back down at his readouts. "I've done a full scan of the wormhole. Everything's within established norms. So far I'm not detecting anything that would explain the lack of gateways in this sector."

"So it's probably something natural to the wormhole?"

Shar's antennae quivered. "We don't even know for sure that the wormhole is connected—it's a vague hypothesis based on circumstantial evidence. I've read the data from Starfleet on the Iconian technology and programmed the *Sungari* computer to compare that to what we receive from these scans to see if there's any correlation. So far, there's nothing showing up on sensors that would prevent the gateways from functioning."

Nog shot Shar a look. "You went over *all* the data?"

"No, I *read* all the data. Twice. Commander Vaughn did ask us to be familiar with it."

Nog blinked. "You read fast."

Shar shrugged.

Nog tried not to let his frustration show. He'd barely had time to look at the data, what with replicating and installing the Shelliak shield modulators, though the latter, at least, he had been able to delegate to other engineers on his staff. Of course, Ezri had to remind him that he *had* a staff to delegate it to. *I'm still thinking like a cadet. . . .*

"With your permission, Nog, I'd like to try a few more specialized scans," Shar said.

It took Nog a second to remember that he needed to actually give the order. "Okay," he said. That didn't sound like an officer, so he quickly added, "Ensign."

Yup, definitely still thinking like a cadet.

After a few moments, Nog asked, "Actually, I do have a question. What's it like?"

"My *zhavey,* you mean?"

"Not exactly. What's it like for *you?*" When Shar hesitated, Nog added, "It's just that, all my life, Father's just been a regular Ferengi—not even that, really. Now he's the most important Ferengi in the galaxy. It's kind of—well, daunting."

"That is a very good word for it," Shar said. "The magnetron scan is negative. Trying a positron scan now."

"Okay," Nog said. "It's funny, but part of the reason I joined Starfleet was so I wouldn't turn out like my father."

That got Shar's attention. "How so?"

"Well, at the time, my father was working for Uncle Quark. He was the assistant manager of policy and clientele."

Shar looked as befuddled as everyone else did whenever they heard that particular title. "What does that mean, exactly?"

Chuckling, Nog said, "In practical terms, it meant that Father did whatever Uncle Quark told him to do." He turned and looked at Shar. "My father is an engineering genius. And he was trapped under my uncle—I didn't want to be like that. I knew I could do better."

"So you did. In fact, I'd say you probably did better than your father."

Nog frowned. "What do you mean?"

"I'm sorry, sir, I spoke out of turn." Shar turned back to his console.

"It's okay, Shar, please—tell me what you meant."

Shar hesitated. "I've seen what your father accomplished once he joined the engineering staff on the station. Those self-replicating mines of his that they put in front of the wormhole probably kept the war from ending badly two years sooner. I just don't see why he would abandon that to go into politics."

Nog adjusted the runabout's position as it started to drift away from the wormhole. "My father has a chance to change the face of Ferengi culture!"

Shar looked back up. "Really?"

"Yes. My father was entrusted with the nagushood and a mandate from former Grand Nagus Zek to bring about major reforms in Ferengi business practices."

At that, Nog thought he saw Shar's antennae move back slightly. Nog wondered if it was an expression of surprise. Shar said, "Well, my *zhavey* was elected to the position of Councillor with a mandate from the Andorian people to improve our trading positions with non-Federation worlds. It hasn't happened yet, and she was elected eight years ago. May your father have better luck." And then Shar smiled.

"I hope so," Nog said in all seriousness. "I think he has the potential to make our society even greater."

"How so?"

Shar seemed genuinely curious, so Nog checked the *Sungari*'s position, and then began to go into a lengthy explanation of the reforms that Grandmother Ishka and Zek had devised and that Father was supposed to put into action.

They spent the better part of the day working and talking about it, interrupted by the occasional monitoring of short-range sensors and Shar's reports of his scans—none of which were of any help regarding the gateways. They paused for lunch—Nog convinced Shar to try a tube grub, which the Andorian didn't like any more than Prynn Tenmei had—and Shar asked more questions about the reforms.

"So women are allowed to wear clothes now?"

"Allowed, yes," Nog said as he washed a tube grub down with a swig of root beer. "Not all of them do, particularly once you get out of the capital city. But more and more are. If nothing else, it's cut down on illnesses—which has the doctors in an uproar."

"I don't understand."

Nog smiled. "Ferenginar in general and the capital city in particular have a very damp climate. Women got all kinds of bronchial infections and things regularly when they'd go out. With more women wearing clothes, they don't get sick as often, so the doctors do less business."

Shar took a bite of his *jumja* stick. The Andorian had made a point of trying other worlds' cuisines— which was why he'd been willing to sample the tube grub—and he had developed a particular taste for *jumja,* much to Nog's abject confusion. "I have to confess, I never would have thought of the economic implications of women wearing clothes on the medical profession."

Laughing, Nog said, "Unfortunately, Father has to. According to his last letter, he's had to sign off on all kinds of concessions to the medical association."

Once they finished eating, they went through the wormhole and ran a few more scans inside, then the same ones on the Gamma Quadrant side. The end result was more of the same.

It took a while for Nog to notice that Shar had never actually answered his question. *That's the second time he's danced around it,* Nog thought. He considered trying again, then decided that, if his friend didn't want to talk about it, Nog would respect that.

As Nog piloted the runabout back into the wormhole, Shar said, "Wait a moment. Computer, is the Kar-telos system within ten light-years of the Gamma Quadrant mouth of the wormhole?"

"Affirmative."

"We are fools. All of us. It cannot be the wormhole that is causing that gap. The *Halloran* fell through a gateway in the Kar-telos system."

Nog blinked. "You're right. It's got to be something else. Well, wait a minute, it could be an unscientific reason." As Nog spoke, the *Sungari* came out the Alpha Quadrant side.

Shar looked at the Ferengi. "What do you mean?"

"We don't know what this area of space was like when the Iconians were around. For all we know, there was some kind of treaty with the people who lived here to keep out any gateways."

Shar nodded. "Good point. Still, I hope they're not

putting too much hope in this. The chance that we'll find the one thing—"

"It's not our place to assume anything, Ensign," Nog said sharply. "We just do what we're told."

"I know, and we're doing it. But it's getting us nowhere. I've done every scan the *Sungari* is capable of."

Nog couldn't help but agree. They'd spent too long at this as it was. "I'm setting course back to DS9. We can look at the data just as easily there—this way we'll free up the runabout for Europa Nova if we need it."

"Wait."

Frowning, Nog said, "What?"

Shar was touching his left antenna. "The Denorios Belt. It's full of tachyon eddies, isn't it?"

"Yes."

"That might be it, then." Shar called up a record on the viewscreen. It was a Starfleet data record—with, Nog noticed, some information removed. "This is the declassified portion of Commander Vaughn's mission to Alexandra's Planet. Tricorder readings showed that for a fraction of a second, there was a disruptive effect on the gateway right around the time they were trying to detect a cloaked Romulan ship."

Nog put it together. "Tachyon bursts are used to detect cloaked ships."

"Exactly. And it makes sense. The wormhole is a local phenomenon. At its absolute worst, it never has any impact on the space around it outside the range of the Denorios Belt."

Picking up the ball, Nog said, "But tachyons move faster than light." He snapped his fingers, a sudden gesture that made Shar jump. "Sorry, but I just remembered something. A couple of years ago, Captain Sisko re-created a Bajoran solar sailing ship."

"Yes, I remember reading about that," Shar said. "What of it?"

"That ship got caught in one of those tachyon eddies and wound up in the Cardassian solar system. Later, the Cardassians admitted that the ship the captain based his design on did the same thing centuries ago."

Shar's antennae pulled back again. "Cardassia is within ten light-years of Bajor. Nog, I believe we have a workable theory."

"Now we just need to test it," Nog said. "And it makes a lot more sense than the wormhole. The belt has always been a navigation hazard. That's why it took so long for anyone to discover the wormhole in the first place." He smiled and added, "Just don't tell Colonel Kira I said that."

Shar frowned. "Why not?"

"Adjusting position for best scanning vector," Nog said, then turned back to the Andorian. "As far as the Bajorans are concerned, the Celestial Temple went undiscovered until seven years ago because the Prophets were waiting for the Emissary."

Shar seemed to consider that. "That's actually a perfectly valid interpretation of the facts. In fact, you could even argue that the Prophets made the Denorios Belt such a navigation hazard in order to keep the temple hidden until the right moment."

Nog grinned. "Do you believe that?"

"Well, I'm not a Bajoran, and I wasn't raised in that religious tradition, so no, but it's an interesting hypothesis."

"So there's no way I'm going to convince you that

you need to live a profitable life so you can go to the Divine Treasury when you die?"

Shar said in all seriousness, "Probably not, no. The Andorian afterlife is a bit more—complicated than that, I'm afraid." He turned to his console. "Computer, do a detailed scan of the Denorios Belt and then run program ch'Thane Gateway One using that data."

"Acknowledged," said the pleasant, mechanical voice.

"Sungari to Deep Space 9," Nog said, opening a channel to ops.

"Dax here. Go ahead, Nog."

"Lieutenant, Ensign ch'Thane and I have developed a working theory for the lack of gateways in this sector. He's running tests now to confirm it, but we're pretty sure it has something to do with the tachyon eddies in the Denorios Belt, not the wormhole."

"Good work, Nog. I'll let Commander Vaughn know."

"Thanks, Lieutenant. How's the rescue mission going?"

"Slowly but surely. The first contingent of refugees are expected within the hour."

"Great. I don't think we'll be at this more than another hour, so the *Sungari* should be available if they need it."

"I'll let Commander Vaughn know that, too," Dax said. Nog could almost see her smile.

Sighing, he thought, *Dr. Bashir is a lucky man.* Aloud, he simply said, *"Sungari* out."

"I think I have something, Nog," Shar said, looking over a readout on his console. "Based on the records from Alexandra's Planet, and also some of Professor

Namthot's notes, a compressed tachyon burst *should* disrupt the gateways, if combined with certain noble gases." With a smile, he turned to Nog. "All those gases are present in the Denorios Belt. We just need to figure out some way to harness them and combine it with the burst. I'm not sure how we could do that, but—"

Nog peered at the readout. "Oh, that's easy. Rig the Bussard collectors on the *Defiant*—or some other starship—for those gases, modify an intermix chamber to infuse the tachyon burst with them, and then run it through the phaser banks—oh, wait." He took a closer look at Shar's display. "No, something like this, we'll need to run it through the deflector array—the phaser banks would burn out after two seconds."

Shar stared at Nog. "If you say so," he said slowly. "One question, though—you said 'disrupt.' Disrupt, how?"

Sighing, Shar said, "I wish I could answer that. We just don't know enough about how the gateways *really* work. All of this is pure theory, but at least it's consistent with the available data. The problem is the unavailable data. That could easily come along and slice off our antennae."

"So for all we know, this tachyon burst will make the gateways belch fire or something?"

Shar's antennae quivered. "Let's not be silly. Still, it's a concern."

"Yes, but it's not our concern. That's Colonel Kira and Commander Vaughn's problem. Are you done here?"

Taking one last look at the data he'd accumulated, Shar said, "Yes, I think I've done all I can."

"Then let's get back. Setting course for DS9."

That's when a strange vessel came out of warp and fired on the *Sungari*.

"Damage report!" Nog cried as he quickly put the runabout's shields up. *What is it* this *time?* he wondered. It all happened incredibly fast. One moment they were alone, the next an odd-looking, oblong vessel ten times the size of the runabout blasted out of subspace.

"Heavy damage to the starboard nacelle," Shar said. "Nothing critical, but we can't go to warp."

"Returning fire." Nog targeted the phasers on the newcomer. *I'm just glad I put off installing the shield modulator on the* Sungari, *or this damage would be a lot worse.*

"Minor damage to their shields," Shar said. "There's no match for this ship in the databank, although parts of it are similar to known ships. Length, two hundred meters, hull composed of a variety of roginium alloys— except for the secondary hull, which is duranium. Their weapons are some kind of directed ladrion pulse."

"Whatever that is," Nog muttered.

Another impact. "Shields at sixty percent. Structural-integrity field weakened."

"Send out a distress call to the station."

"Aye, sir."

Looking down at the console, Nog programmed a random firing pattern that Worf had taught him. It was designed to score multiple hits on enemy shields as hard as possible. The pattern was designed for the *Defiant,* which had more powerful phasers, but the *Sungari* was more maneuverable. After that, he set a course that the computer knew as Kira-Three.

"What are you doing?" Shar asked, sounding concerned.

"Something Colonel Kira taught us about taking on a big ship with a small one."

"Lieutenant, I don't think the SIF can handle this kind of maneuvering."

Another impact. "I know we can't handle sitting here. Implementing pattern."

The runabout moved in a zigzagging spiral pattern around the larger vessel, phasers firing at multiple points on their shields.

"SIF holding," Shar said. "Their shields are weakening."

Just as the *Sungari* came about on its last pass, the enemy vessel fired again.

Several of the aft consoles blew out. Nog's console stopped responding to his commands. The runabout continued forward on its own momentum, Nog unable to control the vessel's movements any longer.

"Shields down!" Shar said over the din of the alarms. "Impulse engines and weapons offline, transporters down, and SIF at fourteen percent." Shar looked over at Nog. "One bit of good news: their shields are down as well. Your maneuver worked."

Nog ground his teeth. "That might mean something if we still had weapons. Did the station get our distress call?"

"Impossible to be sure, but considering that all of our other ships are at Europa Nova . . ." Shar trailed off, then glanced at his console as it beeped. "They're coming around for another pass."

"Ready thrusters," Nog said.

"We can't evade their weapons with thrusters," Shar said.

Nog's left leg started to itch again. "It beats sitting still and waiting for it. Transmit the specs for the tachyon burst to the station in case we don't make it."

"Done," Shar acknowledged. His console beeped again. "They're charging weapons."

Nog closed his eyes.

6

EUROPA NOVA

"COMING OUT OF WARP, entering standard orbit."

Colonel Kira Nerys's fingers flew over the console of the *Euphrates,* suiting actions to words as she led the convoy of nineteen vessels into orbit of the Class-M planet. The world was a bit smaller than Bajor, and looked more blue from orbit than the greener tinge of home—or, at least, parts of it did. As the *Euphrates* and the other ships entered orbit, antimatter waste became visible. Amorphous green material, it clustered in chunks in a close orbit, hanging menacingly over the exosphere.

Kira then looked back down at the screen on her console. She'd been studying the library records on Europa Nova. The planet was pastoral—like

Earth, covered in oceans; like Bajor, awash in vegetation.

Or, at least, she thought, *like Bajor was before the Cardassians.* Seven years later, even with the best efforts of the planetary government and the Federation, Bajor still bore the scars of the previous half-century.

But Europa Nova had been spared those scars. The colonists had built carefully, constructing their small cities in places that could handle the inevitable environmental damage of urbanization with minimal impact on the overall ecosystem, and utilizing the arable land for farms. Five cities were festooned about the landmasses, including one on a remote island. Smaller villages, towns, military bases, and research centers dotted the rest of the two continents.

Kira had been especially fascinated by the cities. Generally, the architectural progression of a city—if it had one at all—was to emanate from the old in the center to the new as it expanded outward. Bajor, for instance, had several cities with millennia-old temples and other older buildings in the middle of town, surrounded by more modern architecture. Europani cities, however, went the other way around: dull, modern, prefabricated structures formed the hubs of the cities—the original, simple constructions of the twenty-third-century colonists who of necessity favored functionality over aesthetics. As the cities expanded and the colony prospered, the buildings became more elaborate and artistic. According to the records, the style was a melding of Earth Gothic and Tellarite *Churlnik*—both involving elaborate decorations on stonework.

The world also had gained an impressively rich cultural and scientific reputation during its first hundred years. Europani duranium sculpture had become especially popular in the last decade or so—there had been an exhibit at the Akorem Laan Museum on Bajor a few years back—and, according to Keiko O'Brien, some of the most important breakthroughs in botany and agriculture of the last fifty years were by Europani.

And these people repelled the Breen. Where Bajor at the height of its renaissance still fell victim to the Cardassian Occupation, where Earth itself had been unable to prevent the sneak attack that had devastated Starfleet Headquarters, this group of humans, who had barely been on their world for a full century, managed to stay out of the Dominion War.

Next to her, Taran'atar said, "I am reading an *Akira*-class Starfleet ship already in orbit. It registers as the *U.S.S. Gryphon.* There are also several non-Starfleet transports—and an increasing amount of theta radiation originating from the antimatter waste field dead ahead."

Kira nodded, then opened a channel. *"Euphrates to Gryphon."*

Turning to the small viewscreen on her left, Kira found herself once again facing the round visage of Captain Elaine Mello.

"Glad to see you, Colonel," Mello said. *"I've been in touch with the Europani authorities, and we started bringing up the sick and injured who can be transported."*

"Good," Kira said.

"Otherwise, they're implementing an evac plan. Wicked efficient, from what I've been able to see so far. They've already gotten most of their children off-planet by using their own civilian vessels, as well as

their military transports. We're only going to have to handle the adults."

Kira breathed a sigh of relief at that—both because the children were already safe, and because it would cut the load the convoy would have to deal with by a third.

Mello went on. *"I'm having a copy of the plan sent to you, the* Defiant, *the* Intrepid, *and the* Rio Grande." Then she frowned, as her gaze moved past Kira. *"Colonel, is that—"*

"Yes, he's a Jem'Hadar. He's a cultural observer, here on my authority."

"If you say so," Mello said, a dubious expression on her face. *"President Silverio said she wanted to talk to you as soon as you were in orbit."*

"Thank you, Captain. I'll be in touch shortly. Kira out." She had been grateful that Mello was going to defer to her command. Since Kira wasn't Starfleet, she had been concerned that the captains would take charge, but it seemed both Mello and Emick considered her the mission commander. She probably had Ross to thank for that, and she made a mental note to mention it the next time they spoke.

Mello also obviously had a war veteran's distrust of a recent enemy, but she was apparently willing to defer to Kira's judgment about Taran'atar as well. Kira could understand the captain's concern, but she also understood the importance of Taran'atar's mission. *Odo sent him to begin bridging the gap between the Dominion and their enemies—former enemies,* she amended. That bridge needed to be built. Kira herself had learned the hard way that not all Cardassians were evil, conquering sadists—*though the species has their share of them,* she thought, an image of Dukat floating unwelcome into her mind. But there were good Cardassians—Ghemor, Marritza, Damar in the end, even Garak, to a degree—and Kira had even helped Damar's resistance movement against the Dominion. If she could put aside her lifelong distrust for all things Cardassian to help Damar, she could put aside the last few years of conflict against the Dominion to help Taran'atar's mission succeed. She owed Odo that much, and more.

Pushing thoughts of her faraway lover to the back of her mind, she opened a channel to the surface. Soon after, a tired-looking human face appeared on the screen.

Had Kira met President Grazia Silverio on the Promenade, she would have pegged the older woman as someone's kindly aunt or grandmother, not a head of state. She had short, curly, paper-white hair, a wrinkled if pleasant face, a bulbous nose, and a jowly neck. The deepest wrinkles were next to the eyes and bordering the mouth, indicating someone who smiled a lot.

She was not, however, smiling now. Her face was long, and her eyes were tired.

"You're Colonel Nerys?" she said without preamble.

"Colonel Kira, actually. Bajoran tradition puts the family name first."

"I'm sorry, Colonel. I'm afraid things are a bit hectic right now."

"Understandable, ma'am."

Silverio waved her right arm. *"Apf. None of this 'ma'am.' Call me Grazia. I've gotten enough 'ma'am' the last few days to last me until I die. Which probably won't be too long now. And before you say anything, I'm not being fatalistic about the radiation—I'm old, that means I'm going to die soon. That's the way of the galaxy. But I'm not going to die today, and neither is anyone else. We didn't fight off the Breen just to let some radiation do us in. You've seen the evacuation plan?"*

"Not yet." She looked over at Taran'atar, who nodded. "We're receiving it from the *Gryphon* now."

"Good. We've gotten most of the children off, as well as about a thousand adults. All together that's about a million that have already made it off-planet."

"That's good to hear," Kira said with a small smile. "They can proceed to Deep Space 9. The station's acting commander, Lieutenant Dax, is coordinating housing efforts both on the station and on Bajor—tell the ships to contact her when they arrive."

Silverio nodded. *"Our treatment facilities could use some assistance, also—we're running out of hyronalin, and our surgeon general tells me that isn't even the best treatment."*

"No, it isn't. *Euphrates* to *Defiant.*"

"Vaughn here. Go ahead, Colonel."

"Commander, have Dr. Bashir contact the Europani surgeon general—"

Silverio said, *"Dr. Martino DeLaCruz."*

Nodding, Kira continued, "Their hospitals need arithrazine. I want him to organize a distribution program. Have him coordinate with the *Intrepid*'s CMO—the *Gryphon*'s handling the evac of the sick and injured, so let them deal with that."

"Understood. Anything else?"

"That's it for now. I'll be in touch shortly. Kira out."

Silverio said with a tired smile, *"Thank you, Colonel. Right now, the remaining population is gath-*

ering in each of the five major cities for mass transport."

"Good. We'll use transporters for as long as is practical. Most of the ships can land—" Kira had made sure that the ten Bajoran ships had atmospheric capability, and the runabouts, most of the civilian ships, and the *Intrepid* all could land as well "—and we'll do that, once the radiation gets past the point where we can use transporters. We also hope to figure out how to cut off the radiation."

"That'd be good. This is our home, Colonel, and we don't abandon it easily."

"You won't have to, ma—Grazia," she amended with a smile. "You have my word, I'll do everything in my power to restore your world."

At that, the president's face blossomed into a smile. *"I appreciate that, Colonel. One other thing. We'd like to get Councillor zh'Thane out of here before the radiation gets much worse. She's our invited guest, after all, and it's bad form to give your guests radiation poisoning. She allowed us to use her own ship to transport some of the children off."*

Kira was impressed—politicians didn't often make that kind of sacrifice, though she supposed the councillor would put the goodwill gesture to use in negotiations. *Not that I'm cynical or anything,* she thought wryly. "Understood. We'll beam her to the *Defiant* as soon as possible."

"Excellent."

"I'll contact you again once I've gone over the evacuation plan. *Euphrates* out."

President Silverio's face disappeared from the screen.

Kira glanced over the evac plan, which was refreshingly well-ordered, and also similar to a standard Federation evacuation agenda—which they no doubt based it on. "Taran'atar, open a channel to all the ships in the convoy."

"Channel open," the Jem'Hadar said after a moment.

"This is Colonel Kira. At the moment, the theta radiation is within tolerances of the transporters, but the level is increasing and we'll lose that ability pretty quickly. For now, we've got five major cities and a lot of other, more rural areas to cover. The *Defiant* will handle L'Aquila. The *Gryphon* will take Spilimbergo, the *Xhosa* will handle Chieti, the *Intrepid* and the *Goldblatt's Folly* will take Padilla, and—" she sighed "—the *East Winds* will take Libre Pista." L'Aquila was the capital city, though the least populous of the five major urban areas—in any case, Kira wanted Vaughn to deal personally with the VIPs who'd be coming up from there, including Councillor zh'Thane. Padilla was the most populous city, and would require two ships. "The *Rio Grande* and the *Halloran* will take the smaller towns on the northern continent, and the *Ng* and the *Euphrates* will take the smaller towns on the southern continent. That still leaves a wide range of rural and pastoral land. Colonel Lenaris?"

The commander of the Lamnak fleet said, *"Yes?"*

"I want you to divide the remaining land into nine areas and dispatch nine of your ships to seek out and transport personnel in those areas. Use your remaining ship to scan the islands."

"Will do."

Kira smiled. Lenaris Holem had been a member of the Ornathia cell during the resistance, and had been involved in the historic Pullock V raid. Later, he'd been instrumental in defusing a crisis in Dakhur Province over the disposition of some soil reclamators. Lenaris himself hadn't made much of his role in that crisis, but those events had led to Shakaar Edon running for, and winning the position of, first minister of Bajor. Kira's former resistance-cell leader had had a most successful reign thus far, and Lenaris's actions had a lot to do with allowing that to come about.

Lenaris was also deeply religious, she knew, as most of his people must also have been, and he probably wasn't entirely comfortable dealing with Kira as one Attainted by the Vedek Assembly. But Kira also knew that Lenaris was too professional to allow any personal feelings to obstruct his duty, especially if lives were on the line. Kira was grateful that the Militia had assigned him to the evac mission. If anyone could get out all the Europani who might still be in the assorted nooks, crannies, trees, and caves of the planet, it was Lenaris.

"You have your assignments—let's get to work. Kira out."

"Colonel, a moment, please?" Vaughn's voice.

"Be right with you, Commander." She closed the general connection, then went ship-to-ship with the *Defiant*. "All right, go ahead."

"Lieutenant Dax relayed a communication from Farius Prime. According to our source there, the Iconians are, in fact, peddling two kinds of gateways. Besides the ones we're familiar with, there are also large orbital ones. Apparently, the original Enterprise *encountered one a century ago on Stardate 5720. I think it's safe to say we've got one in orbit here."*

"All right. Try to get a sensor reading through the theta radiation and see if you can detect the gateway—maybe we can find a way to shut it down before the situation gets worse."

"Aye, sir. Vaughn out."

Kira closed the connection, and said, "Setting course for the southern continent."

"Shields raised for atmospheric entry," Taran'atar said. "There is no indication that the Ferengi's modifications will have any deleterious effect." Then he turned to Kira. "Colonel, may I ask a question?"

"Of course," Kira said, surprised.

"Why did you take command of this inferior vessel instead of the warship?"

Kira smiled. *It figures he'd pick up on that. Sure, I could have taken the* Defiant *myself. It's part of my command, after all. But part of being in command is delegating responsibility.*

She said none of this to Taran'atar, saying instead, "I've always been more comfortable with the runabouts. They remind me of the flitters we flew during the Occupation. The *Defiant's* too much like the Cardassian ships we fought against."

"You prefer the weapon you are used to."

Kira almost smiled. "Something like that. Entering atmosphere."

The viewscreen became all but useless as the *Euphrates* entered a thick cloud layer.

Of course, there was another reason, which she felt it was impolitic to mention directly to Taran'atar. While the Jem'Hadar had proven as good as his word so far—and indeed had been useful both against the renegade Jem'Hadar who attacked the station and on Bashir's enforced errand for Section 31—the fact was that most of the crew didn't yet trust him entirely.

Kira had thought it best to have Taran'atar where she could keep an eye on him, and also keep him from interacting directly with Starfleet personnel who until recently might have shot Taran'atar on sight.

A Starfleet captain would have had Taran'atar on the Defiant, a voice in the back of her head said. *Probably alongside a speech about how we'll never learn to trust each other until someone takes the first step.*

Kira slapped the voice down. *I'm not a Starfleet captain.*

But that single thought brought with it another—one that had been recurring ever since Starfleet had first come to the station more than seven years ago. The thought had become more prominent since Shakaar had informed her how close Bajor was again to joining the Federation. When that happened, the Militia would be absorbed into Starfleet, and all Bajoran officers and enlisted personnel who chose to stay would have to trade their uniforms for another, one that stood not just for one world, but a plurality. It was, she knew, what DS9 had been about from the beginning. In part it was also what Bajor's role in the relief efforts to Cardassia was about, and this mission to help the Europani—Bajor was learning to think outside the confines of one planet and one people. And if that were true, then the next logical step for Kira would be to put on a Starfleet uniform again, as she'd done to help the Cardassian resistance. She recalled vividly that at the time, it had been a strange fit.

But was it the right *fit?*

Her musings were interrupted by Taran'atar. "I have another question, Colonel. You and President Silverio indicated that you intend to restore Europa Nova."

"Of course."

"There's no known way to dispose of theta radiation on this scale. The most efficient course would be to relocate the inhabitants to another planet."

"This is their *home*."

"I don't understand." Taran'atar seemed genuinely confused. "It is simply a planet. To try to restore it is a waste of resources."

Kira shook her head. "There's nothing 'simple' about it, Taran'atar. Saving a home is never a waste."

"Please explain."

She had expected the request to be phrased disdainfully, but Taran'atar seemed genuinely curious. *I guess that comes with age,* she thought with mild amusement. Taran'atar was twenty-two years old, which made him an "Honored Elder" by Jem'Hadar standards. Bred solely for military combat, few Jem'Hadar lived past the age of ten, and fewer still survived even that long.

Kira started several sentences in her head before finally committing to one. "I've spent my life fighting for Bajor. It isn't just a planet I happened to be born on. It's *home*."

"You keep using that word. My home has always been where the Founders tell me to be. A Jem'Hadar's home is his unit."

Seizing on that statement, Kira said, "A people can be defined by where they come from. Who the Bajorans are is shaped in part by our world. It's part of what ties us to the Prophets. The Cardassians didn't belong there, so I fought them. All my life, I've fought *for* Bajor because that is *my* unit."

She thought Taran'atar would grasp the analogy, but he seemed to focus on something else. "You believe caring for your home brings you closer to your gods?"

"I suppose that's one way of looking at it," she said neutrally.

"Yet your gods cast you out."

On reflex, Kira's hand went to her right ear, which had gone unadorned since she'd been Attainted. "Not my gods," she said, quietly but firmly. "Only a few men and women who claim to represent them."

She thought Taran'atar would challenge her statement. Instead, as the clouds outside the viewport cleared, he reported, "Entering lower atmosphere. Setting course for the southern continent."

As the *Euphrates* scanned for life-forms and began beaming people up, nothing more was said about homes and gods. Kira was both annoyed and grateful. Annoyed, because it was in her nature to argue and defend her position, and she was damned if she'd let some Jem'Hadar make light of her devotion to her homeworld. Grateful, because her being exiled from the Bajoran religious community was still an open wound, and the conversation was taking a direction that would surely pour salt on it.

Part of the problem was her own inability to convey her feelings about faith properly. She remembered something Istani Reyla had said to her when she was a child: "One does not explain faith. One simply has it or does not."

And Kira did have faith—in Bajor, and in the Prophets. She always had. It had kept her going during those cold winter nights in the caves, hiding from the Cardassian patrols, with not enough clothes to keep her warm, unable to build a fire for fear of being detected. It would keep her going now, too. *After all, the Prophets didn't "cast me out," Vedek Yevir did. If I learned nothing else from Kai Winn's thankfully brief reign, it's that even the clergy isn't perfect.*

Part of it might also have been that Taran'atar was struggling with his own crisis of faith ever since he returned from Sindorin. Questioning Kira about her own spiritual dilemma was the only way he had to at least attempt to resolve it. He simply wasn't equipped to cope with the doubts that had taken root in his mind. She understood his turmoil; to some degree, she even shared it. But she would never lose faith, never give up.

She wouldn't give up Europa Nova, either. These people, in their own way, fought for their home, same as she always had, whether against the Cardassians or the Dominion, and she would make sure they wouldn't lose it, either.

"Ready to transport the first wave, Commander."

Vaughn nodded to Chief Jeannette Chao as she manipulated the controls in transporter bay one. The *Defiant*'s primary bay was fairly small—there was barely room for Vaughn, Chao, and Ensign Gordimer. The other transporter bay on deck two, as well as the cargo transporter on deck three, were performing similar functions. They would keep going until they had approximately a hundred and fifty refugees, then head back to Deep Space 9 to drop them off.

Getting so many people onto a ship with a normal complement of forty was going to be something of a challenge, particularly when most of them would be the upper echelons of the Europani political structure. The burden on life-support would be considerable. *Still,* Vaughn thought, *"needs must as the devil drives."* Vaughn had also made sure that Ensign Gordimer had issued hand phasers to the security staff, just in case.

Chao manipulated the controls, and seven humans materialized on the platform, along with one tall, familiar Andorian: Charivretha zh'Thane. Her feather-like white hair had been styled in a manner that made her head look like a negative-image *zletha* flower, complete with antennae substituting for the stamen, a blossom with blue petals and a white stem.

At the sight of Vaughn, she broke into a smile. "Elias? Is that really you?"

Vaughn nodded. "Councillor zh'Thane."

"Please, Elias, I'm in no mood for formality," she said in her mildly accented voice as she stepped down from the platform.

Before responding, Vaughn turned to the Europani, most of whom were well dressed and carried themselves with the arrogance Vaughn had come to associate with politicians. *Of course, they're the first to beam out.* To her credit, President Silverio was not among them.

"Greetings and welcome aboard the Federation *Starship Defiant.* I am Commander Elias Vaughn, in charge of this vessel. If you will all please follow Ensign Gordimer, he'll escort you to the mess hall. As soon as we're at capacity, you'll be taken to Deep Space 9."

"The mess hall?" one of the men said—a short, rotund man with receding brown hair and a neatly trimmed beard. "I had assumed we would be getting quarters."

"You will on the station, sir," Vaughn said. "However, the *Defiant* is not equipped with such facilities."

"I've seen Federation starships—you can't expect me to believe that you don't have proper quarters!"

"The *Defiant* is primarily a warship, sir," Vaughn said calmly.

"I'm sure the mess hall will be fine," a tall woman with long, straight, jet-black hair said as she moved toward the door. Others followed suit.

The balding man, however, stayed put. "Commander, do you have any idea who I am?"

"I'm afraid not, sir."

"I am the minister of agriculture, one of the most important people on this planet—"

The long-haired woman rolled her eyes. "Give it a rest, Sergio."

Disregarding this request, the minister put his hands on his hips. "I refuse to be transported on this vessel! I demand to be taken to one of the other starships! One with proper facilities!"

Keeping his gaze fixed on Sergio, Vaughn said, "Chief Chao, prepare to transport the minister back to the surface. Minister, I'm sure you can arrange ground transport to Spilimbergo, which is not very far from L'Aquila. At that point, you can no doubt get on the list for transport to the *Gryphon*. Ensign Gordimer, please see the rest of these good people to the mess hall."

"Yes, sir. If you will all follow me, please," Gordimer said as he led the assorted politicians out of the room.

The minister, meanwhile, had gone pale. "On the list?"

"Someone as important as you can surely arrange for something, sir."

The minister sputtered for a moment, then quickly ran after the departing crowd.

Vretha zh'Thane had remained behind. "Very nicely handled, Elias, as always. But then, you never had any patience with politicians, did you?"

"Chief Chao, please prepare to beam the next wave up. Energize as soon as Ensign Gordimer returns."

"Yes, sir."

Indicating the door, Vaughn said, "Councillor?"

Chuckling, Vretha said, "Of course, *Commander.*" She inserted her arm into the crook of Vaughn's, and walked out the door with him.

"You haven't changed much since the last time I saw you," Vaughn said as they proceeded down the narrow corridor. Allowing himself a small smile, he added, "Except for the hair, of course."

"I needed a change, and I thought a floral hairdo would be fitting for negotiations with a world that prides itself on work in the biological sciences. Where are you taking me?"

"The bridge."

"Really?" Vretha said with a wry smile.

"You're a Federation dignitary. It seems only appropriate."

Again, Vretha chuckled. "The ironic thing is, I was going to make a side trip to DS9 in any case. I wanted to see my *chei.*"

"You'd be very proud. Ensign ch'Thane is a fine officer."

The smile fell, and Vretha's arm tightened in

Vaughn's. "Yes, I'm sure he is. However, there are other—" She hesitated.

Vaughn remembered ch'Thane's comment in ops about not having been home in a while. For the first time, he spoke in a gentler tone. "Vretha, if there's a problem, you can tell me."

They arrived at the bridge. "We'll talk later, Elias," Vretha said with finality—yet also with certainty. Vaughn recognized the tone of a parent whose child was a source of consternation.

Ensign Tenmei vacated the command chair as Vaughn entered. Without even looking at Vaughn, she said, "Sir, we've detected something of interest on the surface." As she took her position at the conn, she activated the viewscreen to show a sensor log. "This is near one of the small towns on the east coast of the northern continent—a place called Costa Rocosa."

The viewscreen displayed a familiar image: the energy signature of a gateway.

Costa Rocosa was on the *Rio Grande*'s agenda. *"Defiant* to *Rio Grande."*

"Bowers here."

"Lieutenant, have you reached Costa Rocosa yet?"

"Not until the next trip, sir."

"Very well." Turning to the crewperson at ops, he said, "Contact the local authorities on Costa Rocosa. Tell them I'll be beaming down to the coordinates of that gateway." Turning back to the conn, he said, "Good work, Ensign. You're in command until I return. Alert Colonel Kira and the other Starfleet vessels to what you've found."

"Yes, sir," the young woman said.

To Vretha, he said as he approached the rear exit,

"Councillor, I think it would be best if you waited in the mess hall with the others."

"Of course, Commander." Vaughn was relieved that she didn't protest, but simply followed him off the bridge.

"Colonel, I have good news and bad news."

Vaughn stood on a large, craggy rock, waves from a reddish-blue ocean crashing only a few meters to his right. Wind blew through his silver hair, sometimes hard enough to cause him to stumble on the uneven ground. That wind also forced him to raise his voice in order for Kira to hear him through his combadge.

Costa Rocosa was aptly named. Spanish for "rocky coast," this fishing town consisted of several well-built stone houses near the coastline, which was composed entirely of rock. *No beachfront property here,* Vaughn observed. The locals had constructed an extensive marina around one of the larger stony outcroppings.

Vaughn's present location was a much smaller outcropping about fifty meters south of that dock. The town had a population of less than a thousand, and it seemed like all of them had gathered near this outcropping since Vaughn had beamed down. One, a tall, skinny, black-haired and -bearded man named Nieto, had identified himself as the mayor and had offered to render any assistance necessary to the commander. Vaughn had thanked him politely and then ignored him and the others while he examined the strange phenomenon on the rocks.

Sitting on the next rock over was, for lack of a better phrase, a hole in space. Through this hole, Vaughn saw not the rocks and breaking waves of Costa Rocosa that he knew to be on the other side of it, but instead an arid expanse of blue sand being blown by winds even harsher than those buffetting Vaughn. A heavy cover of dark red clouds in an even darker sky obscured the sun. At the moment, there was no sign of any life, but Vaughn's tricorder had indicated a thin-but-bearable oxygen/nitrogen atmosphere.

After the tricorder completed its analysis, Vaughn had contacted Kira on the *Euphrates*.

Vaughn continued. "The good news is that this is indeed a working gateway, and it's programmed for a single location." The other gateways that had been discovered tended to be on random settings, jumping from one location to another. Had that been the case, it would have been potentially dangerous for evacuation purposes.

"What's the bad news?"

"As far as I can tell, the location in question is Torona IV—the homeworld of the Jarada."

"And they are . . . ?"

"A fussy, somewhat xenophobic people that insist on very specific protocols. During first contact, the Starfleet captain mispronounced a word in their language, and they went into a twenty-year snit. Relations reopened about twelve years ago, but it's been a struggle to maintain those relations—and they've steadfastly refused to let any aliens set foot on their homeworld. The last people to try were the crew of a transport that needed to make an emergency landing about five years ago. The Jarada fired on the ship and all four crew members died in the resulting explosion. Things have been a trifle sour since then."

Kira spoke sharply. *"Commander, we* have *to use*

that gateway. I just got a report from the Gryphon *that the transporters will be useless in eight hours, which is sooner than we thought. We have to get two million people off-planet with twenty ships that, filled to capacity, will take less than five hundred thousand at a time."*

Vaughn refrained from pointing out that he knew that already. "I don't believe we can risk sending people through the gateway without contacting the Jaradan authorities first."

A pause. *"Agreed. But make it fast, Commander. Do whatever you have to do to convince them to take the refugees."*

"Aye, sir. Vaughn to *Intrepid*."

"Emick here."

"Walter, I need a favor. Your library computer should have records of all the contacts with the Jarada, yes?" The *Defiant,* built for combat, had a very limited library computer, generally only used for temporary storage of mission-specific data. That would change soon enough when the *Defiant* returned to the Gamma Quadrant, but for now, the only permanently stored material tended to relate to military and intelligence matters, not diplomatic ones.

"Of course."

"Could you download it to my tricorder, please?" Quickly, Vaughn explained the situation.

"I don't envy you your task, Elias. The Jarada won't be easy to negotiate with."

"There's no such thing as an easy negotiation, Walter. If there was, you wouldn't need to negotiate in the first place."

"You've gotten cynical in your old age, Elias,"

Emick said with a chuckle. *"You should have the data now."*

"Thank you. Vaughn out."

As Vaughn looked over the material, Nieto approached him again, being helped up the uneven surface with the aid of a young blonde. "Commander, if I may intrude—this thing is a portal to another world, yes?"

"It would certainly appear so, Mayor Nieto," Vaughn said without looking at the taller man. He continued to study the data, running through the pronunciation of the ritual greeting in his head.

"I assume this world is habitable?"

"It reads as Class M, yes."

Smiling under his thick beard, Nieto said, "Then, if I may ask—why the delay in allowing my people to go through it? There would appear to be plenty of space."

"It's an inhabited planet, Mr. Mayor. We need to make contact with the local government and obtain their permission first."

Nieto scratched his beard thoughtfully. "I see. And how long will this take?"

"I can't say at the moment," Vaughn said honestly, frowning at his tricorder. "Sir, if you'd be so kind as to return to your people. I need to finish my preparations for making contact."

"Of course, Commander, my apologies, but please understand my position," Nieto said, and his smile fell. "There is deadly radiation in our sky. Our entire world is rapidly becoming uninhabitable, perhaps permanently. We are a small town, often ignored even during the height of the fishing season. In times like these, it is the small ones who are forgotten. I will not allow that to happen to the good citizens of Costa Rocosa."

Vaughn finally turned to look at Nieto, and he could see the concern in the man's eyes. "I can assure you, Mayor Nieto, that we intend to get everyone off this planet long before the radiation becomes lethal, regardless of how large the town is. However, the Jarada will need to be contacted first. Now please, if you could tell your people what I told you and let me complete my work."

"Very well, Commander. I appreciate everything you are doing for us."

"You're quite welcome, sir. Now, if you please?" He indicated the crowd of Costa Rocosan people, who, Vaughn noticed, were buzzing with more chatter and looked anxious.

With any luck, he can reassure them the way I reassured him, Vaughn thought. *Let's hope that reassurance was warranted.*

Again helped by the blonde, Nieto moved back to his constituency. Turning back to the gateway, Vaughn set his tricorder to boost his combadge's signal. *Here goes nothing,* he thought.

"Attention Jaradan authorities. This is Commander Elias Vaughn of Starfleet, representing the United Federation of Planets." Remembering the Jarada's preference for dealing with those in charge from his recent crash course in Jaradan relations, he added, "And commanding officer of the *U.S.S. Defiant.*" He took a deep breath, then said, *"Ârd klaxon lís blajhblon ârg níc calníc ârd trasulâ rass tass trasulâ."* Wishing he'd thought to ask Kira to beam him down a glass of water, Vaughn cleared his throat before continuing. "As you may be aware, there is an interspatial gateway linking your world with another, a human colony known as Europa Nova. It is through that gateway that I am contacting you now. Europa Nova is suffering an ecological crisis and needs to be evacuated. We respectfully request permission to bring people through the gateway to your world."

A lengthy pause ensued. The sound of the wind combined with the crashing of the waves might have sounded idyllic and peaceful to Vaughn's ears, had they not also been intermingled with the sounds of Nieto speaking to the Costa Rocosans. Vaughn couldn't make out the mayor's words over the din of the natural noises, but the buzz from the crowd itself had dulled, which Vaughn chose to view as an encouraging sign.

"You honor us with the proper greeting," came a haughty voice from Vaughn's combadge. *"For that reason, we will grant you the consideration of a proper warning. Do not set foot on our world, or you will be killed."*

"To whom have I the honor of speaking?"

"You have been given your warning, commander of the Defiant. *"*

Accepting that the Jarada would not identify him- or herself, Vaughn said, "I ask that you rescind it."

"These gateways you describe have caused incursions on our worlds. Three hostile aliens attacked one of our hives on Torona Alpha and destroyed it. No one may step on our soil and live."

Vaughn thought quickly. A humanitarian appeal would do no good—these people had no compunction about firing on a ship in distress. For that matter, during the contact with the *Enterprise,* Jaradan actions almost resulted in the death of four people, including Jean-Luc Picard. Their strategic importance to the

Federation had lessened with the alliance between the Federation and the Romulans during the Dominion War, and no formal treaties had ever been signed.

So what Vaughn was about to do was, strictly speaking, against regulations.

"If you agree to help us, we will share all our intelligence about the gateways. We have encountered them before, and devoted considerable resources to studying them. That study is still ongoing, and we will also share any subsequent data with you. I can tell you this much—the gateways do present a long-term danger to your technological infrastructure, and possibly your very ecosystem. The nature of that danger will also be shared—but only if you agree to accept Europani refugees and guarantee their safety until Starfleet can arrange their transport off your planet."

Another pause. The wind howled louder. Nieto had stopped talking. An especially large wave crashed against a nearby rock and Vaughn—who had gained a fine layer of mist on his person in the time since he beamed down—was splashed with a bit of backwash from it.

"You will share this intelligence before we allow any to step on our soil."

"I will share some of it. The rest will come after the first refugees have passed though the gateway unmolested."

Yet another pause. *"Very well, commander of the* Defiant. *A forcefield has been erected in the area proximate to the gateway. It will accommodate five hundred thousand members of your species. You will send that precise number through and no more, or the agreement will be considered in abeyance."*

Vaughn noticed that the winds on Torona IV had suddenly stopped. "Very well. If any harm comes to those five hundred thousand, we shall likewise consider the agreement in abeyance."

"Any who step outside the boundaries established by the forcefield will die."

"Understood," Vaughn said. *Let's hope Mayor Nieto and his people aren't partial to taking long strolls.* "My thanks to your government. *Trasulâ ríss blajhblon ârd."*

"Again, you honor us with an appropriate salutation, commander of the Defiant. *See that you continue to do us honor and we will not do you harm."*

Letting out a breath he didn't know he was holding, Vaughn tapped his combadge to fill Kira in.

Bill Ross will probably have a seizure when he finds out I agreed to share intel with a semi-hostile government, Vaughn thought grimly. He felt no concern about it, however. It was the only way to save these people's lives.

7

THE DENORIOS BELT

I'M GOING TO DIE, Nog thought.

It was, on the face of it, a stupid way to go: only a few thousand kilometers from Deep Space 9, in a runabout, under fire from an unknown ship. But if AR-558 had taught him anything, it was that the universe was stupid and cruel and arbitrary. So Nog was completely at peace with the fact that—after surviving the taking of the station by the Dominion, a covert mission into Dominion territory, the attack on AR-558, the destruction of the previous *Defiant,* and so much else—he would die under such ridiculous circumstances as this.

His only regret was that he would never find out what happened to Jake.

"Picking up another ship!" Shar said urgently, then looked sharply at Nog and smiled. "It's the *Defiant!*"

Nog looked at his own sensor display. Half the systems were offline, but he could see the *Defiant* bearing down on the enemy vessel.

"I can't get a specific life-sign reading," Shar continued, "but it looks like the *Defiant* is filled beyond its capacity."

"Probably Europani refugees," Nog said in a steely voice. He expected to feel a sense of gratitude that he was likely going to survive. He was relieved that there was still a chance he might find Jake, but for his own survival, he felt nothing.

"Attention unidentified ship," came Vaughn's steady voice over the com system. *"You have fired on a Starfleet vessel. Surrender or suffer the consequences."*

In response, the ship fired its forward weapons on the *Defiant* and its aft ones on the *Sungari.*

"Matter-antimatter containment field weakening!" Shar said over the din of exploding consoles. "And *Defiant* shields are at forty percent!"

Nog winced. His Shelliak modulator weakened the *Defiant*'s shields against directed energy fire, and this ladrion weapon of theirs was a particularly nasty example of the type. And the *Sungari,* of course, no longer had shields. "Eject the core."

"Ejection systems offline." The lights went out. "In fact, at this point, I would venture to say that the entire ship is offline."

Nog looked down at a dark console he could now barely see. Even the emergency lights weren't working. The only illumination came through the porthole from the external lights of the *Defiant* and the unidentified vessel. The *Sungari* was dead in space. If even the emergency systems were out, then the containment field was also down. *Which means that this runabout is a big duranium bomb about to go off. Maybe that's why I didn't feel relieved—I'm not alive yet.*

More illumination as the *Defiant* fired its pulse phasers. Thanks to the *Sungari's* attack, the enemy ship was also without shields. The phaser bolts tore through the hull as if it were tissue paper, and the ship exploded a moment later.

Good, Nog thought, urgently slapping his combadge, *they can lower shields for transport now.* "*Sungari* to *Defiant*. Emergency beam-out."

The room started to fade into a silver haze, then coalesced into the main transporter bay of the *Defiant*. He looked to his right, and saw Shar, who let out a long breath.

From the console, Chief Chao tapped her combadge. "Got them, sir."

"Are they injured?"

Tapping his own combadge, Nog said, "We're fine, Commander."

"Good. Report to the bridge."

"The *Sungari's* about to breach, Commander. You need to—"

"We're aware of the situation, Lieutenant. Remote shutdown isn't working, so we're using the tractor beam to push the ship as far away from the station and the wormhole as possible."

"Still inside the belt, though?" Nog asked.

"Yes. Why?"

Nog turned to Shar. "Will that affect the gases in the belt for the burst?"

Shar shook his head. "It shouldn't."

"Good," Nog said, then he moved to the transporter bay door.

As soon as the doors opened, his sensitive ears were assaulted with a cacophony of sound. Dozens of human civilians were standing in the hallways, along with a few security guards. Nog noticed that the guards were carrying phasers, which he thought might have been a tad excessive. The humans—presumably the Europani refugees—looked tired and scared. Nog couldn't bring himself to be surprised at that.

Shar had an odd look on his face, and one finger brushed against his right antenna. "You okay?" Nog asked.

"Yes, it's just something in the air. This many people crowded together, it changes the nature of the atmosphere. It's usually a bit more—well, sterile than this."

Nog nodded in understanding as he and Shar entered the bridge. Some debris from the enemy ship was visible in the lower right-hand corner of the viewscreen, but its focus was on the *Sungari*. The runabout's running lights were extinguished. A blue tractor beam engulfed the runabout and thrust it away from the debris.

Vaughn fixed his steely gaze upon the two junior officers. "Did they identify themselves at all?"

"No sir," Nog said dutifully. "They attacked without any warning."

The young Ferengi turned back to the viewscreen to see the *Sungari* moving farther away and deeper into the Denorios Belt—before exploding. Sighing, Nog found himself wondering how much longer Starfleet would continue replacing the station's runabouts.

"Set course back for DS9, Ensign," Vaughn said to Tenmei. "We'll collect and examine the debris once we've offloaded the refugees."

A thought occurred to Nog. "Sir, with all due respect—you took a very big risk, engaging in battle with all these refugees on board."

"We were the only option, Lieutenant. There aren't any ships docked at DS9 at the moment, and the station itself is out of range. In any event, there was every chance that the vessel would have turned its attention to the station after disposing of you two. We couldn't take that risk, even with so many civilians on board."

"Thank you, sir." Then remembering the whole reason for their trip to the Denorios Belt in the first place, he added, "Uh, sir, I'm not sure if Lieutenant Dax told you, but Ensign ch'Thane and I have determined a course of action that might disrupt the gateways."

"Thirishar, there you are."

Shar felt like a *grelth* had started weaving a web in his stomach. The voice spoke in Andorii, and it was one he hadn't heard in person for five years.

He turned to take in the unexpected sight of Charivretha zh'Thane, his *zhavey*. She had changed her hair since their last communication, and was as overdressed as her position always required her to be. She was walking with a group of Europani refugees who were being escorted onto the station by Ensigns Gordimer and Ling.

"I wasn't expecting to see you here, *Zhavey*."

She broke off from the crowd to approach her only child. Gordimer gave her a look, then saw Shar. Shar nodded quickly at the security guard, who simply shrugged and resumed his escorting duties.

"I was on Europa Nova. We're trying to convince them to join the Federation, and I was negotiating. Ironically, the Federation's response to this crisis may help me solidify my argument—assuming there's a Europa Nova left when all is said and done." She stared at him. "I didn't realize you were on board. I would've thought you'd have been on the bridge when Elias brought me there."

"I was on the *Sungari*. They beamed me over before it blew up."

"Blew up?" Her voice raised an octave. "Obviously, I should have stayed on the bridge."

Shar's antennae quivered. "It's all right, *Zhavey*, everything turned out fine." He hesitated, and then lied. "It's good to see you."

Vretha's own antennae did likewise. "It's especially good to see you given what happened to your runabout. I was actually going to come to the station after I was done on Europa Nova in any case. We need to talk, Thirishar."

What would be the point? Shar almost said aloud, but he kept the respectful mask plastered to his face. "I'm afraid I can't right now, *Zhavey*. The crisis is not—"

Waving her hand in what appeared to be a dismissive gesture, Vretha said, "Of course not now, Thirishar. You have duties to perform, and I need to check on my ship—I lent it to the relief efforts so they could get the children off-planet right away. We'll talk when we both have time to do so." She stared Shar directly in the eye. "But we *will* talk. We have danced around this subject for far too long."

"Yes, *Zhavey,*" Shar said dutifully.

"You always say 'yes, *Zhavey*' in that respectful tone," Vretha noted, "yet you never change, Thirishar. It is a stalling tactic I will not tolerate any longer."

"I'm sorry, *Zhavey.*"

"No, I don't think you are." Vretha's voice sounded sad now. "And that is a pity." She closed her eyes. "But enough of this. We will speak later. Be whole, Thirishar." With that, she walked off.

Shar struggled to keep his emotions in check. *It would not do to smash a bulkhead right now with all this security and these civilians around.* He latched on to the anger, wrestled with it, and forced it down into the dark corner of his mind where it normally lived— and from which it inevitably clawed its way out every time he talked to Vretha.

Once he felt he was under sufficient control, he also walked off the *Defiant* and into the docking ring corridor, where he saw Nog. "There you are," the Ferengi said. "Was that your—what's the word? *Zhavey?*"

"Yes, it was."

Shar himself hadn't noticed any alteration in his voice at first, but Nog almost flinched from Shar's tone. *Perhaps I haven't buried my anger as efficiently as I believed,* he thought with a sigh. "I'm sorry, Lieutenant," Shar said quickly. "I'm afraid that she does not bring out the best in me."

Smiling, Nog said, "That's all right. C'mon, we need to head to ops to brief everyone on our brilliant theory." As they walked toward a turbolift, Nog added, "Mothers can be difficult. Mine took Father for all he was worth before the marriage contract ended, then remarried a richer man."

Frowning, Shar thought back to the conversations about Ferengi mores that they'd had in the *Sungari*. "I thought Ferengi women couldn't do that sort of thing before the reforms."

"Well, it was her father's doing, really. I think. Honestly, I don't remember most of that—I was very young. Father was destitute after that, and took me here to work for Uncle Quark."

"And now he's the Grand Nagus." Shar considered, then smiled. "It seems to me that your mother should have cause to regret her decision."

Nog laughed. "Probably. I wonder if Father's gotten in touch with her since going home to Ferenginar."

Shar smiled, and he already felt better, the anger well and truly buried now. *This is where I belong,* Zhavey, *not back on Andor—no matter what you or anyone else says.*

He also had to admire Nog's grace under pressure. He hadn't let their life-or-death situation get to him at all. *I suppose that comes of spending most of the war on the front lines.* Shar himself had been fortunate enough to miss any direct combat, spending most of the war working feverishly in a lab.

As they entered the turbolift, Shar said, "Let us go and be brilliant, my friend."

Nog grinned. "Ops."

8

EUROPA NOVA

"Take all transporters offline."

It was an order Kira had not looked forward to giving, but she'd known all along it was inevitable. Antimatter waste now made up an entire orbit of Europa Nova, forming a deadly green ring around the planet. The ring was thickest at the gateway, of course, the point from which the cloud of hazardous material originated, and it thinned as it arced above the planet surface. Now every ship needed to keep its shields up to protect them from the radiation. The concentration was such that, even at the polar regions, transporters were unreliable.

At least Nog's shield modulator is working, she thought, thanking the Prophets for her operations officer's impeccable timing in consummating his business deal just when they needed it most.

The *Gryphon,* the *Halloran,* and the *Xhosa* were on their way to Deep Space 9 to drop off more refugees, and the *Defiant* was already there doing the same. The *Xhosa* had somehow managed to make some extra room, relieving the *Euphrates* of the refugees it had picked up, allowing Kira to remain in charge of the evacuation.

Europa Nova's surface transporters—still operational for the time being—were being used to bring the five hundred thousand the Jarada were allowing to Costa Rocosa to make use of the gateway there.

"Transporters offline," Captain Emick acknowledged, and Colonel Lenaris echoed the reply a moment later, followed by the civilian captains.

"Implement plan B," Kira ordered.

"We've found a landing site for the Intrepid," Emick said. *"It's right outside Padilla. I think we can take the city's remaining population on this run."*

"Good."

"Colonel," Taran'atar said, "I'm detecting a dense concentration of theta radiation in the upper atmosphere."

The voice of one of the officers on the *Intrepid* came through the comlink. *"Confirmed,"* she said. *"A solid mass of waste material has fallen out of orbit. On its present course, it'll land four kilometers due west of Spilimbergo."*

Kira checked the configuration of the convoy. The *Gryphon* had been evacuating Spilimbergo. Between the starship and the assorted private craft, not to mention the earlier evac of the children, a bit less than half of the city's population of three hundred and fifty thousand had been evacuated thus far. Right now, with the *Gryphon* on its way to the Bajoran system, the *Euphrates* was in closest proximity to the threat.

Without hesitating, Kira changed course and reset the shields for an atmospheric entry. "Kira to Bashir."

"Bashir here," said a very tired-sounding chief medical officer.

"Doctor, what would be the effects of a meteoric collision of a mass putting out"—she glanced at her console—"a hundred thousand kilorads of theta radiation four kilometers from a population center?"

"In a word, devastating. I could give you precise figures if you want, but the short version is the population center would be as good as dead."

"That's what I thought you were going to say."

Emick spoke up. *"Colonel, what are you doing?"*

"Saving lives," Kira said. "Doctor, how far from the population center would the waste need to be to minimize the danger?"

"Well, on another planet would be ideal."

"Julian . . ."

"Sorry, Colonel. I would estimate a minimum of a hundred kilometers."

Next to her, Taran'atar said, "I have reconfigured the tractor beam with additional power from the warp drive." He turned to Kira. "I assume your intent is to divert the meteorite."

Grateful for the Jem'Hadar's instincts, she said, "That's the plan. Activate the beam on my mark."

"Why not just destroy it?" Bashir asked.

Emick replied, *"Doctor, if we could just destroy the antimatter waste with phasers, we wouldn't be in this* mess in the first place. Colonel, you sure you know what you're doing?"

"*Euphrates* is the only ship close enough, Captain," Kira said as she guided the ship through the cloud cover. "Our new modulated shields are protecting us against the radiation. As it is, we're cutting it close."

The other *Intrepid* officer said, "*Colonel, I've found a lake about a hundred seventy-five kilometers northwest of Spilimbergo. You should be able to divert the mass there. The only life-form readings I'm getting within a hundred kilometers are flora.*"

Kira found that lake on her sensor display. The locals called it Lago DeBacco. "Got it. Thanks."

"*Good luck, Colonel,*" Emick said. "*With your permission, I'll inform President Silverio.*"

"Thank you, Captain. Kira out."

As the *Euphrates* came out of the cloud cover, Kira quickly ran her fingers over the console, calculating the course she'd need to take. She had to angle her approach just right so that, when the tractor beam was activated, she'd be able to divert the meteorite to the lake in question. It was a delicate piece of navigation, made more challenging by having to account for prevailing winds—which, it turned out, were pretty fierce near Lago DeBacco.

Just like the good old days, she thought with a half-smile. Piloting skimmers around Dakhur Province in the dead of winter, avoiding the Cardassian patrols. No sensors worth mentioning, wind shear way beyond the skimmer's capacity, flying by the seats of their collective pants. All she had to worry about was keeping alive and watching the other cell members' backs, with the assured faith that the Prophets would guide them to freedom if they just kept fighting, kept *believing*. Politics didn't matter. You didn't have to say the right thing or not step on the appropriate toes or go through a chain of command—it was just you, the cell, and the enemy.

As the *Euphrates* neared the mass—which was careening toward the surface at an alarming rate, cutting a trail of green death across the sky as it fell—Kira shook her head at her own wistfulness. *Great, now I'm getting nostalgic for the Occupation. What does that say about my life?*

"Tractor beam ready," Taran'atar said.

It's so simple for you, she thought at her Jem'Hadar companion. *You have your duty, and you perform it. You don't have to worry about what Starfleet will think or what the Vedek Assembly will think or what the Ministry will think or what the Bajoran people will think. You just have to do what you're told.*

Sometimes Kira longed for that kind of simplicity.

The console beeped—they were in range. She waited until the angle of approach was just right, then said, "Activate tractor beam."

As she spoke, she changed course.

Her stomach lurched violently as the runabout—which had been accelerating toward the surface of the planet at maximum impulse—altered its flight path upward.

"Tractor beam holding," Taran'atar said.

Kira could only nod. The bitter taste of half-digested *hasperat* started to well up in her throat. *It's been way too long since I did something like this,* she thought. *Stomach's not used to it. Been spending too much damn time sitting at a desk.*

Taran'atar, of course, did not look in the least bit put out. "We are exceeding the tractor-beam tolerances."

Forcing the *hasperat* down, she said, "Just another six seconds."

The *Euphrates* continued to arc away from the surface, the ship fighting against the momentum of the antimatter waste to which it was tethered. The impulse engines strained, but held.

Then, finally, when the mass had changed course sufficiently to land in Lago DeBacco, Kira said, "Disengage tractor beam."

The *Euphrates* lurched as, no longer burdened with the tremendous mass, its velocity jumped suddenly. Once again, Kira's stomach heaved, but she kept her hands on the controls. Something blew out in one of the aft consoles. She couldn't afford to slow the runabout down, as any moment . . .

A shock wave rocked the *Euphrates* as the meteorite collided with the westernmost side of the lake. Kira was able to remain in her seat, but only barely. *All those years of bouncing around in Bajoran skimmers pays off,* she thought with a bitter smile. The shock wave was considerably less than a direct impact would have been—the *Euphrates*'s tractoring also served to retard the meteorite's rate of descent, greatly reducing the force of its landing.

"Shields have held," Taran'atar said. "No radiation has penetrated. We remain uncontaminated. But this vessel's tractor-beam generator has burned out."

Kira smiled. *We did it.*

Then she put Lago DeBacco on the main viewer.

The smile fell.

Five minutes ago, Lago DeBacco had been a lush, thriving lake. Reddish-blue water flowed gently across, fed from several local rivers that acted as tributaries. An entire ecosystem had lived in it—a teeming mass of plant life.

Now, in spots where the runabout's optical sensors could penetrate the billowing green mist that filled the valley—irradiated water vapor from the lake—the terrain was reduced to blasted ruin. Trees and bushes proximate to ground zero that weren't vaporized were already showing signs of decay from the theta radiation. No one would be able to approach Lago De-Bacco without decontamination forcefields for many years to come.

Europa Nova had its first scar.

Kira swore an oath right there that it would also be the last.

"We are receiving a communication from L'Aquila, Colonel," said Taran'atar. "It is President Silverio."

Sighing, Kira said, "On screen." *Here it comes. The outrage at destroying such a beautiful piece of nature. The anger at not being consulted. I so hate politicians.*

Grazia Silverio's pleasant face appeared on the screen, looking even more haggard than before. The bags under her eyes had doubled in size since Kira had last seen her, and her jowls seemed to droop even more. The theta radiation that they were flying through interfered somewhat with the communication, and the image blinked in and out. *"Colonel, Captain Emick tells me the town of Spilimbergo owes you a debt of gratitude."*

Kira blinked. "Uh—"

"I understand you diverted the meteorite that was

endangering the town at considerable risk to your-self."

"Honestly, ma'am, the only risk was that it would fail to divert far enough to save Spilimbergo. Starfleet makes its runabouts pretty sturdy." That much, at least, was true. The structural integrity field had held up with no sign of strain. If she'd tried that move with one of the old Bajoran skimmers, it would have torn itself apart.

"Apf," she said, waving her arm. *"Don't give me false modesty. The point is, you took the risk, and saved lives. And you got us that gateway at Costa Rocosa. You have my gratitude for that."*

"Thank you, ma'am, although Commander Vaughn found the gateway."

"Grazia, it's Grazia," she said with a tired smile. Then she was distracted by something off-screen. *"What? Oh, all right. I must go, Colonel—there is still much to do, but I wanted to thank you personally. As long as you're in charge, I'm sure we'll get through this."*

With that, she signed off.

As the *Euphrates* came out of the atmosphere and back into orbit, a signal came through from Vaughn, back on the station.

"Go ahead, Commander."

"Good news, Colonel. Lieutenant Nog and Ensign ch'Thane have devised a method of disrupting the gateways—possibly even shutting them down permanently. It's a modified tachyon burst that can be easily done from the Defiant."

"Glad to hear it, Commander. Would we have to do this on a gateway-by-gateway basis or would it knock out the whole network?"

"Ensign ch'Thane seems to think that activating it at one gateway will cripple the entire network at once. That might cause more problems than it solves, of course."

Kira let out a breath through her teeth. Vaughn was right—who knew what kind of uses the gateways were being put to? Yes, the sudden mass opening of the gateways was causing chaos all over the quadrant—if not the entire galaxy—but shutting them down just as suddenly wouldn't necessarily improve things.

On the other hand, the Iconians were, from all reports, lording this technology all over the Alpha Quadrant. It was about time the tables were turned. Besides, the reports Kira had been monitoring from Starfleet indicated that the situation was just getting worse— problems ranging from vandalism to murder to the rekindling of hostilities between governments were rampant. All-out war might well have been the next consequence unless something radical was done soon to stem the tide. Shutting down the gateways might well be it . . . especially if doing so stopped more antimatter waste from coming into orbit of Europa Nova.

Then again, it would also cut off what was rapidly becoming their most important evac point: the gateway at Costa Rocosa.

So, with extreme reluctance, Kira decided that she had no choice but to do something she rarely did: pass the buck. "Run this by Admiral Ross, just in case there's something going on we don't know about that would preclude shutting down the gateways. Besides, we can't do anything until we've evacuated Europa Nova, and that gateway you found is the only way we'll be able to get it done before the theta radiation gets fatal."

"Understood and agreed. I've got a message in to the admiral now."

"Good." She changed the *Euphrates*'s course. "In the meantime, I'm not just going to sit here waiting for another meteorite to endanger the planet."

"I beg your pardon?"

Kira quickly explained about the irradiated mass that had nearly destroyed Spilimbergo. "Since this crisis started, we've been reacting. It's past time we acted. The runabout isn't going to help much with the evacuation—but I can take it through the gateway to the other side and try to cut this off at the source. Somebody's using Europa Nova as their personal dumping ground, and it's going to stop now—before something comes through that we can't stop from killing anyone."

"Very well, Colonel. Lieutenant Nog is modifying the Defiant's *deflector array right now. It'll be ready to emit the tachyon burst as soon as the evac is completed."*

"Good. Captain Emick will be in charge of the task force when I'm gone."

"Understood. Vaughn out."

"Kira to Emick."

"Emick here, Colonel. We've just landed on Europa Nova and are about to begin our evac of Padilla's population. We've also been monitoring your communications. Do I gather that you intend to go through the gateway?"

"Yes, you do," Kira said, getting ready for an argument.

However, it wasn't forthcoming. *"Very well. Anything we can do to help?"*

Breathing a sigh of relief, Kira said, "Actually, yes. You sent a probe into the gateway when we arrived, right?"

"Yes, we did. I'll have my second officer send over the probe's data. The star system on the other side is in the Delta Quadrant. Hang on a second, we might be able to get you some help."

As Kira moved the runabout into a position proximate to the gateway, she said, "I beg your pardon?"

"You familiar with the U.S.S. Voyager, *Colonel?"* Emick asked.

"Of course. They left DS9 before they went missing."

"Right—and they wound up in the Delta Quadrant. I'm having my second officer look up the data from Starfleet's Project Pathfinder— Ah, damn. Voyager's *last reported position is nowhere near where this waste is coming from."*

"Let's hope she runs across another gateway that'll get her home," Kira said.

"Shields are holding against the radiation," Taran'- atar said.

"Good," Kira said. "Setting course for the gateway . . ."

Before she could start the runabout moving, however, Lieutenant Bowers's voice came over the com. "Rio Grande *to* Euphrates."

"Go ahead, Lieutenant."

"Sir, I'm picking up a ship entering this star system—Colonel, it's Cardassian. Galor-*class."*

Kira heard Emick curse. *"What the hell's a Cardassian ship doing here?"*

Kira looked down and saw the same sensor readings that Bowers had picked up. "I haven't a clue, Captain, but I intend to find out. Lieutenant Bowers, status?"

"We're about to head back to DS9 with our refugees, Colonel."

"Stay in-system until we determine what these Cardassians want."

"Aye, sir."

Emick asked, *"Do you want me to cut short our evac?"*

Tempting as it was to add the *Intrepid*'s firepower to her conversation with this Cardassian, Kira had to say, "No, the evacuation takes precedence. Don't worry, Captain, I know how to deal with Cardassians."

"Of that I have no doubt, Colonel. Keep in touch. Emick out."

As Kira brought the *Euphrates* about to intercept the Cardassian, the sensors got a better read on it. As Bowers said, it was *Galor*-class—registry identified it as the *Trager*—and it had seen better days. It was pocked with phaser scarring and had several hull breaches, only two of which were actually sealed with forcefields. The structural integrity field was at about sixty percent of capacity. *Looks like it took a beating during the war,* Kira thought. *And Cardassia doesn't have the resources to do proper repairs, it would seem.* That didn't surprise her. Between the internal strife, with half of the Cardassian fleet turning against the Dominion, the war damage inflicted by the Alpha Quadrant allies—much of the war had been fought in Cardassian territory, after all—and the horrendous retaliation taken against Cardassia Prime by the Dominion, the war had left the Cardassian Union in what could kindly be called a shambles.

The *Trager* took up a position in orbit around the sixth planet. That was, at present, the closest planet in the system to Europa Nova, and also outside Europani space.

She opened a channel. *"Trager,* this is Colonel Kira Nerys in command of this joint Federation/Bajoran task force. What business do you have in this solar system?"

After a moment, a reply came on a standard Cardassian military frequency. A face appeared on the viewscreen.

It was the face of the man Kira Nerys hated more than any other sentient being who'd ever lived—and might ever live. The former prefect of Bajor, the man who had killed millions of Bajorans during the Occupation, the filth who had taken Kira's mother from her family, and the man responsible for the Dominion/Cardassian alliance that led to years of bloody conflict. It was a face she prayed she'd never see again, one that still came to her in nightmares.

"Greetings, Colonel," he said.

"Dukat," Kira said with a snarl, and armed the runabout's phasers.

9

FARIUS PRIME

"Kam, we've lost the signal from Hig's ship."

"Verify that."

"I already have. Their last communication indicated that they were about to destroy the Starfleet ship that was gathering intelligence on the hole in the lattice when another Starfleet ship showed up."

"Then what?"

"Then nothing."

"That's not good."

"I'm fully aware of that."

"Let's hope they were destroyed rather than captured. Do we know what intelligence Starfleet gathered?"

"Hig's ship intercepted a transmission, but they weren't able to forward it to us. All I know is their

123

Ferengi engineer reported that they came up with a way to sabotage the gateways."

"They have a Ferengi engineer?"

"Yes. In fact, he's the nephew of the one negotiating on the Orions' behalf."

"Really? Interesting. Keep monitoring System 418, just in case. The negotiations here are taking far too long."

"Then why bother with them? There are others."

"Because the Orion offer is several orders of magnitude better than anyone else's."

"It may not be worth the risk."

"I'll be the judge of that. You just do as you're told."

Quark popped a tube grub into his mouth. *Things are going well,* he thought. His instincts told him that the Orions had the best offer on the table to the Iconians. *Why else allow it to drag out so long?* Quark knew that people all over the quadrant were clamoring for this technology. Plenty of governments would have made overtures. But no government had the resources of an underworld syndicate—or, rather, they did, but weren't willing to part with them. Quark knew that, and so did Gaila. At this point, the negotiations had boiled down to piddling over minor points. The deal was all but done. Quark could feel it in his lobes.

Indeed, the deal might have been done already, but for Gaila's picking at every point. While Gaila hadn't actively tried to sabotage the negotiations, he hadn't made it easy, either—and there was more to it than simply trying to get the best deal possible. He enjoyed making Quark squirm.

But that only went so far. Like Quark, Gaila was working on behalf of another party, and there was no getting around the quality of the Orions' offer to his client.

They were taking another break before going into what Quark predicted would be the final session. This time, Malic had decided to lay out a buffet of Ferengi food in deference to both negotiators, with some other food for those, like Bajorans and Orions, who preferred blander fare.

Gaila approached the huge ceramic bowl of tube grubs and took a few for himself. "So Cousin Rom is the Grand Nagus now," Gaila said in a conversational tone.

"That's right," Quark said, wondering where Gaila was going with this. *Somehow, I can't imagine he just wants to catch up on family gossip.*

"Grand Nagus Rom. Sounds funny, doesn't it? Aunt Ishka's on Risa with the former Grand Nagus. And I understand Nog's been promoted. All these changes— and yet you still own the same bar you've had for over fifteen years. How many different governments have controlled that station since you set up shop? Three? Yet you've managed to thrive."

"More or less," Quark said, popping another tube grub.

"You'll probably still be running that bar long after your dear brother has been ousted."

That got Quark's attention. "What do you mean?"

"Oh, nothing," Gaila said, pouring himself a glass of Slug-o-Cola. "Just call it—speculation on my part. Zek was able to put forward his reforms because he's Zek. He had the weight of years and experience, and decades of prosperity behind him. What does Rom have?"

A history of being an idiot, Quark thought, but said nothing. Gaila's expression was already saying it quite eloquently.

Gaila took a swallow of Slug-o-Cola. He smiled, wiping some of the green slime of the beverage from his upper lip. Gaila had several smiles that Quark had learned to quantify when they were kids. This was Gaila's "I know something you don't, and I'm not going to tell you what it is" smile. "Mark my words, cousin," he said, leaning close enough to Quark so that the Tholian silk jacket brushed against Quark's own suit. "You can count the years of Rom's reign as Nagus on the fingers of one Daluvian hand."

Daluvians didn't have fingers. Quark grabbed another tube grub.

Not wanting to dwell on this subject, Quark asked, "So how did you wind up negotiating for a dead civilization anyhow? Last time I saw you, you only had seven bars of latinum to your name." That had been the reward Zek had offered for the rescue of Ishka: fifty bars of latinum, which had been split evenly among the six Ferengi who participated in the rescue (after Quark skimmed off a sixteen percent finder's fee, of course).

Smiling his "I'm more clever than you think" smile, Gaila said, "You'd be amazed what you can do with seven bars of latinum." The smile fell. "Unfortunately, my old contacts had dried up. Did I ever tell you how I got that purification squad off my back?"

Quark shook his head.

"I gave General Nassuc weapons—free of charge.

That's why I was destitute when you found me in that holding cell. I bankrupted myself so that mad female could complete her takeover of Palamar. I went through all my cash reserves—I even had to sell my moon before I got enough weaponry to get her to call off the squad." Gaila now took on the "I'm moving in for the kill" smile as he leaned in even closer to Quark and whispered, "She killed ten million people before the civil war was over. The Regent had many friends, it turned out."

The tube grub felt like ashes in Quark's mouth. Quark had set in motion a chain of events intended to keep that very civil war from happening. The death toll was still far less than it would have been if Quark had helped Gaila and his partner Hagath obtain biological weapons for the Regent of Palamar to use against the general. *But still, ten million people. Their deaths . . .*

Quark stopped that train of thought. *Those deaths are* not *on my conscience. Nassuc and the Regent were at each other's throats long before I came along. One way or another, there would have been a war on Palamar. I just did what I could to keep the death toll down.*

Now if I can just believe that, everything will be fine. He grabbed another tube grub, then put it down uneaten.

Gaila was no doubt of the opinion that Quark had let sentiment get in the way of business, but Quark simply could not bring himself to trade millions of lives for personal profit. *Maybe it's years of exposure to the Federation—or maybe that's just the way I am.*

"Sorry, cousin," Gaila said insincerely. "But it was that or death. Not really so difficult a choice."

"Well, it was nice chatting with you, Gaila." Quark started to walk away.

"You know," Gaila said, "the gateways are a lot more valuable to the Orions than they are to the other governments."

Quark stopped. *Now he's going back to business. Interesting.*

"After all, who better to take advantage of the gateways than a decentralized group? It's tailor-made for the Orions. The Klingons, the Breen, the Romulans, the Federation—they'd have to completely readjust the way they live their lives to properly take advantage of the gateways. But the Orions wouldn't have to change a thing. They don't have a homeworld as such, just a network of bases—like this one."

Smiling, Quark said, "If this is an attempt to drive the price down—"

"Merely another observation, cousin."

"You've been full of observations, haven't you?" *Or full of something, anyhow.*

Gaila's shrug was as eloquent as his smile. Then he walked off.

Malic approached, gnawing on some kind of cooked poultry leg. "What was that all about?"

"Just catching up on some family gossip."

Glowering at Quark, Malic said, "I hope that's all it is, Quark. These negotiations have taken far too long. I was under the impression that you were *good* at this."

"I am. So's Gaila. That's why it's taking so long."

"That had better be the only reason, Quark. I'm fast running out of patience."

Only then did Quark notice that the two burly Orions had appeared behind Malic and were now gazing down on Quark. *Is it my imagination, or are their biceps bigger than they were yesterday?*

"Don't worry," Quark said, holding up his hands in as reassuring a manner as he could manage. "I'm confident that this will be the final session and you'll have possession of the gateways within the hour."

"You'd better hope that's the case, Quark. I still have the details of your scheme on my padd, and all it takes—"

"—is a simple command, yes I remember," Quark said with a sigh. "I'm aware of the terms of our agreement, Malic, and rest assured I'll honor it. Seventeenth Rule of Acquisition: 'A contract is a contract is a contract.' " Quark left out the subsequent clause: "But only between Ferengi." It was generally wise to leave that clause out when quoting that Rule to non-Ferengi—it just annoyed them.

Soon, everyone was ready to resume negotiations. Malic, to Quark's surprise, remained in the room, taking a seat in a corner of the meeting room, the two Orions on either side of him. Perhaps because of Malic's presence, the two Iconians—whom Quark hadn't seen since the initial session—also remained, standing behind Gaila. Malic took his personal padd out of his jacket pocket and started making notes onto it.

Tamra took up her position behind Quark, running her hand seductively across the outline of Quark's left ear. *Not now,* he thought, *I don't need the distraction.*

Another Iconian came in and handed a padd to Gaila, then went to stand with the other two.

Unbidden, the image of Rom standing in the bar came into Quark's head. Leeta by his side, Rom was holding the staff of the Nagus. Quark had publicly railed against the Zek reforms that Rom intended to continue. *Maybe that will be enough to keep me from going down with him when . . .*

He cut the thought off and glowered at his cousin, who was reading something on the padd. *I can't believe I fell for that,* he thought, admonishing himself. *I don't know what's worse, that Gaila stooped to try it, or that I almost succumbed to it.*

Aloud, he said, "So, shall we bring this negotiation to a close?"

"Just a moment, Quark," Gaila said without looking up from the padd. Then he finally set the padd down, folded his fingers together, and smiled.

It was the "I'm moving in for the kill" smile again. Quark folded his arms in an attempt at impatience and defiance—but mainly to cover his trepidation. *I don't like this one bit.*

"Tell me, Quark," Gaila said, "how long have you been working for Starfleet?"

Quark burst out laughing. "Working for *Starfleet?* Me? That's ridiculous!"

"Really? Then why is your nephew—an officer in Starfleet—working to sabotage the gateways?"

Quark frowned, genuinely confused. "What're you talking about?"

"We've intercepted a message from a Starfleet vessel called the *Sungari,*" Gaila said, holding up the padd. "Lieutenant Nog in command. The message claims to include the specifications for something that will disrupt the gateways." Looking up at Malic, Gaila said, "Nog is Quark's nephew. Quark is also a known collaborator with Starfleet."

"What?" Quark couldn't believe his ears.

"Three years ago, he worked with Starfleet on a

sting operation to bring down a weapons dealer named Hagath. Two years ago, he bartered a prisoner exchange on Starfleet's behalf involving a Vorta named Keevan."

"Those are lies," Quark said to Malic. Starfleet had nothing to do with either instance, and Gaila knew it—he was there for both incidents, after all.

"Are they?" Malic said quietly. Quark felt his blood freeze. "It would explain why you've been dragging out these negotiations—it allows your friends on Deep Space 9 to find a way to destroy the merchandise."

"They're not my friends," Quark said. His lobes started to ache. This was not going in the direction he'd hoped.

"Really?" Gaila's smile widened, which was never a good sign. "These are the people who kept your bar going when the Ferengi Commerce Authority banned you."

Quark sighed. Technically, of course, that was true—Captain Sisko and the others on the station, even Odo, had provided him with the resources to keep the bar going even when he was forbidden from doing business with any Ferengi.

Malic made notes onto his own padd, then stood up and moved toward the table. "I've been growing more and more suspicious of you, Quark. I have been unhappy with the length of these negotiations—and I was unaware of all these connections you have with Starfleet."

"The negotiations are almost complete," Quark said.

Gaila's smile changed to one of pure viciousness. "I wouldn't presume that if I were you, Quark."

Ignoring Gaila, Quark continued, "And I don't have

'connections' with Starfleet. Yes, my bar is on a station that is jointly operated by the Bajoran Militia and Starfleet, and *yes,* my nephew is an officer in Starfleet—a career path I strenuously objected to, I might add, and which I have never, ever supported. If Nog remained working for me, he'd be making more money and still have the left leg he was born with."

Malic looked at Gaila. "Let me see this transmission."

"Of course." Gaila got up and, smiling his "you're doomed" smile at Quark the entire time, handed the padd to Malic.

Putting his own padd back in the jacket pocket, Malic took the padd from Gaila and examined it. "This is definitely Starfleet, and definitely from one of the runabouts assigned to DS9."

Malic nodded to his bodyguards, and they moved forward and removed sidearms from holsters inside their jackets. Quark recognized the weapons as modified Klingon disruptors, each pointed directly at his head.

Tamra made a squeaking noise.

"You'll either tell the truth, Quark, or you'll die."

As a general rule, Quark found it best to keep negotiations as complicated as possible. It made it easier to find loopholes and get a better deal for himself. This negotiation, however, had just gotten depressingly simple: either tell Malic the truth, or be killed.

For Quark, that was no choice at all.

"All right, all right—I'm working for DS9 security. They sent me here to drag out the negotiations for as long as possible."

Malic shook his head. "And I thought having leverage over you meant I could trust you. I should've known better than to trust a Ferengi."

An Orion pirate is talking to me *about trustworthiness?* Quark thought, but wisely did not say aloud. At this point, saying anything else could prove fatal.

After making a few more notes on his padd, Malic said, "Kill him anyway."

10

EUROPA NOVA

"I BELIEVE YOU'VE mistaken me for someone else, Colonel."

Now that Kira had a moment to take a good look at the Cardassian on the viewscreen, she had to agree. The face and voice were frighteningly similar to Dukat's, but there was a slightly less arrogant timbre to the voice, and his facial ridges, while similar, were arranged a bit differently. Most distinctively, this Cardassian had facial hair, something Kira couldn't remember seeing on any member of the Cardassian military. Two dark tufts extended from the corners of his mouth to his chin in small crescents.

"I am Gul Macet," he continued. *"Skrain Dukat*

was my cousin, and I can assure you, the family resemblance is not something that's done me any favors."

"Surprised to hear a Cardassian say that," Kira muttered.

"I suppose you would be. But my relationship to Dukat has not been a beneficial one—especially of late. It seems that our resemblance has become more pronounced over the last few years. The more famous—or infamous—he became, the more people mistook me for him." He leaned forward. *"I know you have a history with Dukat, Colonel. I would ask only that you no more hold it against me than you would hold it against his daughter."*

Ziyal. "I wouldn't go there if I were you, Macet. What do you want?"

"Simply stated . . . I want to help, Colonel. The Trager *is at your disposal to aid in the evacuation of Europa Nova."*

Letting out a bark of derisive laughter, Kira said, "Out of the goodness of your heart?"

"You've been willing to make use of my services in the past, Colonel—though, come to think of it, you wouldn't be aware of it." Macet's face formed a smirk that was eerily similar to that of his cousin. *"The* Trager *is the ship that destroyed the cloning facilities on Rondac III."*

Blinking, Kira said, "You were part of Damar's resistance."

Macet smiled. Unlike Dukat's smile, which always carried an air of superiority and arrogance, Macet's smile seemed genuine, even warm. *"Why do you think the* Trager *looks like this?"*

135

Taran'atar finally spoke. "You were one of those who betrayed the Dominion."

The smile fell. *"That* would *be your view. You must be Taran'atar, the so-called observer from the Dominion I've heard about. I admire your courage in allowing that creature on your station, Colonel, if not your common sense."*

Ignoring the gibe, Taran'atar said, "Treachery is a poor foundation for trust."

"The traitors were the Cardassians who subsumed our empire to—"

"That's enough!" Kira snapped.

"My apologies, Colonel."

Taran'atar said nothing.

Kira considered Macet's offer. Every instinct told her not to trust him. He was part of Dukat's family. He was a Cardassian gul. *And he had to bring up Ziyal, the bastard.*

That, in turn, was precisely why she couldn't let Macet's accidental relationship—and unsettling resemblance—to Dukat influence her now. She remembered her thoughts upon arriving at Europa Nova the day before, regarding Taran'atar and her feelings toward Cardassians.

She knew the size of a *Galor*-class ship, and had a good idea about the number of evacuees it could probably take on, even one as damaged as the *Trager.* And she thought about the rising levels of theta radiation, the extra time it was taking to get the refugees off-planet, and the scores of people in the rural areas who had proven harder to locate than originally anticipated. Europa Nova apparently had a good-sized contingent of "back-to-nature" types among its population, who were apparently ignoring the orders to abandon their homes, despite the danger, and were proving difficult to find.

"All right, Macet. I can't say I understand why you're doing this, but I'm in no position to refuse, and I don't have time to discuss it. I accept."

"Very well, Colonel. I believe it would be best for all concerned if I remained here and accepted refugees that are brought up from the surface by your task force. The Trager *cannot land, of course, but it would speed up the process, and alleviate the need for your ships to evacuate to another star system once they've reached capacity. I assume you're bringing them to Deep Space 9?"*

"And to Bajor."

Macet nodded. *"Then that would be our wisest course."*

Kira silently agreed. With transporters no longer an option, she had intended to use the *Gryphon* and *Defiant* just as Macet proposed: position them at a safe distance while the *Intrepid,* the *Rio Grande,* and the other landing ships relayed refugees from the surface. The *Trager* would be a big help in that effort.

"Colonel," Taran'atar said, "sensors are showing that the *Trager* is equipped with Dominion technology."

Kira glanced down at the sensor readings. "I didn't know that had been done to any Cardassian ships."

"Some twenty ships were equipped with Dominion transporters and sensors," Taran'atar said. "It was intended to be the first step toward integrating the Central Command vessels with the Jem'Hadar warships. For obvious reasons, the project was never completed, but the *Trager* was apparently one of those twenty ships."

"Your observer speaks true, Colonel. We do in fact have sensors and transporters on par with those of a Jem'Hadar vessel—at least, that was what the Dominion told us," Macet added with another smirk.

Again ignoring Macet, Taran'atar said, "Colonel, if the *Trager* is equipped with Dominion transporters, they will still be viable for another six hours, based on the current rate of increase in theta radiation."

Shooting the Jem'Hadar a glance, Kira said, "Are you sure?"

"Quite sure."

"In that case, Macet," she said, turning back to the viewscreen, "you'll be much better off transporting people from the rural areas. We've had trouble locating all the people in the outlying territories. If you've got better sensors *and* can beam them out . . ." As she spoke, Kira did some quick calculations on her console. *This should cut the evac time considerably.* She was growing ever more concerned as to whether or not they'd be able to get everyone off-planet before the concentration of theta radiation in orbit reached fatal levels.

"I don't think that would be wise, Colonel."

"Why the hell not?"

"Let us just say there is a—history between Cardassia and Europa Nova. Transporting Europani onto a Cardassian vessel without warning would be provocative to say the least. So, for that matter, would be entering orbit of the planet."

"Macet, what are you talking about?"

"I must insist that we proceed with my proposed plan."

"These people are going to die if we don't get them

off-planet within the next day or so, and we can't do it without your help."

"You have my help, Colonel. The only way you will get more help is if you talk to the local government. If they approve of our orbiting Europa Nova and transporting their citizens, I will be happy to do so. But, last time I checked, their military had standing orders to shoot down any Cardassian vessel entering their space. The Trager *has taken enough damage lately, I'd rather not add to it while trying to commit an act of kindness."*

Kira had no idea about any of this. "I'll contact the surface and get back to you. Hold your position until then."

"Of course. And Colonel?"

"Yes?"

"It's a pleasure to be working with you once again."

"I hope I can say the same when this is all over, Macet. *Euphrates* out." She then opened a channel to the *Intrepid.* "Captain Emick, did you monitor that?"

"Yes, Colonel," said Emick, *"and I'm as in the dark as you. I had no idea that there was even any contact between Europa Nova and Cardassia."*

Biting her lip, Kira said, "I'll talk to President Silverio."

She opened the channel, and then was politely told to wait a moment. The president was busy with other duties, but would be with her as soon as possible. While they waited, Kira told the *Rio Grande* to proceed to DS9 with their refugees

As soon as she closed the channel to the *Rio Grande,* Taran'atar said, "You should not trust him."

"Why, because he worked for Damar's resistance?"

"In part."

"I worked for that resistance movement, Taran'atar. Yet you follow my orders."

"I follow your orders because a Founder has instructed me to. I have received no such instructions regarding trusting Cardassian guls who are known betrayers of the Dominion. You don't trust him, either—yet you are willing to give him this responsibility."

"Yes, I am," Kira said. "Because I don't have a choice. Look at the numbers, Taran'atar—we're *not* going to get everyone off Europa Nova in time. We've only got twenty ships and one gateway, and that gateway can only take five hundred thousand people. There's a good chance we won't get everyone off the planet in time. If we accept the *Trager*'s help, then maybe—*maybe*—we'll be able to do it. I made President Silverio a promise, and I'm damned if I'll renege on it because of a Cardassian who reminds me of someone I hate."

"Colonel Kira, I have President Silverio for you," said a voice from the com channel.

Still glaring at the Jem'Hadar, Kira said, "Go ahead."

Silverio looked just as haggard as she had when Kira spoke with her only a few minutes before. *"Colonel, I'm told there's a Cardassian ship in our system."*

"Yes, and they've offered—"

"I want that ship gone, Colonel. I don't care how you do it, but get rid of them." For the first time, there was a hard edge to Grazia Silverio's voice. Gone was the pleasant, grandmotherly tone. Now she sounded like—

Like me seven years ago, whenever the subject of Cardassians came up, Kira thought ruefully.

"Ma'am—Grazia—they've offered to help with the evacuation."

"I don't care if they've offered to scrub out the theta radiation with their teeth, I don't want them in my home."

"They have better sensors and transporters than any of the other ships in the task force—they can still *use* their transporters. If you allow them to go into orbit, they can transport the people in the rural areas that we've been having so much trouble with."

"Colonel, are you familiar with the asteroid belt between the sixth and seventh planets in this system?"

Kira shrugged. "I know it's there."

"When we first colonized this planet a century ago, that was a planet. The only other Class-M planet in the system. We seriously considered starting a second colony there. Thanks to the Cardassians, that's now an asteroid belt. Our military has standing orders to—"

"Shoot down any Cardassian ship that enters your space, I know."

"You know?"

"Gul Macet told me. He knew that, and he came anyhow. Grazia, I spent the first twenty-six years of my life fighting Cardassians—more than that, I spent all that time hating them. Nobody knows more than me what horrors they're capable of, and what they've done. And I'm telling you, we have to let them help. If you turn them away, people are going to die—people who trust you to lead them." She took a deep breath. "Look, if you tell me you don't want them here, I'll tell Macet to go back to Cardassia. But you're going to have to answer to the people who don't make it because you turned away a starship that could've rescued them."

Silverio closed her eyes for a moment. Then she shook her head and waved her arm. *"Apf. Let the ship in."*

Letting out a breath, Kira muttered a quick phrase of gratitude to the Prophets. "Thank you, Grazia."

"No, Colonel, thank you for knocking some sense into this old head of mine. You're right, now's hardly the time to let old hatreds get in the way of good sense. I always thought I had more brains than that."

"As long as you made the right choice in the end, it doesn't matter how you get there," Kira said with a gentle smile. "And call me Nerys. Let me put Gul Macet on." She opened a channel. "Gul Macet, I have President Silverio."

"Gul, I hereby give you permission to enter Europani space. And I thank you for your generous offer."

"You're welcome, Madame President. And may I say that I hope this marks a new beginning in relations between our people."

Kira shook her head. Macet was definitely going to take some getting used to—his voice was *so* like Dukat's. Yet those words out of Dukat's mouth would have had the listener waiting for the other shoe to drop. Macet, though, spoke with a sincerity that Dukat was, as far as Kira was concerned, congenitally incapable of.

"We'll begin scans and beam-outs immediately," Macet continued.

"Good," Kira said. "We're going to investigate the gateway, see if we can stop the radiation at the source. Captain Emick of the *Intrepid* will be in charge of the rescue operation while I'm gone."

"Understood, Colonel. Trager out."

Silverio signed off as well.

"Colonel, I have Commander Vaughn on subspace," Taran'atar said.

"Good timing," she muttered. "Go ahead, Commander," she added in a louder tone.

"Colonel, we're on our way back to Europa Nova. Admiral Ross has given us the go-ahead to attempt the disruption as soon as all five hundred thousand Europani have been evacuated through the Costa Rocosa gateway."

"Good. It'll be at least another three hours before they're all through. That should give Taran'atar and I enough time to check the other side of the orbital gateway."

"Lieutenant Nog says it will take two and a half hours to modify the Defiant. We can aid in the evacuation in the interim."

"Do that. I'll keep in touch. Oh, and we're getting some unexpected help here."

"Colonel?"

"Captain Emick can fill you in. Kira out." Turning to Taran'atar, she said, "Shield status?"

"Modulator is performing as expected."

"Good. Put them on maximum. Setting course for the gateway. Let's see what's on the other side."

II

DEEP SPACE 9

"LIEUTENANT, WE'RE GETTING a message from Vedek Eran."

Ezri Dax stood at the table in ops, looking over the distribution of refugees to the open quarters on the station. Luckily, they had plenty of room to spare, though it meant utilizing some of the quarters that had belonged to station staff and crew who had died in the Jem'Hadar attack a month earlier. Since the quarters weren't needed, the processing of the possessions had been given a comparatively low priority, and had only seriously been tackled in the last week or so. Yesterday, however, Dax had assigned a detail to take care of it, thus providing them with maximum availability.

She had just discovered an anomaly, but set it aside to take the call from Eran Dal. "Yes, Vedek?"

Eran was an older man with a pleasant, round face and a completely shaved head who managed to look exactly like Benjamin and nothing like her old friend at the same time. *Maybe if Benjamin added fifty pounds,* Ezri thought, and had to conceal a smile.

"Lieutenant, we've been having some troubles with the Federation industrial replicators we've been using to fabricate the temporary shelters for the Europani. Is there any way you can provide us with someone to repair them?"

Most of the Starfleet Corps of Engineers crew that had aided in the refurbishing of the station after the Jem'Hadar attack had departed, and the station's own engineering staff was busy with their own duties. Ezri was about to check the duty roster to find a loophole, when she remembered something.

"Hang on a moment, Vedek." She called up a station manifest. Sure enough, there was an industrial replicator on board, tagged for delivery to Cardassia Prime by the *U.S.S. Hood* next week. *If it's just going to sit in a cargo bay for a week, we may as well put it to good use.* She checked another display, and saw that the *Ng* was an hour away from finishing offloading refugees onto the station before heading back to Europa Nova.

"Vedek, I can't spare personnel, but I can give you a temporary replacement. Wait for a signal from Captain Hawkins on the *Ng* in about two hours, and he should be able to bring you a new replicator."

"Excellent. Thank you, Lieutenant."

"Not at all," Ezri said. "It's the Vedek Assembly we

should be thanking for making so much of its land available to the relief efforts."

"It is our pleasure to help those in need, Lieutenant. It was not long ago that we were relying on others for help when our world was devastated. We should never forget that. Eran out."

Eran's face winked out from the screen.

"Are you all right, Lieutenant?" Cathy Ling asked from the operations station.

Frowning, Ezri said, "I'm fine, why?"

"It's just—well, when you were talking to the vedek, your voice seemed to get—deeper. And scratchier."

Smiling her most reassuring counselor smile, Ezri said, "I'm perfectly fine, Ensign. Probably a little rough from all the talking I've been doing." She picked up a padd. "Before the vedek called, I noticed something—the atmosphere was never changed in the suite of rooms the Plexicans were in. We'd better do that before the *Ng*'s refugees try to set up there and find they can't breathe the methane."

Ling nodded quickly. "I'll get a team right on it, sir."

Ezri went back to looking over the status reports. Most of the refugees had settled in as well as could be expected. Many were scared, concerned about what they'd had to leave behind. Some expressed concern about their children—all of whom had been relocated to the Tozhat Resettlement Camp on Bajor. Ezri made a mental note to try to set up a schedule that would allow people to communicate with the camp.

Several had made specific complaints that had been forwarded to Ezri. "Computer, time?"

"The time is 1409 hours."

She still had almost an hour before her subspace

meeting with First Minister Shakaar. As far as she could tell, all the fires had been put out. Ling reported that the off-loading of refugees was proceeding apace. Vaughn had left on the *Defiant* with Nog and Shar's gateway disruption scheme ready to go. Dr. Tarses's last report from the infirmary was that all the cases of theta-radiation poisoning were minor and easily treated—as were the assorted other bumps and bruises that people had suffered during evacuation. She was actually free for the next fifty minutes.

"Ensign, I'll be in the Habitat Ring until my meeting with First Minister Shakaar," Ezri said as she moved toward the turbolift and grabbed a padd with the list of complaints. *May as well give these people's complaints the personal touch. With all they've been through, they deserve the station commander's direct attention.*

Station commander. Ezri surprised herself with how much she liked the sound of that. Most, though not all, hosts of the Dax symbiont gravitated toward positions of authority. In some cases—notably Ezri and Jadzia—that desire didn't seem to come until after joining with the symbiont. Ezri wondered if this inclination was congenital to Dax, or just the combined weight of all those memories of being an authority figure.

Just as she reached the top step of ops's upper level, Ling said, "Lieutenant, there's a personal communiqué here from a Dr. Renhol on Trill."

Damn, Ezri thought. With everything that had been going on, she hadn't made her check-in call with Renhol.

Renhol was a member of the Trill Symbiosis Commission. Ezri had not been a candidate to be joined, and had united with the Dax symbiont in order to save its life. The commission had asked that Ezri check in on a regular basis with Renhol—ideally once a week, but at least once a month, duties permitting. Of course, many on the commission would have preferred to keep Ezri on Trill and have her adjust to a joined life under close supervision, but Ezri was a free citizen and could do as she pleased. *And right now, I'm pleased to be here on the station, thank you very much.* She sighed. *Still, it's been over six weeks.*

"I'll take it in the colonel's office," Ezri said, changing direction.

Ezri went in, took a very deep breath through her nose, let it out through her mouth, and then sat down in Kira's chair. "Put it through," she said, tapping her combadge.

Renhol's angular face appeared on the small viewscreen on the desk. As always, her brown hair was tied severely back. *"Lieutenant Dax. It's good to see you."*

Holding up her hands, Ezri said, "I know why you're calling, Doctor, and I'm *very* sorry, but things have been a little crazy on the station."

"So I've heard. For that matter, so I see—I seem to recall that your uniform was a different color when last we spoke."

Involuntarily, Ezri's hand went up to the collar of her uniform, which was now command red instead of the sciences blue she'd worn ever since graduating from the Academy. "I've switched over to the command track."

"Really? That's rather a major step, don't you think?"

"Yes, it is. But I think this is the right thing for me to do. About a month ago, I wound up in command of the *Defiant* during a combat situation. I realized then that I needed to stop assing around in a fog and put these centuries of experiences to better use."

"Don't you think that's a decision you should have consulted us on?"

Ezri rolled her eyes. "Young lady, I don't need the commission's permission to hold my hand and walk me through every major life decision. I'm a grown woman, and I'm completely capable of making my own choices. Or do I have to consult the commission when I brush my teeth every day?"

Renhol's lips pursed. *"Of course not. But are you aware of the fact that each of those three sentences came from a different host?"*

Frowning, Ezri said, "What?"

"You modulated from Lela to Ezri to Jadzia. For that matter, Torias was fond of the phrase 'assing around,' if I recall correctly. That isn't the way the joining is supposed to work, Ezri, and you know that."

Taking another deep breath to compose herself, Ezri said, "Look, Doctor, I appreciate your concern, but right now I have to deal with a huge influx of refugees from Europa Nova." Quickly, she outlined the situation.

"So you're in charge of the station?"

"At the moment, yes, and I really don't have time to bring you completely up to speed on my life. I promise that I'll contact you again within the next two days, assuming the crisis is resolved."

"I apologize, Lieutenant, I didn't realize my timing was so bad," Renhol said, though Ezri didn't think she was sincere. *"Get back in touch with me again at your convenience—but soon, please. We do need to discuss this."*

"Of course, Doctor. Dax out." She cut the connection.

Stupid, meddling commission. Why can't they just let me live my life?

As she exited the office and headed to the turbolift, she caught sight of Ling. She then remembered what she had said about Ezri's voice getting deeper and scratchier. *That was when I was talking to Vedek Eran—and giving him the speech about how we should thank him. Which,* she realized suddenly, *I did in Curzon's classic "diplomatic mode."*

She shook her head as she entered the turbolift. *I'm just tired—*

—like I was last month when I tapped into Jadzia's memories during sex with Julian? Renhol was right about one thing: it *wasn't* supposed to work that way. Ezri had been content to chalk it all up to a transitional phase she was going through—from a year of stumbling her way through a labyrinth of past lives, to really taking control for the first time. More and more, ever since that terrible day on the *Defiant,* she found herself drawing from the wellspring of her previous hosts to take on greater and greater challenges. And the more she took on, the more she seemed to crave.

What's wrong with that? she wondered, not without some resentment. *Isn't that the point of being joined? To harmonize those life experiences and use them to live up to their combined potential? To be greater than the sum of my past hosts?*

As the turbolift arrived in the habitat ring, she looked over the list, her mind returning to the issues at hand. She decided to simply take the complaints by order of quarters.

On her way, she passed by Ensign Gordimer, who

had remained behind when the *Defiant* left, leading a group of refugees toward Section Nine. She smiled at the line of people who shuffled in a more-or-less orderly manner toward the empty quarters there.

She walked up to Gordimer. "Ensign," she said quietly, "make sure that the last two quarters in this section have been readjusted for humans."

In a whisper, Gordimer reported, "I've already been in touch with Ensign Ling, sir. This group won't need those two quarters, but they should be ready by the time the *Xhosa* arrives with the next batch."

Ezri nodded. "The *Ng*'s refugees are going to Section Twelve, right?"

"Yes, sir."

"Good. Carry on, Ensign."

"Excuse me?"

Ezri turned to see a very short older man. His face was wrinkled, his neck jowly, his snow-white hair thin and wispy, and his skin liver-spotted. Despite this, he did not seem at all decrepit—he walked with as much vitality as Vaughn, even though Ezri figured he had to have thirty years on Elias.

"Can I help you, Mr.—?"

"Maranzano." The deep, rich voice belied the fragile form it came out of. "I just wanted to know—are you in charge?"

Smiling, Ezri said, "Well, I'm presently in command of the station."

"I just wanted to thank you all for your help. I know how difficult this must be for all of you, keeping track of all of us and herding us around . . ."

Ezri couldn't help but laugh. "Difficult for *us*? Mr. Maranzano—"

A woman standing in the queue said, "Oh, don't listen to him, young lady. He just thinks you're pretty and wants to make nice."

Mr. Maranzano turned and gave the woman a dirty look. "I'm not allowed to be nice to a pretty young woman?"

Should I tell him I'm over three hundred years old? Ezri thought mischievously. *No, that wouldn't be fair.* "Well, thanks all the same, Mr. Maranzano, but I think you're the ones who should be thanked. Now please, if you'll go with Ensign Gordimer here, he'll take you to your temporary quarters."

She saw them off, then continued to the nearest quarters containing someone who had relayed a problem to ops.

The first two were minor complaints about the size of the quarters—mostly from people who lived in houses on Europa Nova. Ezri made appropriately conciliatory noises that boiled down to *tough luck,* and moved on.

A heavyset woman answered the third door. "Is everything all right, Ms. DellaMonica?"

"The replicators don't work. I've been trying to make an espresso for the last hour."

"Oh, I'm sorry. Let me take a look." She went inside the quarters, which were also occupied by four other people, all male. All five of them had similar facial features, and Ezri assumed they were related. "Computer," Ezri said to the replicator, "one espresso, unsweetened."

A demitasse cup appeared in the replicator, filled with steaming black liquid. Ezri picked it up. "Looks okay to me."

"Taste it."

Ezri tasted it. It seemed to taste right. But then, Ezri had never been much of an espresso drinker—she put it in the same category as *raktajino,* which she detested—though Jadzia loved it, having been a regular customer at the Café Roma on Earth and its magnificent brew when she was at the Academy. But then, Jadzia also liked *raktajino.*

"It seems fine," she said tentatively.

"It's horrendous!" Ms. DellaMonica cried.

"Ms. DellaMonica, I realize it may not be up to your standards, but replicators are sometimes—"

Holding up a hand, Ms. DellaMonica said, "Lieutenant, I know what you're going to say. 'This espresso is good enough.' Well not for me." She took a deep breath. "Look around you, Lieutenant. What *don't* you see?"

Looking around the quarters, Ezri saw what one usually saw in such places—but saw very little by way of personal effects, which was presumably Ms. DellaMonica's point. "I know that things are difficult, Ms. DellaMonica, but—"

"Do you know what a pietà is, Lieutenant?"

"No."

"It's a religious icon of a woman holding her dead son by the artist Michelangelo. We have a replica of it that's been in my family since Earth's eighteenth century. My *nonna* gave it to me on her deathbed. That pietà means more to us than anything—but we left it behind, because we only had to take the essentials with us. I may never see that statue again, Lieutenant. That's the way the universe works, and I accept that. But, all things considered, I don't think it's too much to ask that at least I can get a decent espresso. This is *not* decent espresso."

Casting her mind over the duty roster for the engineering staff, Ezri tapped her combadge. "Dax to McAllister."

"Go ahead, Lieutenant."

"Could you report to the Habitat Ring, Level Four, Section Forty-Eight and have a look at the replicator, please? The people in the quarters will explain the problem."

"On my way."

The faces of all five DellaMonicas brightened with smiles. "Thank you," Ms. DellaMonica said, clasping her hands together and shaking them over her heart.

"Anything else?"

"Nothing a good espresso won't cure. Without my caffeine, I get cranky."

"Trust me," one of the other DellaMonicas added. "You wouldn't like her when she's cranky."

Ezri smiled. "I get that impression. Don't hesitate to call me if there are any other problems. And Ms. DellaMonica?"

"Yes?"

"We're doing everything we can to get you back together with your pietà and your espresso maker."

"I appreciate that, Lieutenant."

After bidding them a cheery good-bye, she went to the next door.

Without preamble, the occupant, Mr. Pérez, said: "It's too hot in here."

"I'll have the temperature reduced. The last occupants were Ovirians—you know how they like it hot."

"What's an Ovirian?"

"They're from the planet—"

"Aliens? You put aliens in my room?"

"They're simply the ones who had the quarters last."

"I don't want to share my space with aliens."

Ezri took a deep breath. "You won't be. The Ovirians were in here over a month ago."

"If there are any aliens in here, I want to move."

"There are no aliens, Mr. Pérez. It's just you and your brother and sister in here."

"It better be."

The next door: "I've got a terrible rash!"

"Have you been to the infirmary?"

"There's an infirmary here?"

Sighing, Ezri asked, "What type of rash is it?"

"A bad one."

Remembering something Julian had mentioned earlier, Ezri said, "It's probably just an allergic reaction to the arithrazine you were given on the *Defiant,* Mr. Amenguale. You should report to the infirmary right away."

"Where is that?"

"The computer can direct you."

"What computer?"

Ezri quickly described the shortest route from this section of the Habitat Ring to the infirmary, then moved on.

The next door: "Where's the kitchen?"

"These quarters have food replicators."

"What're they?"

Sighing, Ezri tried not to dwell on the irony of explaining the concept of food replicators to someone who lived in a society that relied on them.

"Oh, okay. So how do I cook food, then?"

Ezri explained the concept a second time, which seemed to take, and she took her leave.

The next door: "The lights are too bright."

Next: "These beds are terrible!"

Next: "I can't get the sonic shower to work."

Next: "The lights are too dark."

Next was Ms. Bello, a small, timid-looking woman who said, "Lieutenant, someone stole my necklace."

Before Ms. Bello could elaborate, some insensitive jackass cried out, "How could you let someone steal your necklace? Why were you wearing a necklace anyhow? You knew you'd be crowded in with a bunch of other people and going to a space station! Any idiot knows to keep an eye on your belongings when you come to a space station like this! I can't believe you'd be so *completely* idiotic!"

Ezri realized two things as this diatribe went on. One was that Ensign Gordimer had just turned the corner. The other was that the insensitive jackass was in fact Ezri herself.

"Lieutenant," Gordimer said quickly, "are you okay?"

Catching her breath, feeling like the most horrible person who ever walked the halls of the station, Ezri said, "Yes, I'm fine. Can you do me a favor, Ensign? This woman has had some jewelry stolen. Can you take her statement?"

"Of course, Lieutenant," Gordimer said quickly.

Turning to the small woman, who looked like she wanted desperately to curl herself up into a ball, she said, "I'm very, *very* sorry, Ms. Bello. My behavior was *completely* uncalled for."

Ms. Bello simply flinched and nodded.

Gordimer gave a reassuring smile. "I promise we'll try to get to the bottom of this theft, ma'am."

Again, she flinched. Ezri decided to get the hell away from the woman before she did any more damage.

I desperately need a break, she thought, wondering if perhaps Dr. Renhol didn't have a point.

No, that's silly. I've been dashing about full-tilt since we got the distress call from Europa Nova. I've barely slept in the last fifty hours. I just need to relax. "Computer, time?"

"The time is 1445 hours."

Damn, she thought. *Only fifteen minutes until Shakaar.*

Ezri entered a turbolift. "Wardroom," she said after a moment. That room was likely to be empty—she could get a cup of tea, compose herself, and still make it to ops in time.

As the turbolift wended its way mid-core, she wished Julian had stayed behind. After all, the *Intrepid* and the *Gryphon* had full medical staffs that could work just fine with the Europani medical authorities. But they decided to play it safe and have as many medical personnel available on-site as possible, which certainly made sense. Besides, Simon Tarses and Girani Semna were handling the load back here just fine.

Speaking of medicine, I wonder if Mr. Amenguale actually found his way up to the infirmary. She tapped her combadge. "Dax to Tarses."

"Go ahead." The doctor sounded exhausted.

"You okay, Simon?"

"Nothing eight days of sleep won't cure. What can I do for you, Lieutenant?"

"A Mr. Amenguale should be reporting to you with

a case of arithrazine rash. If he isn't there in the next five minutes or so, send someone from security to find him—I think he might get lost."

"Got it. And hey, you don't exactly sound hale and hearty yourself."

"I promise to get some sleep as soon as I can, Simon."

"Why am I not reassured?"

Ezri chuckled as the turbolift arrived at the ward-room level. "Dax out."

As she exited the lift, she heard the familiar voice of Shar.

"I understand, *Zhavey.*"

"No, Thirishar, I don't think you truly do. You mustn't, if you're going to insist on acting like this."

The second voice wasn't immediately familiar, but given the way Shar addressed her, it must be the infamous Councillor Charivretha zh'Thane. They were obviously right around the corner from where Ezri was walking—or, rather, standing, since she had stopped short of proceeding once she heard the voices.

"I am acting like myself, *Zhavey.* I don't know any other way *to* act. I am sorry for that, but—"

"In Thori's name, Thirishar!" zh'Thane cried out in a voice that, Ezri suspected, had intimidated many on the Federation Council floor, "you cannot afford to take such risks when you *know* what is at stake!"

"Exploring the Gamma Quadrant is hardly a 'risk,' *Zhavey.*"

"Please don't tell me you're that naïve. If you want, I can quote casualty figures on starships exploring un-mapped space for the last two hundred years."

"That won't be necessary."

"Then what will it take?" zh'Thane snapped. "To what part of you should I appeal? Clearly you feel no sense of duty to your own kind, nor to me. You have no fear of what may befall you before the window is closed. Have you even considered what your obstinancy is doing to Anichent, to Dizhei, to Thriss? Are you even thinking about anyone besides yourself?"

There was an unexpected sound, like a bulkhead being struck, and Dax almost moved to see what had happened, to intervene, but the sound of Shar's voice, raised to a hiss and seething with emotion, stopped her in her tracks.

"I have thought of everyone *but* myself my entire life, *Zhavey!* That's how you raised me, isn't it? How *all* Andorian children are raised? We don't live for ourselves, we live for the whole, always the whole.

"You ask me if I love them . . . as if I had a choice. As if every cell in my body didn't long to be among them *every day.*"

"The why are you doing this?"

"Because it isn't working! I've kept track, *Zhavey,* more closely than you imagine. I've seen the numbers, and I see what we're doing to ourselves as a people because of them, because of our desperation to delay the inevitable. We're so consumed with keeping ourselves alive, we have no conception of what we're living *for.*"

"And so your answer is to turn your back to us? On everyone and everything?"

"You don't understand. You never did," Shar said in a deadly whisper.

The last time Ezri had heard an Andorian use that tone of voice was thirteen years earlier, when she was

Curzon. The person to whom the Andorian had spoken was dead five minutes later.

There was a terrible silence. And when zh'Thane broke it, her voice was firm. But also, Ezri thought, tinged with sorrow. "Don't force me to act, my *chei*."

"Stop meddling in my life, *Zhavey*."

"Don't walk away from me, Thirishar!"

Uh-oh, Ezri thought, and she immediately started walking forward in a pointless attempt to cover up her eavesdropping.

Shar turned the corner just as Ezri approached it, and the two almost collided. Shar's antennae were standing straight up, and his eyes—normally the inquisitive eyes of the scientist that Ezri knew quite well from Tobin and Jadzia—were smoldering with emotions Ezri couldn't begin to read.

At the sight of Ezri, though, the antennae lowered slightly, and he regained his composure. "Lieutenant! I'm sorry, I didn't see you there."

A tall Andorian woman with an impressively elaborate hairdo came around the corner, and she was similarly brought up short by the Trill's presence.

Well, this is awkward, Ezri thought. She supposed she should have turned and walked away the minute the first words came within earshot, but her own curiosity—and her counselor's training—had kicked in.

Finally, after the pause threatened to go on for days, Ezri offered her hand to the tall woman. "You must be Councillor zh'Thane. I'm Lieutenant Ezri Dax."

The councillor took it. "Dax—you used to be Curzon Dax, yes?"

"Two hosts ago, yes."

Sourly, she said, "Well, I'll try not to hold that

against you." Turning around, obviously unwilling to air her family's private affairs in public, she said, "If you'll excuse me."

She walked off. Idly, Ezri tried to recall what, exactly, Curzon might have done to offend Andor's representative to the Federation Council. She couldn't remember ever having met her, but that was hardly conclusive—Curzon had annoyed plenty of people he had never met.

Shrugging, she turned to Shar, who looked as unhappy as Ezri had ever seen him. In fact, it was really the first time Ezri could ever remember seeing him unhappy.

Based on the conversation, she could guess why.

"Do you want to talk about it, Shar?"

"I'm afraid I can't, Lieutenant, but thank you for asking."

Ezri thought a moment, then decided to go for broke. "I take it there are three people on Andor waiting for you to come home to take part in the *shelthreth?*"

Shar whirled around, his antennae raised. In a quiet, stunned voice, he asked, "You know about that?"

"I've been around for three centuries, Shar—I've known a few Andorians in my time."

Nodding, Shar said, "Yes, of course you have."

"And I know how important the *shelthreth* is."

Shar's face hardened. "Not you as well, Ezri. I know that I have a duty to Andor. And whether anyone back home understands this or not, I'm fulfilling it in my own way. But now *Zhavey* is making threats."

"What can she do?"

"She can have me reassigned to Andor."

Ezri frowned. "Last time I checked, Federation

Councillors didn't have any influence over Starfleet personnel assignments."

"Respectfully, Lieutenant, I don't think you fully appreciate the power of politics. And she knows Commander Vaughn."

Dax's frown deepened. "You think she'd convince Vaughn to transfer you? I think you underestimate him, Shar. You've been doing superlative work. I ought to know—I sort of used to have the job," she added with a smile.

"Thank you, but unfortunately, I think you underestimate Charivretha. It would be just like my *zhavey* to talk him into transferring me. She might even go so far as to explain why."

"Even if that's true, Vaughn doesn't strike me as the type who'd authorize transfers for personal reasons. And even if he did, I can't see Kira approving it."

"Your confidence is touching, but I've only been here a few months. I haven't done anything to command that kind of loyalty—certainly not enough to refuse the request of a Federation Councillor. Besides, why do you think I'm not on the *Defiant?*"

"That's a good point," Ezri said. "Why aren't you on the *Defiant?*"

"Because *Zhavey* asked the commander to leave me behind so we could talk." Some of Shar's coarse white hair fell into his face, and he brushed it out of the way. "Although the talk accomplished nothing that we haven't already said in our private communications."

Remembering how much more painful it was to deal with her own mother in person than over subspace, Ezri could see Councillor zh'Thane's logic in believing that an in-person plea might be more effective. Saying that, however, would not help matters, so she tried another tack:

"Shar, maybe you should consider what she's saying." At the Andorian's sharp look, she added, "I'm not taking her side. Believe me, I can quote you chapter and verse on the subject of parental guilt and not doing what they expect you to do. I'm not saying you should reconsider your position because it's what your *zhavey* is telling you to do. What I *am* saying is that you should examine the situation without considering her at all. Forget about what she wants. Think about yourself—and think about the three people waiting for you back home. They deserve *some* consideration, yes?"

Shar said nothing.

"Just think about it, okay?"

Sighing, Shar said, "I *have* thought about it. I appreciate what you're trying to do, Lieutenant, but I've already made up my mind. Being in Starfleet is what I want—it's all I've ever wanted, since I was a child. I'm not going to give it up now, and I'm certainly not going to let *Zhavey* hold me personally responsible for the fact that the Andorian species is dying."

12

THE DELTA QUADRANT

THE STARS ARE WRONG.

Kira had that same thought every time she left the Bajoran sector. For years in the resistance, she had depended on the stars in the sky over Bajor. It was better to move at night when they were on the run from Cardassian patrols. Scanners could fail or be jammed, but all she had to do was look up to know precisely where she was. Even when most or all of the moons were visible, she still could see enough of the constellations to orient herself.

In space, it was the same thing. Navigational equipment wasn't always reliable, particularly when you were being fired on. Again, the stars were always there for her—as long as the Prophets provided a view of the other suns in the galaxy, she could find her way.

Before becoming first officer on Deep Space 9, she had spent very little time out of the Bajoran system, and even when she did, she'd had other things on her mind—picking up supplies, or some other errand related to the resistance. For most of the first twenty-six years of her life, the stars as they were seen from Bajor were her anchors. It was something she could depend on in a life that had precious little of that.

The first time she went through the wormhole and into the Gamma Quadrant, the disorientation had been almost painful. Her anchor was gone. Everything was arranged differently, and Kira—at the time, still not accustomed to working with reliable Starfleet equipment—found herself in the uncomfortable position of being forced to depend on technology far more than she was used to.

Now, seven years later, it was hardly an issue. She'd made dozens of trips to the Gamma Quadrant, and had traveled all over the Alpha Quadrant, from Cardassia Prime to Earth. Still, every time she found herself far away from home, there was that feeling that the sky was somehow lying to her.

As the *Euphrates* came careening through the gateway, piercing the the thick green jet that choked the passage, the sky told her a new lie, one as big as the one it told her when she went through the wormhole.

She kept going at full impulse when they cleared the gateway—she wanted to get away from the radioactive waste as quickly as possible. Taking up a position about a hundred thousand kilometers from the gateway, Kira did a sensor sweep.

Her eyes went wide and she felt her jaw go slack. "Oh no . . ."

"I assume," Taran'atar said, "that you have just noticed the waste concentration bearing 273 mark 9."

Kira nodded. "That single mass is putting out more radiation than everything that's in orbit of Europa Nova right now combined. If we let that go through, the planet's as good as dead."

"Can we destroy it?"

Kira shook her head as she studied the readings. "Best we could do is blast it into smaller pieces. Impact damage might be less, but it wouldn't alleviate the radiation." She didn't have to remind Taran'atar that they no longer had a tractor beam, so trying to alter its course as they'd done before wasn't an option.

"Colonel, I'm picking up a vessel," Taran'atar announced. "It's the source of the jet."

"Do you recognize it?" Kira asked.

Taran'atar said, "No. It does not match anything in Starfleet records, nor any ship I have knowledge of." He peered at his sensor readings. "Length, seven thousand meters. Hull is made of an unidentified alloy that appears to include elements of duranium and holivane." Kira had no idea what holivane was and, just at the moment, didn't care. Taran'atar continued, "Indeterminate weapons capacity. They appear to operate on channeled matter-antimatter reactions but, based on what I have been able to read through the interference from the radiation, it's an inferior engine design."

"If they're producing antimatter waste on this scale, that's not surprising. Anything else?"

"Fully ninety percent of the ship is dedicated to cargo space. Based on its size and configuration, I believe the ship is a barge for the hazardous material."

"And they decided they had a perfect dumping

ground." Kira felt revulsion build up in her gut and work its way to her extremities, which she had to keep from shaking. Even at their absolute worst, the Cardassians never did anything so repugnant as to dump highly toxic material into a populated region. "It must've thrilled them when the gateway opened. I wonder if they even bothered to see if there was an inhabited planet on the other side." A brief urge came over Kira to lock the runabout's phasers on the ship and destroy it just to teach these people—whoever they were—a lesson. She set the impulse aside. "What else?"

"There are no docking ports. They also have an unusual shield configuration."

"Unusual how?"

"There are seven of them, though most are offline right now. They appear to have been enhanced in some way. I've never seen a design like this."

Kira noticed that there was none of the scientific curiosity she would expect from, say, Nog or Shar in Taran'atar's tone. He was simply reporting the facts as he saw them.

The Jem'Hadar continued, "At present, most of their systems are offline. I am not reading any life signs."

Blinking, Kira said, "None at all? That ship's got to have a crew of at least several hundred. Could the radiation be interfering?"

"The radiation could not interfere so much as to mask that many life signs, Colonel."

Shaking her head, Kira looked down at the display. They had a little over two hours before the mass would go through the gateway, so there was time to figure something out. *But what? With no tractor beam and no way to destroy it effectively . . .*

Then she noticed something. "I'm reading some debris. Sensors say it's primarily irradiated monotanium—along with organic matter. Looks like a ship was destroyed by the waste."

"A ship with a monotanium hull," Taran'atar mused. "Even the Dominion was never able to refine enough monotanium to make spacecraft from it."

Kira couldn't resist. "Looks like the Dominion doesn't have the market on high technology."

"It would seem so."

Growing serious once again, Kira said, "Still, if even a monotanium ship couldn't hold up to that waste, Europa Nova won't, either."

"There is a *Class-M planet* in this system," Taran'atar said, "less than a million kilometers from our position. There are, however, no high-order life signs."

Kira took a deep breath. "All right, I'm going to assume that *someone* is alive over there." She opened a channel. "Unidentified vessel, this is the Federation runabout *Euphrates*. Respond please."

There was no reply.

"This is the Federation Runabout *Euphrates* contacting unidenti—"

"The tanker's systems are coming online," Taran'atar said suddenly. "Weapons are powering up—"

"Raise shields," Kira said half a second before the weapons fire struck the runabout. She immediately sent the *Euphrates* onto an evasive course that would take them farther away from the radioactive waste.

"Shields at sixty percent," Taran'atar said. "Shall I return fire?"

Kira hesitated only for a second. The Jem'Hadar

was bred for combat. *So why not let him do what he does best?*

"Do it," Kira said, and as she piloted the *Euphrates* away from the tanker, another salvo of weapons fire struck the runabout.

"Shields are down," Taran'atar called over the din of alarms. "Shield generators offline."

"Lucky shot," Kira muttered.

"No, Colonel," Taran'atar said. "That shot was carefully aimed and modulated. Our opponent knew precisely where and how hard to strike."

Before Kira could respond to that, the runabout faded into an incoherent jumble. Her body suddenly felt disconnected from reality. The sounds of the alarms in the runabout faded, the feel of the cushioned seat under her dissolved. It was akin to being transported, but that didn't come with such a feeling of disorientation—of removal from reality.

For a brief instant that felt like it would never end, she was nowhere, felt nothing, *was* nothing.

Then, slowly, her senses returned. Except what she now felt beneath her was hard, cold metal; she was lying down instead of sitting, and her hands were now bound behind her back. Instinctively, she struggled against her bonds, but they did not yield.

She no longer heard alarms, but she did hear the constant thrum of a ship's systems. The ship, however, was not the *Euphrates*. The silvery-blue colors that Starfleet favored had been replaced by dark browns and greens—the latter accentuated by the dim green lights on the ceiling. She saw unfamiliar interfaces and a smaller, cruder style of screen—a rounder design than the usual flatscreen displays Kira was accustomed to. A green-tinged miasma hovered in the very air of the ship, and it smelled like someone was burning plastiform. The gloom was palpable.

Adding to it were the three humanoid corpses which also lay on the deck. Golden-skinned, wearing bulky uniforms, and most in pools of their own greenish-blue blood, these, Kira suspected, were the life signs that the *Euphrates* could no longer read. One appeared to be female, the other two male, one of the latter with thinning hair. All three had been cut to pieces.

If these were members of the crew, they'd certainly paid for the act of dumping their lethal payload on Europa Nova.

Of Taran'atar, she saw no sign.

Then a huge figure stepped into view, walking purposefully toward her. The figure—whom Kira guessed was at least two and a half meters tall, though her worm's-eye view gave her a skewed perspective— wore an imposing uniform of dark metallic armor. Most of its head was covered by a helmet with ridges that began close together at the forehead and spread out and around to the back of the head. The only displays of color beyond the blue-black of the armor were the alien's mottled brown face, the streak of white on either side of the helmet's middle ridge, and the streak of bright red under the leftmost ridge.

The alien stopped, looked down on Kira, and spoke one word in a deep, resonant voice that carried the promise of a painful death.

"Prey."

13

FARIUS PRIME

SO THIS IS IT, Quark thought. *We're going to die.*

What galled him the most was that it was Gaila who engineered this. The beloved cousin to whom he had lent that latinum to get his arms business started—*and this is how he repays me. He undermines a business deal just to take some misguided revenge on me. How could Gaila, of all people, forget the Sixth Rule of Acquisition?* "Never allow family to stand in the way of opportunity."

No, Gaila just sat there, smiling his "I won" smile as if he hadn't just ruined things for his own client. The Iconians would never get a better offer than this. The Orions were not likely to engender much confidence as a potential buyer after killing their own negotiator.

He probably had that same smile on his face after he had Quark's Treasure *delivered to DS9.* Gaila had always claimed that the malfunction that caused the ship to be transported over four hundred years into the past wasn't the result of sabotage, but Quark had never believed it.

One of the two burly Orions looked over at Tamra and smiled lasciviously. "Just so's you know, Quark—after I kill you, I'm takin' the dabo girl for myself."

Tamra smiled right back.

The Orion's face fell. This was not the vacuous facial expression of a woman whose main purpose was to provide distracting eye-candy for the customers. This was closer to one of Gaila's smiles.

Then Tamra grabbed one of those idiotic tassels from her waist and threw it into the middle of the room.

Quark quickly closed his eyes and covered them with his hands. When the flare went off, a huge flash of light filled the room. Quark could see the glow even through his eyelids and hands.

A hand grabbed his left arm and yanked him out of his chair.

He opened his eyes to see the room in chaos. The Iconians, the Orions, and Gaila were all blinking, trying to clear their vision and obviously failing miserably. For his part, Quark was being dragged toward the door.

The only person standing between the two of them and that door was Malic, crying, "Kill them! *Kill them!*"

"I'm blind! I'm *blind!*" one of the burly Orions screamed over Malic's voice. He had, Quark noticed, dropped his disruptor.

The other Orion, though, still had his disruptor, and took Malic's instructions to heart; he fired. Luckily for Quark, he was as blind as his panicky comrade: the shot went about a half a meter over Quark's head.

The blond Bajoran, still dragging Quark with one hand, clipped Malic with her other arm, knocking the Orion to the floor. In the same motion, she bent over and picked up the dropped disruptor.

Another shot flew over Quark's head, closer this time.

"Quark! You won't get away with this, cousin!" Gaila was, Quark noted, facing away from Quark, yelling at a bulkhead.

When they reached the corridor, Quark yanked his arm free. "What took you so long? I was starting to think you were going to wait until he actually pulled the trigger."

Lieutenant Ro Laren glowered at him from under her unnaturally colored hair. "You're welcome, Quark."

DEEP SPACE 9 (FOUR DAYS AGO)

"I've got a little bit of a problem."

It hadn't been easy for Quark to come to the security office. He had, in fact, spent the last day staring at the door to Ro's office, trying to figure out what to do.

Normally, of course, he wouldn't even need an excuse to go to the security office. After all, Ro was there, and that vision of Bajoran loveliness was more than enough reason for Quark to contrive a feeble excuse to drop in.

But this was different.

It had seemed innocent enough when it began nearly two weeks ago. An Orion named Malic had entered the bar with a business proposal: he wanted Quark to negotiate a deal for the Orion Syndicate on his behalf. The terms had been pretty vague at first, as had the payment—all Malic had said was that it would be "worth your while." It wasn't as if the syndicate in general didn't have money, and Malic in particular was obviously a wealthy man, so Quark wasn't terribly concerned on that score. The syndicate had, in fact, turned down Quark's long-ago overtures for membership, so the fact that they were coming to him with a business proposition was enough to get Quark's lobes tingling.

Then came the kicker. Malic explained in very plain, simple terms why this was an offer Quark couldn't refuse. Then Malic departed, promising to return "soon."

Now Quark was scared. He hated being scared—so much so that it rather irritated him how often he wound up feeling that emotion.

In the past, he'd have no one to turn to. His brother had never been the most useful person in a crisis—though even Quark had to admit that Rom occasionally had his moments, for an idiot—and Odo was as likely to toss him into a holding cell as help him out.

But there was a new constable in town, so to speak, and Quark felt confident that he'd be able to appeal to her better nature. *As opposed,* he thought, *to Odo who, let's face it, doesn't* have *a better nature.* Besides, when the renegade Jem'Hadar attacked the station a few weeks back, Quark had saved Ro's life. *It's time I collected on that debt.*

"A problem, huh?" Ro said with her toothy smile.

"This ought to be good." She stood at the rear wall monitors, looking over the current inhabitants of the holding cells. Quark saw the usual bunch of criminals, deadbeats, losers, ne'er-do-wells, and regular patrons of his bar in the screens. Ro turned off the surveillance and the screens went blank.

As she did, Quark started, "There's this Orion—"

"Malic." Ro sat back in her chair and touched the control that closed the door to the security office. "He came to you a few days ago to extort your cooperation in a business venture, and you're expecting him to return at any moment so you can get started."

Quark sighed. He hated when security people did that. They never understood the importance of not letting the person on the other side know that you know more than they think you know.

"Right. And that's my problem."

"Don't want to work for the Orions?"

"Don't want to work for *this* Orion." Quark finally sat down in the guest chair. "You see, I have this friend on Cardassia named Deru. He used to be a glinn in the military, and he was assigned to the station back when the Cardassians ran it. He retired about eight or nine years ago to go into private enterprise. The two of us entered into a business deal about two months ago. We've been arranging to get supplies to people who need it in Cardassian territory."

"Very noble of you." Ro sounded almost sincere. "Or it would be if I didn't know you better than to think you're doing this out of the goodness of your heart."

"I *am* doing it out of the goodness of my heart!"

Quark said indignantly. "What is it about Bajorans that you think that doing a good deed and turning a profit are mutually exclusive?"

"So what's in it for you?"

"Land. See, we divert shipments of relief supplies to certain individuals in return for their land."

Ro's face distorted into a frown. "You kick people out of their homes?"

Quark rolled his eyes. "Don't be ridiculous. We're not doing this to anyone who can't afford it. No, we're getting supplies to the people with excess land. Nobody's being kicked out of their home. Besides, most of this property was damaged during the war. It'll only be useful again with a lot of work—which, I'm sure, some entrepreneuring buyer would be willing to invest in."

"And a Cardassian landowner who's starving to death wouldn't be willing to invest in it, but he might be willing to sell it to somebody like Deru, in order to stay alive," Ro said, showing a keen grasp of the economics.

"Exactly!" Quark said, grateful that she understood. "I knew you had the lobes for this sort of thing."

"Keep my ears out of this, Quark. So let me get this straight. A bunch of Cardassians, who used to be rich, now find themselves stuck with a ton of land, but no way to make use of it. They're also starving to death because the Cardassian economy is in a shambles, or maybe they're sick or injured from the devastation because relief hasn't reached them yet. Along comes Quark—"

"Actually, it's my associate who approaches them."

"Along comes *Deru*," Ro said obligingly, "who

goes to these people, who are used to feeling like they belong to the greatest civilization in the galaxy, and now can't even get a working replicator. And Deru tells them he can get them black-market food and supplies, courtesy of his anonymous, big-lobed accessory—"

"Hey!"

"—and all they have to do is give up all this extra land that they can't do anything with anyhow."

"You make it sound like I've committed a crime," Quark said.

Ro laughed. "If you didn't *know* you'd committed a crime, Quark, you wouldn't be here right now. Because you know damn well that if Malic informed Starfleet or the Cardassian authorities about this, they'd rip your ears off."

"It isn't Starfleet or the Cardassians I'm worried about," Quark snapped. He looked over his shoulder as if he expected someone else to be listening, then turned back to Ro. "It's Garak."

Ro shrugged. "So?"

Quark threw up his hands. "You ever *met* Garak?"

Ro shook her head. "I know he's very involved in the rebuilding of Cardassia Prime. I also know him by reputation, and I honestly don't think we'd ever find your body."

"You see the problem."

"Should've thought of that before you got mixed up with Deru."

"How was I supposed to know that some old Orion would come along and blackmail me with it?"

"Isn't there a Rule of Acquisition about knowing your customers *before* they walk in the door?"

Quark rolled his eyes. "I come to you for help, and you quote the Hundred and Ninety-Fourth Rule at me. Some friend you are."

Ro leaned forward and got serious. "What exactly does Malic want you to do?"

Sighing, Quark said, "He wants me to negotiate a purchase on behalf of the syndicate. I don't know what for."

"I've heard of worse deals," Ro observed. "Maybe you should just take it."

"You don't understand—this is the Orion Syndicate!"

"I know who they are, Quark. I went through Starfleet tactical training, remember? We spent a week just on the syndicate." Ro picked up a padd and started fiddling with it—constantly turning it ninety degrees with her hands without actually looking at it. "You're worried that once the Orions get what they want, they'll tell Garak anyway."

"Something like that."

Now she looked genuinely amused. "You're really scared of him, aren't you?"

"For Gint's sake, Laren, he used to be in the Obsidian Order! Didn't you spend a week on *them* in Starfleet tactical training?"

"No," she said gravely, "it was two weeks." She set down the padd. "All right, Quark, I'll help you. But you have to help me in return."

Quark's eyes narrowed suspiciously. "How?"

"By going through with Malic's negotiations, and helping me to infiltrate the syndicate."

Quark felt his ears shrivel. "Infiltrate? Are you insane?"

Ro keyed a file on her padd and held it up so

Quark could see the display. "Look at this—Malic is on about a dozen wanted lists. Getting close to him—"

Quark stood up abruptly. "I'm *not* going to infiltrate the Orion Syndicate, Laren!"

Ro rose and glowered down at him across the security desk. "Oh yes you are. Because if you don't—I'm going to tell Starfleet *and* Garak you've been exploiting Cardassian citizens."

Falling more than sitting back into the chair, Quark said, "I don't believe this. I save your life, and this is how you pay me back? You help me get out of being blackmailed by Malic by blackmailing me with the same thing?"

"Yes, I know, the injustice of it all." Ro smiled. "Don't look so glum, Quark. Think of the points you'll score with Kira and Vaughn when I tell them that you helped me bring down a major player in the syndicate *and* turned in a Cardassian who is illegally diverting relief supplies to wealthy patrons."

Quark put his hand over his heart. "Are you telling me I have to turn in Deru? Betray my comrade and business partner in order to save my own skin?"

Ro nodded.

"He'll turn me in!"

"Let me worry about that."

Quark knew then that it was over. He had no bargaining position this time. Ro had him by the lobes. *Not the worst position to be in, when you think about it, but still . . .*

"All right, fine. What do I have to do?"

"Exactly what Malic wants you to do. The only difference is, you'll have a dabo girl with you."

Aghast, Quark said, "You want me to expose one of my dabo girls to those Orion lunatics?"

Ro glowered. "Don't be an idiot, Quark. *I'll* be disguised as a dabo girl."

Suddenly getting a very pleasant mental picture, Quark smiled. His right hand brushed across his lobe. "Really?" From the moment he'd met her, Quark had wondered how Ro would look in a dabo girl's outfit. *Maybe this won't be so bad after all.*

When his glazed eyes refocused on Ro, she was scowling at him. "Get your mind out of the waste extractor, Quark. This is business. I'll be by your side at all times. The Orions care—their attitude toward women is even worse than the Ferengi's, so they won't see me as anything more than decoration. If things go well, you'll be out of there with no problems, I'll have some useful dirt on Malic, and I'll make sure Starfleet and Garak don't give you any grief over your little land scheme."

"You're not exactly giving me much of a choice," Quark said pointedly. "All right, it's a deal."

"Good."

"But I think this is insane."

FARIUS PRIME (THE PRESENT)

"I *still* think this is insane."

Quark ran after Ro through the corridors of the Orion ship. Alarms blared loud enough to hurt Quark's sensitive ears.

Two Orions came around a corner. Ro took them out with two well-placed shots before they had the chance to fire their weapons.

"Nice shooting," Quark said. He noticed that they were headed farther away from both the ship's transporter and the hangar bay. "Where are we going?"

"We need to be near an outer bulkhead. The inner sections of the ship are shielded against transporters."

"Why not just go to the ship's transporter?"

"Because then there'll be a record, and they'll know where we went."

"Oh."

Ro bent over and took the Orions' disruptors. She stuck one in the waistband of her slitted pants and handed the other to Quark.

The Ferengi looked at it as if it were someone asking for a handout. "What am I supposed to do with this?"

"Take a guess."

Reluctantly, Quark took it. Since it was of Klingon design, it didn't have a safety, so Quark handled it as if he feared the slightest touch would trigger it.

While Quark weighed the risk of putting the weapon in his jacket against holding it and accidentally blasting a hole in the bulkhead, Ro took a moment to admonish him. "Oh, and by the way, the reason it took me a minute to throw the flare is because I frankly didn't expect you to cave in so easily."

"What're you talking about? I was following the terms of Malic's oral agreement. Malic said to tell the truth or die, so I told the truth."

Ro shot him a dubious look.

Quark sighed. "Fifteenth Rule of Acquisition, Laren: 'Dead men close no deals.' It's not my fault that Malic changed the terms of the deal at the last minute and decided to kill me anyhow."

They turned a corner. A turbolift door opened on an Orion male, escorting a scantily clad Orion female. The female—who was a full head taller than the male—was practically draped all over him. She wore what appeared to be rags, but Quark recognized the custom tailoring at work. *Obviously the male has a thing for women in dirty rags and she's dressing for the part.*

At the sight of Ro's disruptor, the male screamed, which surprised Quark—he'd expected the scream from the female.

"Back inside," Ro snarled.

The female quickly backed into the turbolift. The male just stood there, screaming. He was worse than the alarms.

"Stop," Ro said, putting the disruptor to the Orion's head, "screaming."

The male fell silent and went into the turbolift. He did blubber a bit, though.

Once the doors closed, Ro said, "Take us to deck seventy-one."

Quark frowned, confused—then he remembered that the ship's computer would probably only accept commands from certain Orion males. No female, and no Ferengi—not even one working for the Orions—would have access.

At first, the male didn't reply, busy as he was with his blubbering. Ro again put the disruptor to his head. "D-d-d-d-d-deck seventy-one," he finally said.

The turbolift moved. As it did, Ro removed another of her tassels. There was a small button on it, which she pressed.

"What's that do?" Quark asked.

"Scattering field. It should block any attempts the Orions make to divert the turbolift."

"Should?"

Ro shrugged. "If this were an ordinary Vulcan ship, it would, but I don't know what kind of modifications they made."

Soon, the question was academic. They arrived on deck seventy-one—the ship's lowermost deck—and the doors opened.

Half a dozen Orions were waiting for them.

Ro immediately put the disruptor to the female's neck. "Let us go or the slave gets it."

"Are you insane?" Quark whispered. "She's just a female."

Snarling, one of the Orions said, "Lower your weapons."

Slowly, and to Quark's abject shock, the Orions did so.

"Try anything," Ro said, "and I blow her pretty head off, understood?"

"Just don't hurt her," the Orion said.

Ro moved down the corridor, guiding the female in front of her with the disruptor, still at her neck, and pulling the male along behind her. Quark followed behind the male.

As soon as they got close to the Orions—who parted to let them pass—Ro tossed the male in the direction of three of the Orions.

One of them immediately punched Ro's former hostage in the gut. "Alhan, you idiot!" another one said. "How could you let Treir be captured like that?"

Alhan was unable to reply, as he was too busy coughing up blood.

Quark quickly followed Ro and Treir. Now he understood Ro's logic—Treir was valuable merchandise. The Orions couldn't afford for her to be harmed. Alhan, on the other hand, was just another Orion male, and by allowing himself to be captured, his value to his fellows had plummeted to nothing. Once again, he admired Ro's grasp of business matters. *So rare to find a female who understands—especially a female Bajoran.*

From behind him, Quark heard one of the Orions' voices. "Malic, they've got Treir." A pause. "I *know* she's not to be harmed, but they're going to get away."

They turned a corner, out of sight of the Orions. Quark could still hear the Orion talking to Malic.

"All right," the Orion was saying as Ro stopped walking and—still holding the disruptor to Treir's neck—removed the last two tassels from her waist. She threw the first one back around the corner toward the Orions. The one speaking to Malic was suddenly cut off by a noise that sounded to Quark like five phasers firing at once.

Then silence.

"What was that?"

"Concussive grenade. Should keep those six out for a while."

"You couldn't do that before he told Malic we were here?"

As she pressed a control on the final tassel, which caused its base to split open, Ro said, "You really can be a whiner, can't you? We had to get out of range."

Ro removed a Bajoran communicator from inside the tassel and tapped it.

As soon as she did, the corridor shimmered, faded, and re-formed into the flight deck of a small spacecraft of Bajoran design. About the size of a small Starfleet shuttlecraft, the ship seated two fore and two aft.

A Bajoran woman in a red Militia uniform and with the rank insignia of a sergeant vacated the pilot's seat. "Who's your friend, Lieutenant?"

"She was a hostage," Ro said, removing the disruptor from the woman's neck. "Luckily, they didn't call my bluff when I said I'd blow her head off."

Treir, for her part, had kept a remarkably calm expression on her face from the moment she first saw Ro with the disruptor. Once she dropped out of the role of being Alhan's lover, her face had gone surprisingly neutral.

Quark asked, "Where are we?"

"A Bajoran Militia flitter," the sergeant said.

"I *know* it's a Bajoran Militia flitter," Quark said impatiently. "I mean *where?*"

"Farius Prime's innermost moon." Ro touched the flame gem on her necklace. Her hair returned to its natural black color. "Ychell Mafon, this is Quark—Quark, this is Sergeant Ychell. I had her hide out here as our escape route."

"Nice of you to tell me ahead of time," Quark muttered.

"Don't push it, Quark, or so help me—"

Quark rolled his eyes and shut up.

Turning to Treir, Ro said, "As for you—you're free to come with us. You can start over in the Federation or on Bajor. You don't have to be a slave anymore."

Treir smiled. "Did it even occur to you that I liked being a slave?"

Ro blinked. "Honestly? No, it didn't."

"You're lucky, then, that I didn't. On the other

hand, no one ever gave me a choice in the matter. Besides, Malic treated me very well."

"Well, Malic doesn't own you anymore."

Again, Treir smiled, this time a wry one. "Malic may have something to say about that."

Ro settled into the pilot's seat. "He has to find us first." She indicated the two rear seats. "Get in the back. You too, Quark. We need to get back to DS9."

"What's the point?" Quark asked, taking his seat. "I'm doomed anyhow. You may as well give me back to the Orions."

"What are you talking about?"

"You heard Malic. All it takes is one command into his padd, and Garak will know all about my role in that land deal."

Ro reached behind her back and took something out from under the rear part of her waistband. She smiled broadly. "You mean this padd?"

Quark saw fighting Aldebaran serpents and a nude Orion woman. His mouth fell open.

So did Treir's, but unlike Quark, she was still able to formulate words. "That's Malic's padd! How did you—?"

"I grabbed it out of his pocket when I knocked him down in the meeting room. Not only are you safe from the Orions, Quark, but I'm betting there's enough information in this thing to bring Malic down—and maybe the whole syndicate."

A huge sense of relief spread over Quark. "So Garak won't find out?"

"Well, I never said *that*."

Quark eyes went wide. But before he could pursue the matter, Ychell announced, "Lieutenant, the Orion ship has started a search pattern. They're going to find us soon. We need to get out of here. I've got a course set for that hole that your transport came through—the one that goes to the Clarus system."

"Let's do it," Ro said, getting into the pilot's seat. She touched a few controls, then turned back to Quark and smiled. "I wonder if Malic made a copy . . ."

Quark felt his lobes shrivel.

14

THE DELTA QUADRANT

"THEY WERE DIVERTING PREY."

The giant indicated the fallen aliens with one gauntleted hand. Kira looked once again at the three butchered corpses she shared the floor with. *Diverting* wasn't the first word that came to mind. It was possible, of course, that these aliens were tougher than they looked, but Kira couldn't imagine they were so vicious that it was necessary to slaughter them.

"But only just," the being amended. "It was their ship that was the true enemy. I had hoped that a vessel capable of withstanding an attack such as mine and causing my own vessel's destruction would be crewed by the worthiest prey."

That explains the debris, Kira thought.

He started to pace around the bridge. "Instead, I found them to be soft and weak. Not worthy of a hunt." The creature pounded a fist on a nearby console, denting the metal. "My ship was destroyed. My trophies, my weapons, my *life*—all of it wiped away by these insignificant creatures."

"They were fighting for their lives, what do you expect?" Kira found herself saying.

As if she hadn't spoke, the alien went on. "After I killed them all, I waited. I knew this ship would not stay unmolested for long—not with such volatile cargo. So I awaited fresh prey." He once again looked down at Kira. "Then you came."

"You tie up all your prey before you 'hunt' them?" Kira mocked, testing her bonds. "Some predator."

The insult slid right past the alien. "No, you are bait. Just as this ship sat idle as a lure, so will you."

"A lure for what?" Kira asked angrily, already knowing the answer.

"The other one. I beamed two over from your ship, but only one is here. The other one is somewhere on the ship. Eventually it will show itself."

Taran'atar, Kira thought. *He must've shrouded when we were beamed off the* Euphrates. Jem'Hadar were born with the ability to cloak themselves, rendering them invisible both to the naked eye and most scans. The ability required most of their concentration, which meant they couldn't actually fight while shrouded. Kira hoped Taran'atar was scouting the ship, then waiting for the right moment to attack. "You're wasting your time," she said. "He's probably long gone."

"He's near," the hunter said with certainty. "I can feel it in the— *Ooof!*"

That last word was spoken as he was tackled from behind by Taran'atar, who solidified half a second before striking.

While both aliens crashed against the deck and began struggling for the upper hand, Kira managed to roll over to a nearby console. Bracing her back against it, she pushed herself upward to get into a crouching position, and then stood upright, quickly taking stock of her surroundings.

The room, which she assumed was the tanker's bridge, had two entrances—one, a closed door on the far side, the other, an open hallway right behind her.

A very large handheld weapon, easily twice the size of a Starfleet phaser rifle, was lying on the deck beyond the combatants, out of her reach. *Not that I could use it with my hands tied behind my back, but . . .*

The alien had gained the advantage, pinning Taran'atar to the deck. Kira saw an opportunity and sprang forward, pivoting on her left leg, spinning and landing a kick to the alien's helmeted head.

Her teeth clenched. It was like kicking a stone wall, and she suspected only her boot's padding kept her from breaking her foot.

It did, however, surprise the alien enough so that Taran'atar could fling him off. The alien crashed against a instrument panel, sending sparks flying. The Jem'Hadar leapt and stood in front of Kira, deliberately placing himself between her and their foe.

The alien slowly rose and faced them. Now that they were all standing up, Kira saw that the self-styled hunter was indeed tall, but not quite the giant she had thought him to be—Kira estimated he was a bit more than two meters in height.

The alien smiled in a manner that reminded Kira far too much of Dukat. "At last," he rumbled. "Worthy prey."

To Kira's annoyance, Taran'atar had thrown the alien closer to where his rifle lay. If he grabbed it while they were in the room, they were dead.

"Move!" she barked, leading Taran'atar to the open hallway behind them.

Without a instant's hesitation, Taran'atar followed.

"I had the chance to explore this deck before I attacked the Hirogen," the Jem'Hadar said as they ran side by side down the corridor.

So that's what he's called. "Fine, take point."

He led them through a maze of corridors. Everywhere they went, Kira found more bodies like the three on the bridge: gold-skinned, wearing the bulky uniform, and bleeding from dozens of wounds each.

Taran'atar led them into what appeared to be a maintenance tunnel. He shut the hatch and locked it, showing an impressive aptitude for equipment he'd never seen before today.

Once the door closed, Kira turned around. "Can you do something about these bonds?"

Taking Kira's wrists in his scaly hands, Taran'atar said, "I believe so. This may hurt."

"Just do it."

Taran'atar grabbed the bonds, the sides of his hands pressing up against Kira's wrists. He pulled for several seconds. She gritted her teeth against the pain that shot through her shoulders as the bonds finally gave in to the Jem'Hadar's strength, and her arms were suddenly wrenched apart.

She flexed her shoulders. "Thanks. Now then, you obviously know who this guy is."

"I know of the species from an encounter a Jem'Hadar unit had with a Hirogen ship several hundred years ago. Back then, they were nomadic hunters with an impressive level of technology."

"Judging from what I've seen and heard, I'd say they still are," Kira said. "I take it from the way you shut the door so easily that you had a chance to examine some of the ship's systems?"

"Those that still function, yes. It did not take long, as very few of the systems are functioning at all. Propulsion, weapons, and tractor beams are inoperative."

"So we can't try to draw the waste back into the cargo hold?"

"No, Colonel."

Kira pounded the bulkhead with a fist. "Dammit!" She reached for her phaser—and found that it wasn't there. "I don't remember him taking my weapon."

"He didn't. My rifle didn't materialize with me when we were taken to this ship. Our energy weapons are either still on the *Euphrates* or dispersed."

Kira tapped her badge. "Kira to *Euphrates*. Computer, two to transport to the runabout."

The computer's voice was barely audible through a burst of static. *"Unable to comply due to theta radiation interference."*

Kira muttered an Old High Bajoran curse that her brother Reon had taught her when they were kids. "Computer, scan this vessel. Is there anywhere aboard we can go where the interference is weak enough so transporters can penetrate?"

"Negative."

She thought a moment. Obviously the transporters on this ship could penetrate the theta radiation, otherwise the Hirogen could never have beamed them over. Besides, these people had reason to make their transporters more resistant to radiation interference than Starfleet ever did, if they lived with this toxicity every day. "Can you locate the transporters here?"

"Affirmative."

Kira looked around. There were no working terminals, and she didn't have a tricorder. "Locate the nearest one to these coordinates."

"The nearest transporter to your location is in the fore section of deck twelve."

"And where are we right now?" Kira asked impatiently.

"In the middle section of deck two."

"Can you read any life-forms aboard this vessel?"

"Life-sign scan inconclusive. Two life-forms are assumed based on combadge signals of Colonel Kira Nerys and Taran'atar."

Kira repeated the curse, and cut off the transmission. Then she looked at Taran'atar. "Do you still have your *kar'takin?"*

"Yes." Taran'atar reached behind his back and unsheathed the thin-bladed weapon that Jem'Hadar generally carried as backups in case their energy weapons failed or were sabotaged.

"Good. We don't have any way to track the Hirogen—and he's a trained hunter. Do you know any way to go down ten decks from here?"

"No," Taran'atar said, "but I believe it should not be difficult to find one. With respect, Colonel, I should take the point."

Kira was unaccustomed to letting others put themselves in danger on her behalf. Unfortunately, in this particular instance, Taran'atar was the only one who was armed. "After you."

Taran'atar led them down the corridor, his *kar'takin* held in a defensive position. Kira followed close behind, feeling naked without a weapon. No rifle, no hand phaser, not even a blade. *Hell, at this point, I'd take a club.*

Finding access to the lower levels proved easier than she expected; they discovered a narrow, vertical shaft that was propped open by the corpse of one of the tanker crew.

"Were you able to find any working terminals?" Kira asked as she and Taran'atar moved the body out of their way and onto the deck. "Find out who these people are?"

"No."

Shaking her head as she peered into the shaft, she said, "It's ironic. When we first arrived, I wanted to kill these people. Now that they're dead—I actually feel sorry for them." A ladder on the far wall of the shaft went up one level to deck one, and went down farther than Kira's eyes could see. The shaft was illuminated only with the same dim green lights that the rest of this deck was bathed in.

"Whoever they are," Taran'atar said, "their battle is done, and they did not reclaim their lives. Our battle is not yet over."

"Damn right it isn't," she muttered as she clambered into the hatch and set her feet down on one rung of the ladder. Taran'atar followed a moment later.

Kira couldn't read the writing on the shaft wall—in

the dim light, she could barely even see it—but she counted her way down past each of the identical hatchways until she reached what should have been the twelfth deck from the top.

Unfortunately, this hatch was not propped open by a gold-skinned corpse. Simply pushing on the handle didn't budge it. She tried pulling it, but that didn't work, either.

"Give me your blade," she said, reaching up.

Taran'atar handed the *kar'takin* down, hilt-first, without comment. *There are times when his unquestioning obedience is really refreshing.* For all that Starfleet insisted on military protocol, their officers had a tiresome tendency to question everything. It was a nice change to work with someone who just did what he was told.

Hooking one arm and one leg through the ladder's strut, she used the thin blade to try to pry the door open. Her leverage was awful, and the best she could do was bend the metal slightly outward.

That should be enough, though. Handing the Jem'Hadar his weapon back, she asked, "Taran'atar, do you think you can pry the door open with that handhold?"

"I believe so."

Kira climbed down several more rungs to allow Taran'atar access. Grimacing slightly, the Jem'Hadar grabbed at the bent metal and pushed against it. He peeled back the hatchway, the sound of the distorting metal disturbingly loud in the shaft. He then went through the opening he'd made, the edges of the torn metal tearing at his dark coverall. Kira, who was much smaller, was able to get through a moment later without any damage to her uniform.

Deck twelve looked very much like the one they had just come from: same green lights, same browns and greens in the décor, same nonfunctioning equipment, same miasma. The only improvement was that the burning smell didn't make it down this far.

As Taran'atar led the way toward the ship's fore, Kira tapped her combadge. "Computer, can you pinpoint the exact location of the transporter room on deck twelve of this vessel?"

The static was less here than it had been on deck two. "*Negative. Theta radiation prevents a precise reading.*"

"Figures," she muttered. "We'll just have to try all the doors in the forward section until we find one."

The first two doors they came to seemed to be locked. Taran'atar pried them open to find that they were storage rooms.

The third opened when they approached. At the sight of what was inside, Kira gasped. She tapped her combadge again. "Computer, can you scan the equipment in this room?"

"*Negative.*"

"Is the shield generator somewhere in the forward section of deck twelve?"

"*Affirmative.*"

She looked at Taran'atar. "If this is what I think it is . . ." She knelt down in front of one piece of equipment.

The room was lined with machinery that looked enough like a shield generator to satisfy Kira—especially given the device that was attached to one of the consoles. The device was very obviously of a different design than the rest of the ship. It had a sleeker interface, a different control layout, and a different type of display screen from everything else on the tanker.

It was also very familiar.

"I was right," she said after examining it. "This is just like the shield enhancers we had in the resistance." She looked up at Taran'atar. "Under normal circumstances, our little ships couldn't hold up to the Cardassian warships, but we were able to enhance our shields. This is very similar to something that one of the other cells came up with for our sub-impulse raiders."

"With respect, Colonel, we must find the transporter and—"

"Help me remove this."

"Colonel, the Hirogen may arrive at any time to—"

So much for unquestioning obedience. "Taran'atar, this may be what we need to save Europa Nova! Now help me remove it!"

Taran'atar glared, then said, "As you command."

As she started undoing connections, she said, "It'll still be another three hours before all the Europani going to Torona IV will be through the gateway at Costa Rocosa. The *Defiant* can't disrupt the gateways until then. That huge mass of waste will go through in less than two hours. If we attach this shield enhancer to the *Euphrates*, it may just boost Nog's shields enough so that we can use the ship to block this gateway completely. It won't just stop the mass, it'll stop more of the irradiated material from going through and give our people more time to evacuate." She had removed all the rear connections by the time she finished the sentence.

Taran'atar undid the last of the side connections, and the two of them gently set the enhancer onto the floor. Kira looked around, and found a handle. Awkwardly, she picked it up with both hands. *These people also designed it to be portable. Smart move.* When Kira's resistance cell acquired the enhancer, the first thing Kira had said was it needed to have a handle on it so it could be carried more easily—without that handhold, it needed two people to move it. This one was heavier than the one they'd had in the resistance, but still manageable.

The Jem'Hadar moved to assist her, but she shook her head. "No. I'd rather you kept your hands on your weapon. Let's find that transporter."

The fourth door opened as they approached, and it appeared to be the transporter. Kira lugged the enhancer to the platform while Taran'atar sheathed his *kar'takin* and went to the controls.

"I have locked on to the *Euphrates.*"

"Good. Get up here."

The Jem'Hadar did not move. "If we both beam off the tanker, the Hirogen will simply beam us back. One of us must remain behind to distract the hunter while the other installs the shield."

Kira stared at Taran'atar. The Jem'Hadar, typically, betrayed only one emotion: resolve. Taran'atar knew that there was only one decision Kira could make here. He was armed and could shroud, and therefore had the best chance against the Hirogen. Kira knew the shield enhancer and how to install it—she'd done so once while under fire from Cardassians, she could certainly do it in a Starfleet runabout that was much more receptive to adaptive components than Bajoran sub-I's.

But she hated the idea of leaving someone behind. With the runabout's transporters unable to pierce the radiation, she'd be unable to beam him back to the *Eu-*

phrates, or even return to help him once her task was done. "That thing out there will probably kill you."

Unsheathing his *kar'takin* and holding it across his chest, Taran'atar said, "I am already dead. I must go into battle to reclaim my life. This I do gladly because I am Jem'Hadar."

As if I needed reminding, Kira thought.

"You must fulfill your oath to President Silverio, Colonel. And I must fulfill the one I made when the Founders gave me life."

Kira took a deep breath, then nodded. "Energize."

Taran'atar set the controls. Then he looked up. "One more thing, Colonel. When the Founders sent me on this mission, I thought that my gods had cast *me* out. I have since learned that I was wrong."

Then he finished the sequence, and both the Jem'Hadar and the tanker's transporter room disappeared, replaced by the interior of the *Euphrates.*

Sighing, Kira thought, *Every time I think I have that Jem'Hadar figured out, he goes and surprises me.*

"Computer," she said, then hesitated. She was about to ask for a full damage report, but that would take too long. "Status of shields and propulsion."

"Shields inoperative. Warp drive functioning at eighty-two percent of capacity. Impulse drive functioning at seventy-four percent of capacity."

"Reason for shield failure?"

"Power conduits one through four have been irreparably damaged. Six microprocessors have failed."

"If the conduits are replaced, will the shields function?"

"Affirmative."

"Do we have four replacement conduits on board?"

"Affirmative."

"Thank you, Nog," she muttered. Then, removing her uniform jacket and setting it on one of the chairs, she set to work.

Within twenty minutes, she had replaced the conduits. "Computer," she said, "prepare shield generator for installation of additional equipment."

This certainly brings back memories, she thought, as she looked for an appropriate access port. The last time she had to install one of these, it was in the midst of a firefight. She, Furel, Lupaza, and Mabrin were supposed to rendezvous with Shakaar at Singha when the Cardassian scout ship found their flitter. They had just obtained the enhancer, and Kira had been forced to connect it and use it without testing—all in about five minutes, while under fire. It only worked part of the time, but that was true of everything on that ship.

Unbidden, the voices of her fellow resistance fighters sounded in her head.

"They're coming around for another pass. Hurry up with that evasive course, Lupaza."

"I'm moving as fast as I can, Furel. The controls are sluggish."

"I'm gonna slug you in a minute."

"They're firing!"

"Shields are down to fifty percent!"

"Nerys, if you don't get that damn thing installed in another minute, there won't be any shields for it to enhance."

"I'm working as fast as I can, Mabrin. Anytime you want to climb under here and help out . . ."

Kira smiled as she attached two more leads to the generator. So many memories—liberating Gallitep and freeing those poor laborers from their deadly mining duties, the attack on Gul Pirak, the destruction of the Seltran mine. Most of all, she remembered Lorit Akrem taking her twelve-year-old self to meet Shakaar Edon for the first time in the caves of the Dakhur Hills.

It was all so much easier, then. Shakaar gave us our orders, and we fought. We knew who the enemy was, and we went after them.

She stopped what she was doing, and shook her head. "What the hell am I thinking?" she said.

"Please repeat instruction," the computer droned.

Ignoring the computer, Kira snarled and threw herself back into the shield enhancer. *How screwed up is my life that I'm looking back* fondly *on the resistance? Now I'm feeling nostalgia for Gallitep?*

I wish Odo were here.

She stopped working. *Dammit,* she thought, furious at her own weakness. *I promised I wouldn't let myself do that. Odo did what he had to do. I* know *that.*

But she could always talk to Odo. Even before they became lovers, he had always been there for her when she needed him. And if he wasn't available for whatever reason, there had always been someone—Jadzia Dax, Bareil Antos, Tiris Jast, even sometimes Captain Sisko, when she could get her mind around his being the Emissary.

But Odo and the captain were gone, perhaps never to return. Jadzia, Antos, and Tiris were dead. Ever since becoming station commander, Kira had been putting more distance between herself and her officers, even the ones she'd known for years. She admired and respected Vaughn, but they were still getting to know each other. She'd also recently put a huge strain on her friendship with Kasidy.

And since I became Attainted, most Bajorans can't even bear to look at me.

What was it Benjamin once said? "It's lonely at the top." But dammit, even he had Dax—either one. Not to mention Jake and Kasidy. Who've I got?

"*Warning—power requirements of enhancement module exceed current capacity.*"

"Dammit," she muttered. She had been hoping that Starfleet's adaptable engines would be able to handle it. But this enhancer was designed for that beast of a tanker out there, not something as small as the *Euphrates*.

That can't be it, she thought. *There's got to be another way.* "Computer, is it possible to divert enough power from other sources to the shield generator to allow it to function?"

"*Affirmative.*"

Another thought occurred. "Can it still be done if impulse power is left active?"

"*Affirmative.*"

"Good. Do it."

"*Unable to comply.*"

She closed her eyes. *Take it easy, Nerys, you can't punch the computer.* After taking a deep breath she asked, "Why not?"

"*In order to comply, life-support must be terminated.*"

"There's always a catch," she muttered.

"*Please restate request.*"

"Never mind." She searched around the enhancer, and found an inhibitor switch that would keep it from activating when it was hooked up. "Computer, time?"

"The time is 1242 hours."

She stood up. *Little more than an hour before that mass goes through.* "Computer, begin recording a message."

"Recording."

Placing her hands on the back of one of the side console's chairs, Kira took a moment to compose her thoughts. "This is Colonel Kira Nerys on the *Euphrates* contacting all vessels at Europa Nova. The radiation is coming from a cargo tanker that's dumping antimatter waste from its hold into the gateway. The crew of the tanker is dead, killed by an alien who is currently engaged in combat with Taran'atar. There's a concentration of toxic material bigger than anything that's gone through the gateway so far, coming through in one hour. I'll be using the *Euphrates* to block that and any further waste with the help of a shield enhancer I salvaged from the tanker." She took a deep breath. "In order for this enhancer to function, I'll need to shut down life-support. I'll therefore be evacuating the *Euphrates* and taking my chances on the fifth planet in this system, which is Class-M." *Not much choice; with the transporter useless and no docking ports on that thing, there's no way for me to return to the tanker on my own.* "As soon as it's feasible to attempt the disruption of the gateways, do it, regardless of whether or not Taran'atar or I have returned. That's an order." She took another deep breath. "Computer, end message. When the *Euphrates* approaches the gateway, broadcast the message every two minutes."

"Affirmative."

She sat at the helm and set a course for the fifth planet.

As the runabout descended into the atmosphere, Kira programmed a course that would take the *Euphrates* on autopilot back to the gateway. The ship would take up position at the threshold, then activate the enhancer and expand the shield envelope to maximum, with the impulse engines working to hold the runabout in position regardless of any force arrayed against it. After all, it would do no good to have that chunk of waste push the runabout through the gateway.

The viewport showed an arid desert of a planet. The vegetation was sparse at best, and there were few bodies of water around. Kira did an intensive scan, and found a location that was near a freshwater lake and that also registered a survivably low temperature. Unfortunately, that spot was currently in the early morning, so the temperature would probably increase significantly before long, but she didn't have time to search for the perfect place to land.

Once she set down, she got up to inspect the runabout's emergency kit. Everything seemed to be present and accounted for, and then some. *Starfleet does believe in overcompensating, don't they?* A small army could subsist on the combat rations, and Kira had to wonder if both a temperature control unit *and* an expandable shelter were necessary. The quick diagnostic she ran showed that the small communications module was in working order, and the medikit had been stocked with arithrazine. The Hirogen had indeed dispersed her phaser, so she took a Starfleet-issue one from the weapons cabinet—then took a second for good measure, as well as a tricorder.

She opened the hatch. A blast of heat assaulted her face, a dry wind pushing her back from the hatchway.

The air smelled stale and uninviting, and Kira was grateful that she hadn't bothered to put her uniform jacket back on, though she had tied it to her waist.

Everywhere she looked on the ground was sand, broken very rarely by bits of plant life, and the one freshwater lake that she had made sure to land near. It was flat land, with the only variations being the curvature of the planet itself. Not even any hills or mountains or sand dunes in sight. It was almost like a negative image of Europa Nova—where that world was the picture of luscious beauty, this was quite possibly the bleakest planet Kira had ever seen.

And I'm stuck in this place in order to fulfill my oath to save the other one. To think, some people believe the Prophets don't have a sense of humor. Well, they do, and it's a black one. My life is proof of that.

She tapped her combadge, and her hand almost slid off it, it was so covered in sweat. *And I've only been here a minute.* "Computer, activate program Kira-One."

At those words, the hatch to the runabout closed. As soon as it locked into place, the runabout lifted off into the cloudless blue sky. Kira watched it ascend for as long as it was in sight, then tracked it with her tricorder while it remained in range—which wasn't long at all.

Now I just have to hope that my plan works.

She checked the tricorder. Theta radiation was already contaminating the atmosphere—that clear sky was working against her—and with the gateway blocked up, it was only likely to get worse.

Kira gave herself a dose of arithrazine, then got started setting up the shelter.

Within two minutes she had to stop. Sweat plastered her uniform to her body and dripped down into her eyes. Kira worked hard to keep herself in shape, and so little physical effort should not have exhausted her so quickly. She grabbed a bottle of water from the emergency kit and drained the entire thing in one gulp. It helped only a little.

This is gonna be fun, she thought grimly. Then she got back to work on the shelter, moving more slowly this time, conserving her energy, praying that Taran'atar would win his battle.

And that she would win hers.

15

EUROPA NOVA

"COMMANDER, WE CAN'T DO THIS."

Vaughn didn't bother to turn the *Defiant*'s command chair around at Bashir's outburst. "What in particular is it that we can't do, Doctor?"

Bashir stepped between Vaughn and the conn. He was holding a padd in his left hand and pointed at the viewscreen with it as he said, "This! All of it! I had hoped that the *Trager* and the gateway to Torona IV would make a difference, but I'm afraid they won't. The *Trager* is transporting people more slowly than anticipated. Each wave of evacuation is taking twice as long as the previous one. This relay method of the *Trager* and *Intrepid* picking people up and passing them off to the other ships is not what one would call expedient."

"We're not exactly overburdened with alternatives, Doctor," Vaughn said dryly.

"I'm aware of that, but—" Bashir sighed. "We had a chance when we started, but with the tortoise-like pace we've been going at, I'm afraid those chances have dwindled to nothing. People are going to die!"

Vaughn simply stared at him. "We had this conversation in ops, Doctor. The chances were poor to begin with. We don't give up because the math is bad."

"I understand that, sir, but we have a bigger problem. Have a look at this." He handed Vaughn the padd.

Looking down at the padd, Vaughn saw a familiar-looking sensor reading from the *Gryphon*, then handed it back to Bashir. "Yes, I know. Captain Mello told me about this an hour ago."

Bashir looked incredulous. "If that mass comes through the gateway—"

"I'm aware of the danger to Europa Nova. Tell me, Doctor, do you have any actual business on the bridge besides telling me things I already know?"

"I'd like to know why I wasn't informed of this! And I'd like to know what's being done!"

His voice as calm as Bashir's was frantic, Vaughn said, "Colonel Kira and Taran'atar have gone through the gateway to try to stop the radiation at the source. Since you've been occupied with coordinating relief efforts, keeping you briefed wasn't a priority. Neither is panicking, nor flailing about in outrage. We'll deal with the problem."

A voice sounded over Bashir's combadge. *"DeLa-Cruz to Bashir."*

"Bashir here. What is it, Martino?"

Vaughn was impressed—and grateful—that Bashir

and the surgeon general of Europa Nova were on a first-name basis. His predilection for histrionics notwithstanding, Bashir was a damned efficient doctor, and the treatment of the sick had been handled very well on this mission.

"Julian, did you remove the arithrazine stock from Spilimbergo's hospital?"

"Of course not."

"Well, it's gone. And I've got hundreds of people here that need treatment."

"Doctor, this is Commander Vaughn. The *Intrepid* is supposed to be landing within the hour to take the remaining population of Spilimbergo." While Kira's diverting of the waste to Lago DeBacco saved Spilimbergo from any immediate danger, the level of exposure made that city's evacuation a priority. Unfortunately, the proximity of that waste meant that even the *Trager*'s transporter wasn't reliable, so the *Intrepid* was tasked with evacuating Spilimbergo as fast as possible.

"I'm aware of that, Commander, but some of these people can't wait an hour."

Bashir looked over at the command chair. "Commander, with your permission, I'd like to have the *Chaffee* bring down some of our arithrazine stock to Spilimbergo."

Vaughn nodded. "Granted." He turned to the conn. "Ensign Tenmei, can you please handle that?"

Prynn said nothing, but simply nodded, got up, and approached Bashir.

"Martino, one of our shuttlecraft will deliver your arithrazine within twenty minutes," Bashir said.

"That's fine, Julian, but I'm also a bit concerned with who might have stolen it. Arithrazine has to be

administered very carefully. If some amateur is passing it out . . ."

"We'll keep an ear out for it, Doctor," Vaughn said. "Thank you for bringing that to our attention, however. *Defiant* out."

Bashir then spoke with Prynn about the particulars of bringing the arithrazine down on the *Defiant* shuttlecraft.

Nog announced, "Incoming message from the *Gryphon,* sir."

"On screen, Lieutenant."

The viewscreen shifted from a view of the planet to the face of Elaine Mello. "What can I do for you, Captain?"

Mello broke into a smile. *"You can enjoy the good news I'm about to give you, Commander. Colonel Kira did it. The toxic stream coming through the gateway has reduced by ninety percent."*

"That *is* good news."

Bashir, having finished his conversation with Prynn, said, "That'll improve the chances that we'll be able to evacuate in time." For her part, Prynn left the bridge without a word.

"We're not sure exactly how she did it—sensor readings are still pretty spotty—but Dr. Bashir's right in that it should buy us some more time."

Nog looked up from his console. "Commander, we're getting an incoming message from the *Euphrates.*"

"On audio, Lieutenant."

Kira's voice was barely recognizable—and not consistently audible—over the static from theta-radiation interference. *"This is Colonel Kira Nerys on the* Euph . . . *fleet vessels at Europa Nova. The radia . . . antimatter waste from its hold into the gate-way. The crew of the tanker is dead, killed by . . . ger than anything that's . . . using the* Euphrates *to block that and any further waste . . . eed to . . . fifth planet . . . soon . . . it is feasible to attempt the disruption of the gateways, do it, regardless of whether or not Taran'atar or I have returned. That's an order."*

"Can you clean that message up, Lieutenant?"

"I'm afraid that is the cleaned-up version, sir. It's broadcast twice since the radiation levels decreased, and the first transmission was the better of the two."

Vaughn scratched his beard thoughtfully. "Keep an ear out for more repetitions. With the radiation decrease, we might get a better signal. Some of those gaps were too damn long."

Nog nodded. "Yes, sir."

"Captain Mello, I assume you got that message, as well?"

"Yes, Commander. And to answer your next question, we've still got two hours before we've hit our quota for the Jarada." The *Gryphon* security chief had taken over supervising the evacuation at Costa Rocosa.

Turning back to Nog, Vaughn asked, "Will the tachyon burst be ready by then, Lieutenant?"

"It should be, sir." Nog hesitated, then added, "Sir, I'd feel better about it if Ensign ch'Thane were here to look over the specs one more time. It was his design. May I ask why he didn't accompany us?"

"You may *not* ask, Lieutenant," Vaughn said without looking at the engineer. That was all he planned to say on the subject. He had ordered ch'Thane behind as a favor to Vretha. He wasn't happy about it, and Nog's concern was understandable. But then he thought about his just-departed daughter. *I'm not going to keep a parent from trying to reconcile with her child. Especially given what's at stake. I just wish it were that easy for me to order Prynn to talk to me off duty.*

"*Spillane to Mello.*" The voice was coming through the bridge speakers.

"*Mello here.*"

"*Captain, we've, ah, got a bit of a problem down here.*"

Lieutenant Ann Spillane was Mello's chief of security, so "down here" was Costa Rocosa. *That's not encouraging,* Vaughn thought.

"*There's a Europani down here,*" Spillane continued, "*holding five people hostage along with six crates of arithrazine.*"

Bashir looked up at that. "There goes Martino's arithrazine," he said quietly.

"*He just showed up with a ship and the drugs, grabbed five people who were about to go through the gateway to Torona IV, and blocked the way. He says he'll release the drugs and the people if we let him and his family through to Torona IV.*"

Nog muttered, "So why not just let them through?"

Mello apparently heard him, because she said, "*Because the five-hundred-thousand-person limit the Jarada put on us is pretty strict, and all those slots are taken. I take it no one's willing to give up their slot, Lieutenant?*"

"*That's the kicker,*" Spillane said. "*He won't let anyone give up their slot—says he doesn't want anyone else to suffer because of him. He just wants to add him, his wife, his mother, his five kids, and his sister*" *to the group—and he'll kill the hostages and destroy the drugs if we don't let him."*

"Interesting method of not letting people suffer," Bashir said. "Especially if he's blocking the gateway."

Vaughn stood up. "With your permission, Captain Mello, I believe I can handle this."

"Granted."

As he moved to the door, he said, "Doctor, you're with me. I'll need you to deal with the arithrazine when we're finished. Lieutenant Nog, you have the conn."

It only took forty minutes for Vaughn to fly the *Sagan,* the *Defiant's* other shuttlecraft, to Costa Rocosa. Bashir spent the time contacting Dr. DeLaCruz to inform him that he had a promising lead on that missing arithrazine, and then checking the radiation levels to make sure that none of it penetrated the shuttle's enhanced shields.

Vaughn scanned the area in search of a decent landing spot. When he had beamed down the last time *(Was that only yesterday?* he thought; *seems like decades . . .),* there seemed to be a paucity of places to land on the uneven ground near the gateway. *And if this hostage-taker has a ship, he's probably used one of those places already.*

That last assumption turned out to be false. The Europani hostage-taker had landed his ship—a small atmospheric pod about five meters long—right on the rocky outcropping and was using it to block the gateway.

I see how this got out of hand. He was sure Spillane was a completely satisfactory security chief, but one person with a hand phaser, no matter how talented, was hardly in a position to stop an unannounced pod from landing wherever it wants.

A quick sensor scan revealed that the pod had four landing struts meant for resting on solid, even ground, and that only two of them had any kind of solid support. One plan immediately presented itself: destroy that support—either by phasering the struts or the rock under them—and get the hostages out in the confusion. That was a last-resort plan, as it carried the greatest risk, and one Vaughn dearly hoped he wouldn't have to implement.

He picked up approximately five thousand human life signs in the vicinity. Most were congregated just to the east of the gateway outcropping. There were another nineteen near the gateway, one of whom wore a combadge whose signal corresponded to Lieutenant Spillane.

He landed the *Sagan* in a clearing about twenty meters from the gateway in a flat area atop a rock. Then he rose and went to the weapons locker. As he removed a hand phaser, Bashir said, "Do you think it's wise to go into a hostage negotiation armed, Commander?"

Vaughn ignored the question as he opened the hatch. The early-evening wind blew fiercely into the cabin. Bashir approached the hatch alongside Vaughn. He peered out and saw the almost sheer drop. The flat part of the rock on which they'd landed was no bigger than the *Sagan* itself.

To Bashir's credit, he kept pace with Vaughn as they clambered down the steep incline without once making a tiresome comment about the first step being a doozy—a remark which Vaughn had fully expected the doctor to make. Bashir found handholds with all the assuredness and athleticism of a well-trained climber. Idly, Vaughn wondered how much of that was truly training and how much was Bashir's genetic enhancements—then decided that it didn't really matter.

Once they reached bottom, it was a short walk to the scene. The crowd was being kept at bay and in relative order by the Costa Rocosan police force. Based on the reports, they were the only locals still present. Mayor Nieto had been the first one through the gateway, along with other members of the police force, and they had taken over the organization of the refugees on the Jaradan side of the gateway. The thousand inhabitants of the city were next. After that, there had been a steady flow of Europani from the nearby principalities, organized by the local police and Lieutenant Spillane.

Spillane herself stood with two Europani police officers about ten meters from the pod. As the *Sagan*'s sensor readings had indicated, the pod was right in front of the gateway.

Standing in front of the pod was a short man with long black hair. He looked determined. Behind him were eight other people, ranging in age from mid-thirties to about eight years old—presumably the family he wished to take with him—who all looked more worried than anything. Next to him were five adults—three men, two women—who looked scared to death.

"What is that he's holding?" Bashir asked, squinting at the hostage-taker.

"I think it's a Starfleet phaser," Spillane said. She was a slim human woman. Her long blond hair, currently tied back in a ponytail, had been matted down by the local humidity. "But I don't remember ever seeing one that—well, bulky before."

"That's because its type was taken out of service before either of you were born," Vaughn said. "That's a standard-issue Starfleet hand phaser from around the turn of the century." He turned to Spillane. "Report, Lieutenant."

"Nothing's changed since I contacted the *Gryphon*, Commander."

Nodding, Vaughn said, "Very well. Doctor, I want you to take a precise sensor reading of the vicinity and tell me the concentration of theta radiation in the area in front of the gateway. Triple-check your findings before you report them to me, understood?"

"Of course," Bashir said, sounding confused.

Keeping his phaser holstered, Vaughn stepped toward the outcropping. "Good evening, sir!" he called out.

"Uh, hello," the man said after a moment.

"My name is Elias Vaughn. I'm with Starfleet. We seem to have a bit of a problem, and I was hoping you could help us out with it."

"There's—there's no problem. Are you—you in charge?"

"Yes, sir, I am. May I ask your name?"

"M-my name is—is Tony Fusco."

Vaughn inclined his head. "A pleasure to meet you, Mr. Fusco. Where are you from?" As he spoke, Vaughn took a closer glance at the weapon. *That's definitely an old Starfleet phaser. Looks just like the one I was issued when I graduated from the Academy, almost eighty years ago.*

"My—my family and I are from Spilimbergo. We—we just want to go through the portal!"

Letting out a breath, Vaughn said, "That may be difficult, Mr. Fusco. You see, the people on the other side of the gateway are a bit—fussy. Dangerously so, in fact. The *Intrepid* has been evacuating Spilimbergo, I'm sure—"

"I—I—I—I *can't* go *up* there." Fusco shook his phaser with each emphasized word. "You don't—you don't know what it's *like* up there."

"Up where?"

"*Space!* It's all so—so—so *open!* There's—there's nothing around you, you just get billions of kilometers of nothing before you even come—come close to getting near anything and I *can't* go *up* there."

Hell and damnation, Vaughn thought, *a space case.*

"We're going to try to work this out, Mr. Fusco. Just wait here and please don't hurt anyone."

"I—I don't want to hurt anyone, b-but I *can't* go *up* there, d-do you understand?"

Holding up his hands in a conciliatory gesture, Vaughn said, "I understand completely, sir. If you'll just give me a moment to consult with my people, we'll see what we can do to accommodate you."

He climbed back down the outcropping. Bashir, Spillane, and the police gave him an expectant look.

"Agoraphobic. Violently so. The idea of being in space terrifies him so much that he'll do anything to avoid it."

Bashir nodded. "He must have seen this gateway as a golden opportunity."

"Until he realized that nobody from Spilimbergo got on the list of five hundred thousand going through. What did your tricorder readings tell you, Doctor?"

"Hm? Oh, the radiation levels are at seven hundred rads at the moment, though that amount is climbing, obviously."

Vaughn let out a small sigh. "Oh, good, I was worried that this was going to be difficult."

He turned around, saw that no one was standing closer than half a meter from Fusco, raised his phaser, and fired.

In the instant it took the beam to reach him, Fusco's expression changed from agitation to shock. Then he fell to the ground.

Spillane and Bashir had similar looks of shock on their faces. The latter spoke. "Commander, with all due respect, you took a terrible risk! What if his finger had spasmed on the phaser and fired?"

"I'm sure it did." With that, Vaughn walked back toward the pod.

Bashir frowned as he followed. "What?" Behind him, Spillane and the two officers did likewise.

"I told you, that phaser is Starfleet issue from eighty years ago. Those models were especially susceptible to ambient radiation—anything over five hundred rads and they misfire."

They arrived at the pod. The officers immediately escorted the Europani—both the hostages and Fusco's family—off the outcropping.

Vaughn took the phaser out of Fusco's hand, which still had a surprisingly firm grip on the weapon considering the wielder was unconscious. He pointed it at Bashir and fired. As expected, nothing happened, though the doctor did flinch. "You see? That design flaw's not in later versions, of course . . ."

Shaking his head, Bashir asked, "Why didn't you say that's what you were planning in the first place?"

Vaughn smiled. "Because, Doctor, when they make

you a commander, they take the bone out of your head that makes you explain orders."

"Point taken." Bashir said.

Vaughn looked at the pod. "Lieutenant Spillane, do you think you can fly this thing?"

With a wry smile, the young woman said, "It's been a few years, sir, but I think I can hop it out of the way at least."

"Good, get to it." He tapped his combadge. "Vaughn to Lenaris."

After a moment, the Bajoran's voice came over the speaker. *"Lenaris."*

"Colonel, when are you scheduled to return to Bajor?"

"We're receiving refugees from the Trager *right now. We'll be at capacity in about ninety minutes."*

"So what's your ETA to deliver the refugees to Bajor itself?"

"Call it 2530 hours."

"Thank you, Colonel. Dr. Bashir will be bringing you nine additional passengers, one of whom will be fully sedated for the journey."

"Understood. I'll notify Gul Macet of the change."

Turning to Bashir, Vaughn said, "Doctor, I want you to find something that will keep Mr. Fusco sedated until at least 2530. I don't want him to wake up until he's back on a planet."

Understanding, Bashir smiled and nodded. "I'll take care of it, sir."

"Good. Let's get out of the pod's backwash so the lieutenant can take her up."

It took a moment for Vaughn to convince the Costa Rocosan police to remand the Fuscos into Starfleet custody, but ultimately they didn't want to deal with any more than they already had on their hands. By the time Bashir and Vaughn had gotten the entire Fusco family and the crates of arithrazine onto the *Sagan*, the evac had resumed under Spillane's watchful eye, the Fusco family pod tucked safely out of the way.

The Fuscos themselves were abject in their apologies for their patriarch's behavior. Vaughn listened patiently to their complex explanations of his rather simple psychosis. Soon enough, they were transported to Lenaris's ship, and Vaughn took the shuttle back home.

"The arithrazine we recovered can replace the stock Ensign Tenmei brought down from the *Defiant*," Bashir said.

Vaughn just nodded as he guided the shuttle into the bay.

As soon as Vaughn walked onto the *Defiant* bridge, Nog vacated the command chair and said, "We just received a message from the *Gryphon*, Commander. The last of the five hundred thousand allowed by the Jarada have been evacuated through the gateway."

Settling into the chair, Vaughn said, "Were you able to get a clearer message from Colonel Kira?"

Nog shook his head. "No, sir."

Vaughn sighed. "Very well. Prepare the tachyon burst."

"Sir, Colonel Kira—"

"Colonel Kira," Vaughn interrupted, "specifically said to try the tachyon burst as soon as it was feasible, regardless of whether or not she and Taran'atar had returned. Are you questioning her orders, Lieutenant?"

"No, sir," Nog said reluctantly.

"Good." Vaughn was grateful that Prynn hadn't yet

returned from the surface. No doubt she'd have some choice words on the subject of condemning people to their deaths. To the officer who'd replaced her at conn, he said, "Take up position forty thousand kilometers from the mouth of the gateway."

"Aye, sir," the conn officer said.

Nog manipulated the controls of his console. "Tachyon burst ready on your orders."

"Consider the order given, Lieutenant."

A burst of light shot from the *Defiant*'s deflector array and struck the mouth of the gateway.

As soon as it did so, the gateway seemed to light up with a rainbow's worth of bright colors. Vaughn had to avert his eyes from the viewscreen.

Then the gateway went dark.

"Radiation levels at the gateway's perimeter have reduced to zero percent," Nog said, "and we're no longer reading the Delta Quadrant. Power output of the gateway is zero." He checked another reading. "Power output on the Costa Rocosa gateway is also nil, sir." Turning toward the command chair, Nog smiled. "We did it. The gateways have been shut down."

16

THE DELTA QUADRANT

KIRA LOOKED DOWN at her tricorder readings. *Not good,* she thought. The radiation levels were increasing dangerously. If she stayed here too much longer, no amount of arithrazine was going to help her.

She had drained the emergency kit's water supply. The cooling unit in the shelter was at maximum. Kira knew she would have to leave the confines of the shelter to get more water from the lake, but just the act of walking would drain her—she had barely been able to get the shelter constructed, as the heat only intensified with the passing of time. Soon it would be midday. Kira wondered how well the cooling unit would hold up.

She hadn't heard anything from Taran'atar. The Jem'Hadar was far too much a creature of duty—the moment he was able, he would contact her to announce his victory. The fact that he hadn't done that yet meant either the fight was still going on—or he had lost.

Damn you all, she thought at the Hirogen and the owners of the tanker and everyone else in this quadrant. *Didn't the Borg come from this area of space? Damn them, too. Hell, the Iconians also probably came from around here.*

Checking her tricorder again, she saw that the radiation would be at fatal levels in two hours. The intensity had been rising exponentially, and her arithrazine would be all but useless before those two hours were up. A blister started to form on her hand, and she injected another dose of arithrazine, figuring she had nothing to lose.

Kira then did something that the Vedek Assembly had judged her unworthy to do with other Bajorans: she prayed.

Or, rather, she tried to.

On many occasions in her thirty-three years of life, Kira Nerys had been sure she was going to die. From the resistance to the Dominion War, her life had been fraught with danger, and she had long ago made peace with the fact that she was not likely to die of old age in her bed.

When circumstances permitted, Kira had always prayed on those occasions. She had faith in the Prophets, and in prayer she took comfort in the idea that her life had some meaning to them, that she had made some contribution to their grand design. And she always believed that if the path they had guided her on had finally come to its end, her death wouldn't be a vain one. Those prayers were always heartfelt and came easily to her.

But this time, the words wouldn't come. She had been a devout follower of the Prophets her whole life. *Is this how I'm to have that faith rewarded? Dying on an arid wasteland, alone in a Starfleet shelter tens of thousands of light-years from home, theta radiation chewing up my cells and spitting them out?*

True, her actions might well lead to saving Europa Nova, something she swore she would do no matter what.

But I don't want to die like this. Not here, not this way—and not Attainted.

Then her tricorder beeped.

Worried that it would show her that the levels of radiation had increased yet again, she was surprised to discover that it was instead registering a familiar energy signature half a kilometer distant.

A gateway.

A gateway here, on the surface of the planet where she'd taken refuge. A gateway that didn't exist a moment ago, suddenly appearing in her hour of need.

Why? What does it mean?

Ultimately, it didn't matter. Whether it was dumb luck from the Iconians or deliverance from the Prophets, Kira had a way off this death trap of a planet.

It took only a minute to compress the shelter into its backpack form, but Kira almost succumbed to heat exhaustion just by performing the act of picking it up and shrugging into it. She walked slowly to the lake and proceeded to refill the kit's water containers. The lake was, of course, warm, but Starfleet built its kits well. Within seconds, any water she bottled would be refrigerated to five degrees.

She then set off in the direction the tricorder had indicated.

Five minutes later, Kira was ready to collapse. But she soldiered on. The gateway would take her away from here.

After another five minutes, she did collapse. She only took one moment to compose herself, then gathered every muscle in her sun-battered body and hauled herself to her feet.

Her vision blurry from the sweat that poured into her face, she finally gave up and dropped the shelter from her back, hanging on only to the water.

Ten minutes later, she collapsed again.

The Prophets have given you a sign! her mind yelled. *They haven't abandoned you! But you have to get to the gateway. So move it!*

Again, she gathered every muscle. Again, she got to her feet.

She didn't know how long it was before she drained the water supply. Or, for that matter, when the blisters started breaking out all over her skin. She didn't have the wherewithal to check her tricorder to see how bad the radiation was. Every fiber of her being was focused on the overwhelming task of putting one foot in front of the other.

After what seemed like an eternity, she saw it.

It floated in the air over the endless expanse of sand.

Dimly, in the small part of her mind that was able to focus on something other than moving forward, Kira remembered that the ground-based gateways tended to do one of two things: jump randomly from vista to vista every couple of seconds, or, like the one at Costa Rocosa, stay fixed on one location. This one, however, was different: it jumped back and forth between only two destinations.

The first was ops on Deep Space 9.

The other was the comforting light that Kira Nerys knew in her heart belonged to the Prophets.

Each time the vista switched to the light, Kira felt her heart beat faster. *This is it. The Prophets are calling to me. My road is at an end.*

But when it switched back to DS9, she wavered. *You can go back home.*

To what? Pain and hardship? The disdainful stares of most Bajorans? The headaches of running the station? Making life-or-death decisions about everything from attacking Jem'Hadar to Section 31 nonsense to rescue operations? To a life of losing everyone I care about?

When she was within a meter of the gateway, it lit up with a rainbow's worth of colors. Kira had to avert her eyes from it.

Then it went away. Kira saw nothing in front of her but the endless sand.

Her outrage giving her strength that the heat of the planet had drained out of her, she took out her tricorder and scanned the area in front of her. The gateway's power reading, according to the tricorder, was nil. The hand that held that tricorder was now covered in cracked skin and red-and-green blisters.

On many occasions in her thirty-three years of life, Kira Nerys had been sure she was going to die.

This time, it seemed, she was right.

17

FARIUS PRIME

"APPROACHING THE HOLE."

Smirking at Ychell's choice of words, Ro said, "It's called a gateway, Sergeant."

Ychell shrugged. "Whatever. So far, no sign of pursuit, but that could change at any moment."

Ro nodded, then looked back at her two passengers. Quark was fidgeting nervously, no doubt still worried about Malic. Ro supposed she shouldn't have said anything about the possibility of copies—from all accounts, Malic was the type to keep information to himself as much as possible.

Treir sat passively, looking surprisingly unconcerned.

Ychell obviously noticed Ro staring, because she asked, "What're you going to do with that one?"

Shrugging, Ro said, "Not sure. It's funny, she didn't even flinch when I put the gun to her neck. I mean, she couldn't have known I was bluffing."

"She's been a slave all her life, Lieutenant. She may not know how to be anything else."

Ro sighed. "Maybe. For now, let's just go through that gateway and—"

Suddenly, the gateway lit up with a rainbow's worth of colors. Ro winced.

Then it went dark.

"I'm not reading any power signature from the gateway," Ro said, looking down at her instruments.

Ychell looked at hers. "I'm not picking up the Clarus system anymore, either."

"Dammit."

"It gets better," Ychell said. "The Orions have found us. Two of their fighter ships are on an intercept course."

18

THE DELTA QUADRANT

THE ALPHA SMILED for the first time in a long time. *At last,* he thought, *worthy prey.*

As the alpha worked his way through the corridors of the Malon tanker in search of the Jem'Hadar, he chastised himself for his own carelessness. He had grown overconfident.

For far too long, he had been on his own. He had had no real choice—everyone with whom he'd crewed had been too weak, too slow. They hadn't been worthy of his hunting skills and made the hunts so much poorer.

So he had chosen to fly alone. And he had been much more successful.

There was no sign of the Jem'Hadar on this deck.

He climbed down the access shaft to the next one, holstering his rifle on his left shoulder.

After a time, the thrill of the hunt had started to wane. It became too easy. He'd hunted for so long that no prey presented a true challenge. He had grown soft and careless. So careless that he had allowed the cargo of those Malon fools to destroy his ship.

Everything he had was in that ship: his trophies, his food, his triumphs, his war paint, most of his weapons—his entire life. All he had left was his rifle, his armor, and himself.

Perhaps this is all I truly need. Perhaps this will allow me to restore my own glory, by reducing the hunt back to its essence.

He saw a shadow move behind one of the bulkheads.

Prey.

The alpha moved slowly toward the shadow.

As he approached, the shadow took on the form of one of the Malon fools.

I thought I had destroyed all of them, the alpha thought angrily.

"Please, gods, don't kill me, please don't kill me!" the Malon cried as he stepped into the open. He had blisters on his skin.

This prey is weak to be susceptible to so minor a thing as theta radiation, the alpha thought with disgust. *It isn't even worthy of being hunted.* This one was as bad as the tanker captain—she had pleaded to the alpha about a mate and offspring, as if the family structure of prey was of any relevance. He had particularly enjoyed slicing her open.

However, the alpha did not have time to kill this one with his blade as he did the others. With the press of a button on its rifle, he blasted the Malon into atoms. The Malon screamed for as long as he could before he discorporated.

The alpha forgot about the Malon and turned his mind back to thoughts of the Jem'Hadar.

How long has it been since we hunted one of these magnificent creatures? Engineered by their primitive gods to be the perfect soldiers. They are among the worthiest prey the Hirogen have ever sought.

They were from a part of the galaxy where few Hirogen had traversed. Their presence here was a surprise, since the portal that had opened in this star system did not open to the region where the Jem'Hadar came from. Either their empire had expanded, or these portals were more widespread than the alpha had thought.

When the alpha came to the room with the shield generator, he noticed that a component was missing. *The prey has been in this room.*

The prey had also been in the next room over. The transporter logs showed that someone had transported one person and one piece of equipment to the prey's vessel. The Malon computer did not recognize the life signs, but the alpha knew that it was not the Jem'Hadar. No doubt the other, less significant prey had taken the shield modulator.

The alpha cared little for the petty concerns of prey. He no more cared about what it was doing with the shield modulator than what the Malon prey did with their meaningless cargo. All that mattered was the hunt.

The prey has been here. But the trail is cold now.

The alpha moved on to the engineering deck. Here,

he found plenty of the corpses he had left behind on his last trip through this ship.

But of the Jem'Hadar there was still no sign.

Soon, the alpha had checked every cranny of the Malon tanker. *How has the creature managed to evade me? Not only is there no sign of him, there is no sign he has been anywhere, save the bridge and the transporter.*

It has been too long since we hunted these creatures. There is obviously missing intelligence about them that I need for the hunt.

If he still had his ship, he could check records of previous hunts. But that was lost to him. All he had was his instincts.

That should be all I need.

He returned to the bridge. Some of the equipment on this ship still worked. The alpha would make use of it to find his prey and destroy it.

Taran'atar had followed the Hirogen throughout the ship, watching as the alien hunter tried in vain to track the Jem'Hadar. He had watched as the Hirogen checked every portion of the tanker, pausing only to kill one native who had somehow escaped the predator's prior rampage.

Remaining shrouded had proven to be the right course of action. The Hirogen had an extraordinary tracking ability—without any apparent aid from mechanical devices—but could not detect Taran'atar as long as he remained shrouded.

What had started as a simple stalking strategy soon became a handy delaying tactic. After all, the important thing was to keep the Hirogen occupied while Kira installed the shield enhancer onto the *Euphrates* and used it to block the gateway. The only flaw in the plan was that Taran'atar could not contact Kira to keep her apprised of his progress—the Hirogen could easily have had some way of detecting transmissions.

Still, this was the way that best served Kira. Ultimately, that was what mattered.

His assignment to the Alpha Quadrant had been a difficult thing for Taran'atar to accept, particularly being assigned to the command of Colonel Kira. After all, she had fought hard against the Dominion, and was even intrumental in its defeat. Kira was also like no Vorta Taran'atar had ever served under. Most Vorta were weak fools—self-serving at best, incompetent at worst. Taran'atar had obeyed them only because the Vorta served as the voice of the Founders. But Kira was no one's functionary. She did not just command, she led. She did not react, she acted. She did not direct battles, she fought them.

Taran'atar had fought alongside thousands of Jem'Hadar, and grown to respect many of them, for they had been true soldiers of the Dominion. Kira Nerys was the first alien he had ever met that he could truly call a soldier.

The Hirogen had gone through the entire ship. Taran'atar could not be completely sure of what the alien's facial expressions signified, but he was fairly sure that the creature was growing frustrated. He headed back up from the engineering section toward the bridge.

This may require a change in strategy. It was possible that the Hirogen was planning to use the ship's equipment to supplement his own tracking skills. Taran'atar's understanding about this ship's level of technology was still incomplete, but considering that it had transporters that could penetrate Starfleet shields, sophisticated tactical equipment was not unlikely.

Of course, he thought, *they also have such primitive warp engines that they still produce antimatter waste.* This was why the Dominion's way was so much better: everyone in the Dominion benefited from the technological advances of all its component parts. Such inefficient disparities as the owners of this tanker had did not exist.

Sure enough, the Hirogen arrived at the bridge and began to manipulate the controls of one of the consoles. He had holstered his rifle across his left shoulder.

The rifle is the key, Taran'atar thought. *With it, the Hirogen has the clear advantage.* The Jem'Hadar's sole weapon was his *kar'takin,* which the Hirogen had thought so little of that he hadn't bothered to remove it from Taran'atar's person as he had his phaser.

The initial strike was the most important: to land as devastating a blow as possible while he had the element of surprise. Striking at the armor would be pointless—as strong as his blade was, Taran'atar seriously doubted it could penetrate. The rifle itself was probably similarly difficult to damage. That left only two viable alternatives: the Hirogen's face, and the strap holding the rifle.

Possibly they are the same alternative, he thought as he studied the battlefield. The Hirogen currently stood at the center of the bridge, operating what appeared to be a general-purpose operations console. The console was a circular island in the middle of the control room—which, like those of Jem'Hadar ships, had no chairs.

Taran'atar took up position on the side of the console opposite where the Hirogen stood. Then he stepped backward as far as he could and unsheathed his *kar'takin*, directing his thoughts at the Founders.

I am Taran'atar, and I am dead. I go into battle to reclaim my life. This I do gladly, for I am Jem'Hadar. Victory is life.

He ran toward the console, leapt on top of it while lifting his *kar'takin* over his left shoulder, unshrouding as his concentration shifted to combat mode, and brought the weapon down.

The Hirogen fell back, one hand reaching up to cover his lacerated face, the other groping for the rifle that fell clattering to the deck, its shoulder strap severed cleanly.

Little blood flowed from the wound, and Taran'atar didn't allow his foe a chance to respond. He leapt onto the Hirogen, dragging him down and away from the fallen rifle. The pair fell to the deck, much as they had the last time Taran'atar attacked, only this time the Jem'Hadar was on top.

Again he attacked the Hirogen's face with the blade, but this time he thrust straight downward, aiming for the alien's right eye.

Unfortunately, the Hirogen clapped his gauntleted hands over the *kar'takin*, halting its downward motion. Taran'atar struggled to push the blade downward, but the Hirogen's strength was tremendous.

The hunter swung both arms to one side, pushing Taran'atar off balance and forcing him to release his hold on the *kar'takin*. The blade spun away as Taran'atar tumbled off his opponent and fell into a roll. He came up to his feet as the Hirogen did likewise.

The rifle was on the far end of the bridge out of

reach of both combatants. The *kar'takin*, however, was close enough that the Jem'Hadar was willing to take the extra second he needed to reach it and arm himself, especially given how he expected the Hirogen to respond.

Sure enough, the Hirogen got to his feet and pressed a control on his right wrist. A long, straight blade extended from the underside of his gauntlet. The part closest to the Hirogen's palm was shaped differently—a grip, Taran'atar realized as the Hirogen's large hand clasped around it. *Clever design. The blade is still attached to his armor, so there's no risk of him dropping it, but it has a grip that provides him with better leverage.* The blade had to be either flexible or collapsible, but Taran'atar could not count on that meaning that it was weak. The Hirogen were an ancient species, that much he knew, and Taran'atar had to assume that any civilization capable of refining monotanium into hull metal could also manage comparable metallurgy in the creation of hand weapons.

Holding his *kar'takin* in front of him, ready to strike or parry at a moment's notice, the Jem'Hadar focused on his primary advantage: Hirogen were more interested in the hunt than the victory—but Jem'Hadar knew better. In a hand-to-hand fight, the Hirogen's size and armor gave him an edge over Taran'atar. Armed combat leveled the playing field to some extent—how much would depend on the Hirogen's skill. Taran'atar had already known that the Hirogen carried an edged weapon—it was what he used to kill the owners of the tanker—and Taran'tar also knew that if he came at the Hirogen with a blade, the Hirogen was likely to respond in kind.

The two circled each other on the spacious bridge, each ready to strike at a moment's notice, neither willing to make the first move.

"Curious prey," the Hirogen said. "You yourself set the terms for combat with blades, yet you do not attack. Instead you wait—try to gauge my own attack even as I wait to gauge yours."

Taran'atar said nothing. Speaking during battle was pointless unless one was giving orders to one's troops. Taran'atar had no troops, so he remained silent.

"Do you not speak, prey?"

Again, Taran'atar said nothing. *Let the hunter rant all he wants.*

They continued to circle each other. Taran'atar watched for any sign in the Hirogen's eyes that he would strike, but all the Jem'Hadar could read was curiosity.

Then the Hirogen did something unexpected: he smiled.

"Very well, prey. If you will not strike first, I will."

In the back of his mind, Taran'atar had wondered if perhaps this hunter was simply incompetent. After all, he had lost his ship to an inferior foe. And now he announced his attack so that Taran'atar had plenty of time to parry the downward strike at his head.

Another thirty seconds of sparring, however, disabused him at least of the notion that the Hirogen had no weapons skills. He was as good as Taran'atar with his weapon, and the Jem'Hadar found himself unable to move onto the offensive. He was able to counter each of the Hirogen's attacks, but his foe was too fast to allow Taran'atar ever to strike back.

The weapons clanged against each other, the sound

of metal colliding with metal ringing through the otherwise silent bridge. The combatants soon fell into a rhythm. The Hirogen's thrusts were fast, strong, and powerful, but predictable. He never varied the pattern—a simple right-left-forward progression that he stuck to without deviating. Unfortunately, being able to predict the strike only meant Taran'atar could raise a defense against it. The Hirogen presented no opening to take the offensive.

Taran'atar soon realized that—collapsibility or flexibility notwithstanding—the Hirogen's blade was as strong as the Jem'Hadar's own weapon, and since it was attached to the armor, there was no way Taran'atar would be able to disarm him. *So I must turn his unity with his sword to my advantage.*

Looking around, Taran'atar saw that the Hirogen was maneuvering the fight toward the rifle. *I cannot allow that.* The minute one of them was able to get his hands on the rifle, the battle was over.

When the Hirogen made one of his right swings, Taran'atar overstumbled to his left after parrying, and continued backing away in that direction. This also sent Taran'atar in the direction of one of the secondary consoles against the wall. *Ordinarily, backing into a wall would hardly be an optimum strategy . . . but this might provide me with a path to victory.*

Right-left-forward, right-left-forward.

The first Vorta that Taran'atar had served under as a Sixth had been fond of dances performed by a minor Dominion species known as the Thepnossen. When he first saw them, Taran'atar had thought their movements to be foolish and wasteful, and he had been equally foolish in voicing these thoughts in the presence of the Second. He had been reduced to Seventh for the infraction—had the First or the Vorta herself heard him, he might well have been killed. He had learned that day to be more prudent when speaking his mind. Until now, he had only thought of those dances as a reminder of the discipline.

Now, however, he and the Hirogen were engaged in a dance that was eerily similar to that of the Thepnossen.

But unlike those choreographed moves, which were consistent and constant, Taran'atar was, as he was backed closer and closer to the console against the wall, noticing a change to the Hirogen's pattern: each forward thrust was lower than the last. The lower thrusts made Taran'atar's parry—which, on the forward thrust, required him not to just block the strike but push the sword away—more difficult, and gave him less time to mount a defense against the next, right thrust.

Right-left-forward, right-left-forward, right-left-forward, left—

Left!

Taran'atar had thrown off the forward thrust and had already raised his *kar'takin* to block the expected attack on the Hirogen's right. But the Hirogen switched to a left thrust. Taran'atar attempted to switch over, hoping that the Hirogen's enforced right-handed attack (thanks to his sword being attached to his right arm) would slow his attack to the left enough so that Taran'atar could block.

The Hirogen's blade cut through the Jem'Hadar's coverall and into his scaly skin, slashing his right bicep.

But, while there was pain, it was not enough to be distracting. While Jem'Hadar could, of course, feel pain—it was necessary to insure survival—the

Founders had designed their nervous systems with a very high threshold for it. A cut to the arm was nothing.

So it was a simple matter for Taran'atar to thrust his *kar'takin* forward with his left hand toward the Hirogen's face. The hunter saw the attack coming, but with his blade still embedded in Taran'atar's arm, he could not back away in time. Taran'atar made a second gash across his foe's face, but again, not deep enough to kill.

The Hirogen pulled his sword out of Taran'atar's arm as if he were sawing the limb off, causing more damage, and then backed away. The arm felt sluggish, and Taran'atar knew that he could not depend on it. He switched from using the *kar'takin* two-handed to holding it in his left hand.

Taran'atar was now standing directly in front of the console he'd been backing toward.

They stood facing each other for a moment once again. "Clever prey," the Hirogen said as dark blood trickled down his cheek.

He then thrust his sword forward, even lower than he had in previous strikes.

Rather than parry it, Taran'atar instead leapt into the air. The Hirogen stumbled forward, and his sword went straight into the console.

The Jem'Hadar came down from his leap onto the Hirogen's head, using it to flip through the air and land on his feet behind his opponent. His hope that his foe's embedded sword would carry an electrical charge through the armor was not realized—either the Hirogen missed a power junction or the metal was nonconductive. But for the moment, at least, the Hirogen was stuck.

And Taran'atar now faced the rifle on the far side of the bridge.

Knowing he only had seconds before the Hirogen pried his sword out of the console, Taran'atar ran for the energy weapon, which he estimated to be ten meters away.

At eight meters, the Hirogen growled.

At six meters, he heard a metallic snap that rang through the bridge even louder than the clashing blades had.

At four meters, the Hirogen's armored form collided with Taran'atar's back, sending them both sprawling.

The Hirogen grabbed Taran'atar's good arm and twisted, forcing the Jem'Hadar around and onto his back. Taran'atar could see that the Hirogen had broken the sword off—a very short, jagged edge protruded from the hilt.

His mouth spreading into a rictus, the Hirogen started pummeling the Jem'Hadar's face with both hands. Blood from the alien's face dripped onto Taran'atar, mingling with his own.

Taran'atar's vision began to blur.

Suddenly, the pummeling stopped. Through a haze, Taran'atar saw the Hirogen get up.

No.

The Hirogen was moving toward the rifle. *I won't allow that. I won't be defeated.*

Taran'atar gathered every bit of strength he had left as he forced his arms to brace himself. He gathered every millimeter of faith in the Founders and willed his legs to move. He gathered every shred of duty and made himself stand upright.

The image of the Hirogen was still blurry to his

eyes, but Taran'atar could see that the alien had stopped and was regarding the Jem'Hadar with surprise. "Resourceful. But this hunt is over."

For the first time during the battle, Taran'atar spoke. "Not . . . while . . . I . . . live."

And then he leapt at the Hirogen. The attack was without grace, without subtlety. It was simply brutal.

The hunter again fell to the deck. Taran'atar punched the Hirogen at the alien's face wound.

Taran'atar kept on, kicking the alien twice in face and chest. Growling, the Hirogen twisted the Jem'Hadar off balance. Taran'atar toppled to the deck—

—and saw the rifle within reach.

Reaching out with his good arm, he managed to snag the broken strap in his fist. But before he could pull the weapon toward him, the Hirogen's boot came down on his arm.

A klaxon started to blare. He had no idea what it signaled, and it hardly mattered now.

But the sound caused the Hirogen to turn, shifting his weight just enough for Taran'atar to yank his arm free and pull the rifle toward him.

But then the Hirogen knelt down hard, his knees impacting Taran'atar's chest. The Jem'Hadar found it hard to breathe.

"I repeat," the Hirogen said, "this hunt is over."

With that, the Hirogen stabbed Taran'atar in the chest with the jagged edge of his broken sword.

19

FARIUS PRIME

"I DON'T LIKE THIS."

"I'm not really interested in what you like, Gen. We've come this far."

"Kam, the gateways have gone offline! And I haven't the first clue as to why."

"Probably that sabotage they developed in System 418. Have you had any luck getting them back online?"

"No. That's why I said I didn't like this. I think it might be prudent if you return to the ship."

"It would be dangerous to leave now. The Orions are a suspicious people by nature, and they've already been betrayed by their own negotiator. We can't risk their discovering our deception."

"If you say so."

"Yes, I do. Meanwhile, get those gateways working again. Coordinate with the other pods—we can't permit a perception of anything other than complete control."

"Of course, Kam. I'll keep you posted."

"Good."

"Sensors are picking up a Bajoran Militia craft near the gateway—pursuit ships have been dispatched. And the gateway has gone offline!"

Vincam's first sentence was the only piece of good news Malic had received since before the "final" negotiation with the Iconians had begun. He stood on the bridge of his ship, having left the Iconians and their Ferengi in the conference room under the watchful eyes of his two bodyguards. Up until they'd allowed Quark and his dabo girl (or whoever she was) to escape, the guards, Werd and Snikwah, had been Malic's most trusted employees.

The bridge had a simple, logical layout—one would expect no less from Vulcan ship designers—with three tiers. Command was on the top tier, with primary operations on the second tier closest to the commander, secondary operations on the third—near enough to be accessible but out of the way when not needed. Vincam sat at the communications console just under the command chair next to which Malic was standing. He had chosen not to sit in the chair, as he didn't intend to remain on the bridge for all that long.

What had started out as a simple business transaction was getting irritatingly more complicated. Quark had betrayed him. That dabo girl was either Starfleet security or Bajoran Militia—given the class of ship they'd just detected, not to mention the fact that she took Treir hostage, the latter was more likely. Hostage-taking wasn't Starfleet's style.

Now this.

"What do you mean the gateway has gone offline?"

Vincam finally looked up from his console and turned around to face Malic. "Just what I said. There's no power reading from the gateway, and we're not reading the Clarus system on the other side." His console beeped and he looked back down at it. "Gatnir is reporting—that gateway he took to Ferenginar went offline, too." Looking back up, he continued, "And I've monitored half a dozen other communiqués— Starfleet, Klingon Defense Force, Federation civilian, Ferengi Alliance, Romulan—that indicate that other gateways have gone dead. I've picked up one message on a Starfleet frequency—this appears to be the result of something one of their ships is attempting at Europa Nova."

Damn them, Malic thought. *No doubt this is the very same sabotage that Quark's accursed nephew dreamed up.* "It's time I had a conversation with these Iconians. I'll be in the conference room."

Loga spoke up from the sensor console. "Malic? I'm getting life-form readings on the Bajoran ship— two Bajorans, one Ferengi, and one Orion. They're also retreating into the asteroid belt."

Snarling, Malic said, "They still have Treir." Turning back to Vincam, he said, "Make sure the pursuit ships are told that the Bajoran ship is to be disabled— not destroyed. If any harm comes to Treir, the person responsible will be expected to compensate me for her full value, understood?"

Vincam nodded.

Malic turned toward the lift and reached into his pocket to make notes into his padd.

His hand felt only the fabric of his inner pocket.

For almost a hundred years, Malic had thrived. He'd started out as a simple deckhand on a ship belonging to the famed pirate Tu. Nobody there would take him seriously—he was viewed as being useless owing to his lack of height. Determined to prove himself, he quit Tu's ship and went to Finneas XII. He started working for Zil, one of the more talented enforcers in the syndicate and the man who controlled pretty much the entire planet. Malic had made his height work for him by his ability to fit into odd places to scout and spy. What Zil had never suspected was that Malic didn't just spy on people Zil had told him to spy on, but also on Zil himself. Soon enough, he had gathered enough information to take Zil—who had been skimming off the top of his fare to the syndicate for years—down.

Malic's only mistake had been to trust others. Although technically he was the one who brought Zil down, others had taken the credit by altering the data he had gathered to make it appear that it had been someone else's intelligence. Malic had been rewarded in other ways, but not with the credit he deserved.

So after that, he made sure that all the information he gathered was all in one unimpeachable source. He had spent all the money he had and more on a special padd that was genetically coded so that it could not be used by anyone but him. The information on that padd was sacrosanct, and could only be traceable to him. He upgraded the padd every chance he got, making sure that its security was the best that money could buy. And, with the information he gathered on it used to his own ends, the amount of money in question soon became considerable.

Still, no security was perfect, and Malic had been careful to guard the padd with his life. He'd never let it out of sight in the near-century that he'd owned it except when the upgrades were performed. Besides a record of all his transactions and business arrangements, the padd contained dirt on several other prominent syndicate members, half a dozen officials from virtually every major Alpha Quadrant government, most of the people Malic had done business with over the years, and Malic himself.

So to not feel it in his pocket now . . .

While quickly checking his three other pockets, he whirled and bellowed, "Loga! Turn on the tracer for my padd, now!"

Loga nodded and operated his console. Then his face went almost yellow. "Uh—you're not going to like this."

Clenching his fists hard enough that he could hear his rings scraping against each other, Malic said, "Where is it?"

Turning to Malic, Loga said, "You're *really* not going to like this."

"I like your procrastinating even less," Malic said in a low, menacing tone.

"It's on the Bajoran ship."

Several thoughts went through Malic's head at once, from disbelief to outrage to anger. *That damn dabo girl, whoever she truly is.* She had knocked the wind out of him when she tackled him, and had apparently managed to make off with his padd. *If she is*

Starfleet—or if she turns it over to Starfleet—it will be the end of me.

Looking at the communications console, Malic said, "Vincam, add this to the message regarding the penalty for any harm coming to Treir: the pilot responsible for disabling the Bajoran ship and bringing its contents directly to me will be rewarded with a hundred bricks of gold-pressed latinum."

Vincam's eyes went wide, and it took him a moment to recover his wits enough to send the message.

Malic then left the bridge, ordering the turbolift to the conference room. Initially, he had been concerned with how to conclude these negotiations in light of Quark's sabotage. However, the Ferengi, damn his ears, had actually negotiated a good deal for them. True, the actual process had taken longer than necessary—and Malic had his suspicions as to how that was accomplished—but the deal itself was a solid one.

This new wrinkle about the gateways, however, gave Malic a concern regarding the Iconians themselves. From the first time they approached him two weeks previous, Malic had never gotten the feeling that they were as—well, *old* as they said they were. Admittedly, one could hardly judge what a member of an ancient civilization would truly act like—Malic hadn't met all that many, after all—but something about these Iconians felt wrong.

Let's see how they react to this latest news.

He arrived at the conference room to see Werd and Snikwah standing on either side of the doorway, Klingon disruptors in their hands, though lowered. That was on Malic's instruction—he was taking no chances. The head Iconian, Kam, and his aide Pal, were standing in the same spot in the back of the room where they had been when Malic left. The Ferengi Gaila was currently at the buffet table, stuffing tube grubs into his mouth.

"Would you care to explain," Malic asked the room in general—he didn't care if it was Gaila or the Iconians who answered, as long as someone did, "why the gateways have all gone offline?"

The Iconians's facial expressions were as bland as ever, but Gaila's eyes went wide. "What?" he said through a mouthful of grubs.

Kam spoke up quickly. "It is nothing to be concerned over. We wish to conclude these negotiations."

"These negotiations will not be concluded until I have a satisfactory answer as to why the gateways are all dead."

Smiling a small smile, Kam said, "We said from the beginning that we would not reveal all the secrets of the gateways to you unless and until you consummated the deal."

"And I'm telling you now that no deal will be consummated until you explain to me why a relative of your negotiator has sabotaged your product."

Gaila, who had by this time swallowed the tube grubs, actually smiled at that. "If you're referring to young Lieutenant Nog—why would you assume that our family relation is meaningful?"

"For the same reason you assumed that his relationship to Quark was meaningful. You proposed that as sufficient reason to discredit him as my negotiator—I am starting to wonder if it is equally sufficient to discredit you."

"*Malic.*" It was Vincam's voice.

"Excuse me a moment," Malic said. "I must speak with my bridge. In the meantime, see if you can concoct a compelling reason for me not to have all three of you shot."

With a nod to his bodyguards, Malic moved toward the exit. As the doors parted, the two large Orions raised their weapons, and Malic could hear Gaila gulp.

Malic went to an intercom. "What is it, Vincam?"

"The gateways just came back online. They were only down for about ten minutes. As far as Loga can tell, they just seemed to reboot."

"Very well."

"There's more. We've been monitoring the Iconian ship. They've been doing the exact same thing we've been doing—examining it with sensors. And they've been in constant contact with the two in the conference room."

"That's to be expected."

"Yes," Vincam said, and Malic could hear the pride in the younger man's voice, *"but we finally were able to break their code."*

For the first time in several days, Malic smiled.

"Kam, the gateways are back online."

"Good work."

"It wasn't my work! I think they just rebooted and came back online."

"We'll take what we can get. The Orion is suspicious of us. We have to inform him that this was our intention all along."

"How you coming along with that code, Ychell?"

Ro asked the question as she maneuvered the

fighter through the asteroid belt. Already a skilled pilot, she had learned every trick in the book for evading capture during her time with the Maquis—and, in fact, had taught them a few tricks before the Jem'Hadar all but wiped them out.

Memories of a raid on a Cardassian supply depot came unbidden to Ro—piloting that ancient crate that was called the *Zelbinion* for reasons no one in her cell could adequately explain. They had been chased into an asteroid belt then, too, the depot's guard ships flying around in a standard search pattern while Ro kept the *Zelbinion* out of their sensor field.

That in turn led to another memory, of piloting another ship—one that didn't even have a name— through a field of antimatter mines laid by the Jem'Hadar en route to Osborne's World. They lost a lot of good people on that mission. In fact, if it hadn't been for Jalik's sacrifice, they all would have died . . .

Ychell suddenly spoke, forcing her to put those bad memories aside. "I don't think I can do it, Lieutenant," she said.

"You need a code broken?"

Ro looked back briefly to see that Quark had moved to stand between the pilot and copilot seats, then turned back to her console as she said, "Quark, get back in the rear."

"I need something to do, Laren. Besides, I'm an expert codebreaker."

Ychell made a dismissive noise. "Expert? I spent most of my time in the resistance cracking Cardassian codes."

Quark waved a hand dismissively. "Any idiot can crack Cardassian codes."

Before Ychell could respond, Ro said, "Sergeant, let him have a shot at it. We've got nothing to lose, and I'd really like to know what's in all the com traffic we're picking up."

Glowering at Ro, Ychell said, "Fine. I'm transferring access to the com systems to the aft panel." With a sneer at Quark, she said, "Have a party, Ferengi."

Quark gave her an equally mocking smile back and went back to the aft compartment.

"Why do you allow him such familiarity? Hell, why do you let him stay in business? He worked for the Cardassians—and for the Dominion when they took over."

"You should know better, Ychell. He was part of the resistance movement that kicked the Dominion off the station," Ro said as she maneuvered around one particularly large asteroid. Sensors said it had a high enough magnetic content that it should confuse the hell out of the Orions. "And his bar serves an important social function."

"If you say so. I never went much for the type of socializing that goes on in those establishments." She checked her console. "I'm picking up two Orion pursuit ships nearby—the others are still outside the asteroid belt."

Ro studied the sensor readings. "Well, if they've found us, they're hiding it well. That's a pretty standard search pattern. We ought to be okay here for a few more minutes at least."

"I broke the code!" came a triumphant voice from the rear of the fighter.

Ychell whirled around. "What!? That's not possible!"

"Let me rephrase," Quark said as he bounded triumphantly back to the fore. "I broke one of the codes.

That's why you were having trouble, Sergeant, there were two different codes there—the Orions' and the Iconians'."

"Which one did you break, the Orions'?"

"No," Quark said, to Ro's surprise, "the Iconians'. You should be getting a translation of the last five minutes' worth of com traffic on your panel, Sergeant."

Ychell looked down. "Looks like it, yes. It—" Her eyes went wide. "Interesting."

"What?" Ro asked.

"If I'm reading this right, Lieutenant, these aren't the Iconians at all."

Ro repeated, "What!?"

"They're still transmitting—I'll put it on audio."

"You're lying."

Kam had just spent several minutes explaining what had happened to the gateways, that it was a simple maintenance cycle, and Malic's reaction had been those two words.

He stood between Werd and Snikwah in the conference room. The bodyguards had their disruptors trained on the two Iconians and the Ferengi, who were now all standing against the wall together. The Iconians looked as unconcerned as ever, but Gaila seemed a bit panicky.

"I don't think you even were the ones who opened the gateways," Malic continued. "I think this was all part of an elaborate plot on the part of the two Ferengi, the Bajoran Militia, and perhaps Starfleet to undermine the Orion Syndicate. Well, your accomplices will be captured soon enough." *They had better be, at least,* he thought, remembering his stolen padd. "And we have our weapons trained on your ship."

"There's no need for these hostilities," Gaila said. Malic could hear the Ferengi attempt to keep his voice calm, but he was failing. "We can discuss this like rational beings."

Malic snorted. "The time for discussion is over. It's obvious that you withheld intelligence on the gateways, not as a bargaining tactic, but because you didn't have that intelligence. It's also obvious that you didn't know about the gap in the gateway lattice in the Bajoran sector—otherwise you wouldn't have dispatched a ship there as soon as we brought it up. And it's equally obvious that you have no idea why the gateways went offline, nor why they came back online. You've lied to us. The syndicate doesn't appreciate being made fools."

"We haven't made fools of you!" Gaila said quickly. "It was Quark! He made fools of all of us! He's a crafty one, my cousin. But I can assure you—"

"Be silent, Ferengi. I have learned the hard way not to trust the mouthings of anyone from your wretched species." He turned to the Iconians—or whatever they truly were. "Well, Kam? Have you nothing to say for yourself?"

Kam simply regarded Malic with the same calm expression that never seemed to leave the alien's face. "Are you familiar with subvocal communication?"

Frowning, Malic said, "No."

"We perfected it some time ago. I have been in constant communication with my ship while we have been speaking. They have armed their weapons. You will allow us safe passage back to our ship and then allow us to leave the Farius system, or we will destroy you."

Malic didn't need a century of experience in business to know when someone was talking a better game than they could truly play. "Don't be fooled by the fact that this vessel was constructed by pacifists, Kam. It is more than armed enough to eliminate your ship." He turned to Werd and Snikwah. "Kill them all."

Then the lights went dead.

The darkness was short-lived, as the room was lit by a rather spectacular explosion from one of the walls. Malic heard someone scream, but he couldn't tell if it was the Ferengi, one of his own people, or one of the aliens.

Vincam's voice sounded over the speakers. *"We're under attack!"*

"We've got to save Gaila."

Ro turned in surprise at Quark's statement. "I beg your pardon?"

"He's still on that ship," Quark said, pointing to Ro's tactical display. "The Orions and the Iconians—or whoever they are—"

"They're called the Petraw," Ychell put in, "based on these coms we've been intercepting."

Nodding in acknowledgment, Quark said, "They can kill each other for all I care, but we have to save Gaila."

"Not that I disagree with the sentiment or anything, Quark," Ro said, "but why this sudden outburst of compassion? Gaila was the one who betrayed you in there."

Quark just shrugged. "That was just business. He's still family."

"Isn't there a Rule about how family should be exploited?"

Smiling, Quark said, "And how am I supposed to do that if he's dead?"

"Lieutenant," Ychell said, "the pursuit ships are breaking off—they're heading back toward Malic's ship. Probably to help out against the Petraw. That firefight is getting worse. Both ships have taken heavy damage."

Ro looked down at her own console. As it happened, the most direct course from their current position in the asteroid belt to the gateway—which had gone back online only ten minutes after shutting down—involved going straight through the battle between the Petraw and the Orions. The only way to go fast enough to escape their notice would be to go in a straight line at near-lightspeed. *So that works out fairly nicely anyhow . . .*

"Sergeant, can this crate do a near-warp transport?"

Ychell whirled toward Ro. "You're kidding, right?"

"I'm dead serious."

Snorting, Ychell said, "Bad choice of words, Lieutenant." She took a deep breath. "I suppose it's possible, but I've never done it."

"I have," Ro said confidently. Of course, that was on the *Enterprise*—a top-of-the-line Starfleet ship that was designed for those kinds of maneuvers. In fact, the operation had been performed at least once before she'd signed on. In addition, back then she'd been working in concert with Miles O'Brien, an expert in transporter technology.

She set the course she'd need to take in order to make this work. *I just hope the gateway doesn't wink out on us again.* "Can you get an accurate life-form reading from the Orion ship?"

Ychell nodded. "Scanning for Ferengi life-forms now." A pause. "Got him."

"Good," Quark said, "let's move while he's still alive."

Without looking up, Ro said, "Quark, get back aft. The ride's gonna be a little bumpy. You and Treir need to strap in."

Quark didn't look terrifically pleased by the notion of a bumpy ride, but said nothing as he moved back aft.

"Course set," Ro said and looked over at Ychell.

"Transporter standing by."

Ro took a deep breath, and remembered something one of her Academy instructors always said right before flight simulations. "Here goes nothin'."

Gaila ran.

He had no idea where he was running to, but he thought remaining in a dark room waiting for one of the two moon-sized Orions to shoot him was not in his best interests. So he made a dash for where he remembered the door being, was favored by that door opening at his approach, and proceeded to run down the hallways, which were now lit only by green emergency lights.

Escape pods, he thought. *That's what I want. They have to have them here. No self-respecting Vulcan would build a ship without escape pods. Wouldn't be logical.*

Gaila did not allow himself to think that getting rid of them might have been one of the (several) modifications Malic had made to the ship.

This is all your fault, Quark. Every time I turn around, you're there to thwart me.

A small voice in the back of Gaila's head reminded him that it was Gaila's own actions that led to this particular state of affairs, in his attempt to take his revenge for Quark's indignities. After all, if it hadn't been for Quark, Gaila would still own a moon. But if it hadn't been for Gaila, the Orion ship probably wouldn't be falling apart around him right now.

And then there's the Iconians. If they really are the Iconians. Not only did I break the Sixth Rule to get revenge on Quark, it's looking like I broke the the Ninety-Fourth as well. Cost me a perfectly good client, too.

Or maybe not so perfectly good, if Malic's suspicions were right. Frankly, Gaila didn't really care much one way or the other if they really were the Iconians or not. They'd paid him half up front, and that—along with most of the other seven bars of latinum he'd gotten from Zek—was safe in a despository. *All I need to do is live to get off this ship, and everything will be fine. I'll live without the rest of Kam's fee. I won't live if I stay here any longer.*

He turned a corner to see a male Orion who looked like he'd been worked over by a particularly cranky Klingon standing there.

Regarding him with two eyes that were half-swollen shut, the Orion asked through his split lip, "What're you doing here?"

"Trying to find the escape pods. Didn't you hear the order to abandon ship?" The first sentence was truthful, the second somewhat less so.

"Abandon ship?" The Orion started to quiver. Gaila supposed his eyes might have widened in shock if they weren't so swollen. "No, I didn't hear that! Follow me, the escape pods are this way."

Gaila smiled. *That's more like it.*

As they moved as one toward a turbolift, a voice from behind Gaila cried, "There he is! Good work, Alhan."

It sounded like one of Malic's bodyguards. *Damn,* Gaila thought. *Almost made it.*

He turned around and saw that it was indeed one of Malic's two mountains. He was aiming his disruptor right at Gaila's head.

So this is it, he thought. *I'm going to die.*

Then, suddenly, Gaila found himself looking down at the bodyguard from what felt like inside the ceiling.

That rather bizarre sensation only lasted an instant. Then the world dissolved into a confused mess before coalescing into the very face Gaila had imagined himself punching repeatedly only moments before.

"Quark."

"Good to see you too, Gaila."

He looked around to see that he and Quark, along with a Bajoran sergeant, an Orion slave girl, and Quark's dabo girl—who was a brunette now—were crammed into the flight deck of a Bajoran Militia flitter. "Where are we?"

"A Bajoran Militia flitter," Quark said.

"I *know* it's a Bajoran Militia flitter," Gaila said impatiently. "I mean where?"

"On our way to the Clarus system, and then to DS9. Oh and Gaila?"

"What?"

"You're welcome."

Gaila's stomach hadn't felt this unsettled since the last time he had to eat cooked food in order to suck up to a potential client. He looked past Quark's self-satisfied smile to the viewscreen to see that they were indeed heading to the gateway in this system—which would take them to Clarus.

The Bajoran sergeant spoke up. "The Orion ship's shields just went down. The Petraw are firing again."

Then she touched a control and the image on the viewscreen changed to an aft view, showing the small ship commanded by Kam doing as the sergeant had indicated.

"Petraw?" Gaila asked.

Quark's oh-so-smug smile widened. "You mean you didn't know that you weren't working for the Iconians? Well, I'm surprised, Gaila. These Petraw were running such a weak scam that I thought for sure you'd be involved."

"Very funny, Quark. Their latinum was good enough regardless of—"

Gaila was interrupted by the rather impressive sight of Malic's ship exploding in a fiery conflagration.

"Well, if Malic did have a backup of that padd, it's gone now."

"Any sign of the Petraw ship?" the erstwhile dabo girl asked the sergeant.

"Negative. They could've warped out under cover of the explosion." The sergeant then looked up. "Entering the gateway now."

As usual, there was no real sensation of travel. Unlike wormholes or transporters or warp drive or any other method of getting somewhere fast, the Iconians had built their portals with a minimum of bells and whistles. One moment they were in the Farius system, the next they were in the Clarus system. No disorientation, no disruption of the very air, just a simple movement from one place to the next.

"Set course for DS9," the dabo girl said, holding up a padd. "I want to get to work on cracking this thing." Gaila realized after a moment that it was Malic's padd, thus explaining Quark's comment about a backup.

He then looked at his most hated cousin, who still hadn't lost the smug smile. "You saved my life."

"Looks like I did, yeah." Quark put his hand on Gaila's shoulder. Gaila looked at it with all the disdain he could muster—which right now was considerable— but Quark did not remove it. "Don't worry, Gaila. I promise not to ask for too much to settle the debt."

"And you have Malic's padd."

"Mhm. All in all, it's been a good day for me."

"If it's all the same to you," Gaila said, taking a seat next to the Orion slave woman—who had been watching the exchanges between Gaila and his cousin with a level of amusement that Gaila found inappropriate in a female—"you can drop me off at Clarus IX. I have no interest in accompanying you to that wretched station."

The dabo girl turned and smiled in a way that Gaila hated even more than he hated Quark's. "This isn't a ferry service, Gaila. We're heading to DS9, so that's where you're heading. If you have a problem with that, we can always send you back where we found you."

"Look—" Gaila started, but Quark interrupted him.

"I don't think you've been properly introduced. Gaila, this is DS9's new security chief, Lieutenant Ro Laren."

Gaila shot Quark a look. "Security chief?"

Quark nodded.

Sighing, Gaila leaned back. *I suppose it won't be so bad. I don't have any outstanding warrants or bad business contacts on Bajor.* "Fine," he said. "I'll arrange transport on DS9."

"Good luck with that," Ro said, still smiling. "Right now, DS9 is chock-full of refugees from Europa Nova. I doubt there are any quarters available."

"Oh don't worry, cousin," Quark said quickly. "I'd be more than happy to put you up in my quarters for a very reasonable fee."

Gaila looked up at his cousin for a long time before coming to a realization.

"I hate you, Quark."

20

EUROPA NOVA

"COMMANDER VAUGHN, the last of the refugees have been evacuated from Europa Nova."

At Nog's words, a cheer went up from all around the *Defiant* bridge. Vaughn did not join in that cheer, but he did smile. There had been several hundred cases of theta-radiation poisoning, but—between the efforts of Bashir and Dr. DeLaCruz on the surface and the sickbays of both the *Intrepid* and the *Gryphon*—none of those cases were fatal. The combined efforts of the five Starfleet ships, ten Bajoran ships, one Cardassian ship, one gateway, and the assorted civilian and Europani military vessels had resulted in a complete evacuation of the adult population.

And not a moment too soon, as the regions directly

beneath the mouth of the gateway—which included the large cities of Spilimbergo and Chieti and half a dozen smaller towns—were at fatal levels of exposure at this point.

The cheering continued for several seconds. Prynn got up from the conn and gave Nog a hug. When the embrace broke, Prynn found herself looking right at Vaughn in the command chair.

Vaughn was expecting a look of disdain or annoyance, so he was rather surprised when Prynn actually smiled at him and nodded her head.

He returned both the smile and the nod, and with that, she went back to the flight controls. Vaughn had no idea if Prynn was just feeling giddy from the success of their mission or if she was truly softening in her attitude toward him. He hoped for the latter, but he was cynical enough to believe it was more likely the former. *Still,* he thought, *it's a step. And not a small one, either.*

When the din finally quieted enough to speak over, Nog said, "According to Captain Emick, President Silverio was the last person to board the *Intrepid.*"

Vaughn nodded. *Good for her,* he thought. *The captain should be the last one off the sinking ship.* "That's excellent news, Lieutenant. Open a channel to the entire convoy, please."

"Yes, sir," Nog said, returning to his console. "Channel open."

"This is Commander Vaughn. Excellent work, all. We still have a long way to go, but the most important thing—getting the Europani out of danger—has been accomplished. At this time, we will prepare to bring the last remaining refugees to Bajor and Deep Space 9. Lieutenant Bowers, you and the *Rio Grande* will remain behind and await any new signals from Colonel Kira or Taran'atar."

Vaughn hesitated. It galled him that he could do no more than that. It had also galled Nog that the gateways had come back online after only being off for ten minutes. While it did leave the door open, so to speak, for Kira and the Jem'Hadar to return, it also meant that Ensign ch'Thane's solution was not the cure-all they'd hoped for. He wished he could inform Nog of the eyes-only communiqué he'd gotten minutes before from Bill Ross, telling him that the disruption of the gateways had been useful in exposing the "Iconians" for the frauds they truly were. Apparently, the people peddling the gateways—under false pretenses—were known as the Petraw, and their helplessness in the face of the temporary disruption proved their undoing.

At least, when the gateways had come back online, the *Euphrates* was still there blocking the radiation, keeping the Europa Nova situation from getting even worse. There was still the matter of somehow disposing of all this theta radiation—but that was a solution for more scientifically bent minds than that of Elias Vaughn.

Prynn said, "The convoy is getting into formation for the return voyage, Commander." A pause. "Except for the *Trager.*"

They weren't part of the original convoy, Vaughn thought. "Open a channel to the *Trager,*" he said, standing as he faced the viewscreen.

Gul Macet's image was suddenly looking back at him. *"What can I do for you, Commander Vaughn?"*

"I merely wish to confirm that you'll be joining the convoy back to DS9, Gul."

"Of course, Commander, I simply was not sure where, precisely, to align myself."

"Have your conn officer coordinate with Ensign Tenmei."

Macet nodded. *"Very well."*

Vaughn was about to order the connection cut, then hesitated. *Oh what the hell,* he thought, *you've been wanting to ask him since they got here.* "If you don't mind my asking, sir—why are you here?"

At that, Macet threw his head back and chuckled. *"Not an unreasonable question under the circumstances, Commander."* His face grew more serious. *"Are you familiar with a former Starfleet captain named Benjamin Maxwell?"*

In fact, Vaughn had known Ben quite well when the latter was a junior officer, though he'd lost track of him by the time he made captain. The erstwhile commanding officer of the *Phoenix* had been court-martialed and imprisoned following his attacks on several Cardassian ships. Maxwell had been convinced that they were carrying weapons, in violation of treaty, and had taken matters into his own hands.

Aloud, Vaughn simply said, "Yes. And to answer your next question, I know why he's now a former captain."

"I was assigned by Central Command to work with a Starfleet ship to track Maxwell down when he went rogue. That ship was the Enterprise.*"* Macet took a deep breath. *"I did as I was told, and we were eventually able to stop Maxwell before he murdered any more citizens of Cardassia. But the strange thing was—Maxwell was right. Those ships were carrying weapons. I did not agree with the actions of Central*

Command in that case, but I was a good soldier, and said nothing, not even when Captain Picard told me that he knew the truth.

"I learned an important lesson that day, Commander, and that lesson is why I am here today. You see, both Maxwell and Picard knew that we were violating the treaty. But where Maxwell's reaction was to madly destroy our ships, Picard's was to work to preserve the peace."

Macet took another deep breath and folded his arms. *"My people have been too much like Maxwell of late. We have worked against the galaxy. At a time when the entire Alpha Quadrant united against a common threat, we alone stood with the threat—well,"* he added with a smile, *"we and the Breen. We did not realize our mistake until it was too late. Now many of us—including myself—believe that we are better off trying to become part of the quadrant once more. We were a nation to be reckoned with once, Commander. If we are to be so again, we must work with our neighbors to preserve peace, not against them in conflict. You may consider this,"* he said, holding his hands outward, as if to encompass the entire convoy, *"the first step on that road."*

Vaughn nodded. At worst, it was a good speech. At best, it was an encouraging sign for the future of both Cardassia and the Alpha Quadrant. "Thank you for your candor, Gul Macet."

"You're welcome."

"And perhaps when we arrive back on Deep Space 9, we can discuss future steps on that road of yours."

"I would like that, Commander. Trager out."

Macet's image disappeared. As Vaughn returned to his chair, a voice from his right said, "Weird."

"What's 'weird,' Lieutenant?" Vaughn asked Nog.

"He looks so much like Dukat. When I first moved to the station as a boy, Dukat was the prefect of Bajor. He was always coming into Uncle Quark's bar. I used to be scared of him. Later on, I hated him. Seeing someone who reminds me so much of him . . ."

"There's an old human saying, Nog—don't judge a book by its cover. You of all people should be aware of that. Give Macet a chance to prove himself."

Nog nodded. "Oh, I will, sir. But it's still going to be weird."

"Convoy is in position, sir," Prynn said before the conversation could continue.

"Very well, Ensign. Ahead warp six."

21

CARDASSIA PRIME

"THIS PRICE IS OUTRAGEOUS, DERU."

Deru sighed at the face of the Kobheerian on his personal com unit. He'd been going around in circles with him for almost an hour now over the price of the land he and Quark had acquired on Chin'toka IX. He got up from his chair—which was comfortable in theory, but after sitting in it for an hour his back was starting to ache. He paced around the sitting room of his large house, the maroon walls covered with Bajoran paintings he had taken during the Occupation.

Riilampe was an entrepreneur Quark had brought in. He claimed to be looking for landowning opportunities, and was therefore perfect for the operation Deru and Quark had going. The price he had offered was of course three times what Deru and Quark had paid that retired gul for it (they had paid in *kanar* and *taspar* eggs).

"The price is commensurate with the value. Think about it, Riilampe—this land is arable. Cardassians all over the union are starving. Replicators can't handle all of it—farmland is going to be immensely valuable. In fact, I could easily justify charging more, if it weren't for—"

"If it weren't for the battle damage," the Kobheerian interrupted.

Deru sat back down. "And the amount we lowered the price is about what it would cost to restore the scarred topsoil to proper form. I know Quark went over all this with you before, and when you arrive at Deep Space 9—"

"The Ferengi hasn't gone over anything with me. I haven't been able to get through to him for a couple of days. I've also been turned away from DS9. Some kind of crisis—they're not letting anyone on-station."

Frowning, Deru said, "That's odd. Perhaps—"

"I'll be on Cardassia Prime in two days, Deru. We'll finalize the deal then, all right?"

"So you accept this price?"

The Kobheerian hesitated. *"Provisionally. Let me look over the deal memo one more time."*

"You won't regret this, Riilampe. You're getting in on the ground floor of one of the best land-development deals of the century."

Laughing, Riilampe said, *"You've been hanging around that Ferengi too long—now you're starting to sound like him. Screen off."*

Deru's com went dark. He then entered some commands into his computer.

Odd, he thought, *that he couldn't get through to Quark. Wonder if it has to do with that emergency. Not to mention all those rumors of strange portals opening up all over the galaxy . . .*

Ah, well. Not my concern.

In the middle of his file update, the screen went out. So did the lights, plunging his house into utter darkness.

Damn, another power outage. I thought they'd solved the power problems. That, he supposed, was wishful thinking. The Dominion had inflicted obscene damage onto Cardassia Prime, and even well-to-do citizens like Deru had had to live with this sort of thing. He walked toward the window—

—to see that the other nearby houses all had power.

The emergency power kicked in. It wasn't enough for him to get his computer back, but at least now there were lights, albeit dim ones, and the doors would work. *I can't believe that just my house had an outage. It's not like I haven't kept up with my payments. Somebody's going to answer for this.*

He walked out to the hallway, and thence to the front door.

It opened to reveal the smiling face of a Cardassian that Deru recognized immediately. He'd never met the man, but it was impossible for anyone living on Cardassia not to know him.

Former agent of the Obsidian Order. Living for almost a decade in exile on Terok Nor—or, rather, Deep Space 9. And the man now spearheading the rebuilding of the Cardassian Union.

"Garak." Deru's voice sounded hollow to his own ears.

"Good evening, Mr. Deru," Garak said in a most pleasant, affable tone. "I've only just become aware of your charming little enterprise here . . . and I believe we need to have a little chat."

Deru swallowed hard.

22

DEEP SPACE 9

"EXCUSE ME, but how long am I supposed to stand here?"

Ro Laren rubbed her temples. Never a particularly religious person, right now Ro would happily worship the great god Ho'nig if they would just take this damn Orion woman away from her.

They'd returned to DS9 to find absolute chaos. Intellectually, Ro had expected this—Ychell had received coded updates from Dax on the Europa Nova situation, and Ro had talked with the lieutenant directly when they were en route from Clarus—but she hadn't been emotionally prepared for the reality of the station being so completely inundated with refugees. From the minute she arrived, all her deputies had questions and Dax had half a dozen tasks that needed Ro's attention.

Pointedly, none of the Starfleet security people came to her with questions or requests. Most of them treated her with indifference at best, which was to be expected given Ro's somewhat rocky Starfleet career—and just at the moment, it meant that one less set of people was harassing her.

Unfortunately, every time she looked up, she saw a green torso standing in front of her desk. The Orion woman who dressed in a skimpy outfit carefully tailored to look like rags would not leave her office.

"Treir, I'm really busy now. Can't you go somewhere else?"

Indicating the Promenade with one hand, Treir asked, "Where, precisely? I'm not exactly dressed for walking around in public."

Ro looked up. Treir had a point. Although the outfit did technically conform to Bajoran decency statutes, about seventy percent of the Orion's green flesh was exposed, and her presence on the Promenade would cause a stir to say the least.

"And," Treir continued, "I don't have a change of clothes. In fact, I don't have much of anything now, thanks to you."

Ro ran her hands through her increasingly tousled black hair. "If you want to go back and sift through the debris of Malic's ship for your personal belongings—"

"Very funny. The point is, Lieutenant, I had a life until you hijacked me into your harebrained scheme."

Aghast, Ro said, "You were a slave!"

"I was well treated, fed four exquisite meals a day, given luxurious quarters, and I was damn good at what I did. Then some Bajoran woman needs a hostage, and my life's turned upside down." She put her hands on her hips and glowered at Ro with a stare that reminded the security chief that this woman was almost two heads taller than Ro.

"Look, I'm sorry about that, but—"

Treir snorted. "No you're not. I know your type, Lieutenant. You think you've done me a big favor. Well, you haven't."

Throwing up her hands, Ro said, "You're right, Treir. I should've left you on Malic's ship so you could've died when the Petraw blew them up. What was I thinking?"

"Oh, please," Treir said, rolling her eyes. "You didn't take me hostage to save my life, you took me hostage because it was the only way you could get off the ship safely. And you knew damn well that I'd be more valuable as a hostage than Alhan. Did you for one second think about what your actions would mean to me?"

During Treir's tirade, Quark approached the entrance to the security office. "Lovers' spat?" Quark asked as he entered, smiling lasciviously.

Glowering, Ro said, "Quark, I really don't have time for—"

"Actually, I have a solution to your problem."

Indicating the pile of padds on her desk with a sweeping arm gesture, Ro asked, "Which one?"

"This one," he said, putting his arm around Treir.

That one gesture had a remarkable effect on Treir. Her face transformed from angry to seductive—even though it looked to Ro like all she did was lower her eyelids slightly. She draped herself over Quark, which was no mean feat, since the height differential between her and the Ferengi was even greater than it was with Ro.

"What did you have in mind?" Treir asked. She had lowered her voice half an octave, and spoke in a breathy whisper.

Quickly, Ro said, "Quark," in as menacing a tone as she could manage.

Quark straightened—at least, as much as he could with a two-meter-tall woman hanging all over him. "Calm down, Laren. I actually have a business proposition for you, Treir, if you're interested."

As quick as that, Treir extricated herself from Quark's embrace and took a step back, transforming from a seductress into something more akin to a Federation negotiator. Ro found herself wondering which one was the real Treir, suspecting it might well be something else entirely.

"Go on," Treir said expectantly.

"Well, as it happens, I haven't been able to find a decent dabo girl to replace the one who married my brother and moved to Ferenginar. How'd you like a job?"

Ro couldn't believe what she was hearing. "You want to hire her as a *dabo girl?*"

"Why not? She's definitely got sex appeal, which is the only skill she'll need. She'll earn her keep. Plus it gets her out of your hair."

"And you get to fulfill your lifelong dream of having an Orion dabo girl."

Grinning, Quark said, "Exactly. So everyone wins."

"Excuse me," Treir said, "but I haven't said yes yet."

"Oh, come on," Quark said in what Ro was quickly

coming to recognize as Quark's best wheedling tone, "what could possibly be better?"

Treir laughed. The breathy whisper a thing of the past, she said sharply, "Listen to me, you little troll, I was the most respected of Malic's women. I had my pick of clients, I had the second-best quarters on the ship, I had clothes, jewelry—"

Quark grinned. "No you didn't. Malic had all those things, and he let you use them."

Ro almost cheered.

"Maybe." Treir seemed to concede very reluctantly. "But now you're making me work as a dabo girl on some backwater station run by Starfleet and Bajorans."

This time, Ro rolled her eyes. "Nobody's *making* you do anything, Treir. You're free to go wherever you want, do whatever you please." Grabbing a padd at random off her desk, she added, "And the only condition to that is that it isn't in my office. Now, if you'll both excuse me . . . ?"

Treir went back to standing with her hands on her hips. Ro looked up at her face, which seemed to be wrestling with the decision, even though, to Ro's mind, she really only could make one.

Finally, Treir threw up her hands. "Fine. It's not like I've got a lot of alternatives, thanks to you," she said with a glare at Ro.

Biting back a retort, Ro said, "Good luck."

Quark's grin widened so much that Ro was sure his head would split in half. "Come along, my dear," he said, offering his arm. "We'll get you a proper dabo-girl outfit and get you started."

Smiling a vicious smile right back, Treir said, "No, you'll get me some real clothes and then we'll talk about the terms of the employment contract—over a dinner that you're buying."

Ro chuckled as she opened the door to let them out. *At least she's not letting Quark play her for an idiot.* Whatever Treir's other qualities, she wasn't just a mindless slave. Hell, she seemed to enjoy it.

Treir stopped in the doorway and turned around. "Oh, Lieutenant?"

Looking up at her, Ro said, "Yes?"

"Have you ever heard of the Hinarian coding system?"

Ro frowned. "It rings a bell."

"You may want to use it when you're trying to crack the code for Malic's padd."

With that, she and Quark exited the security office.

Ro stared after them for several seconds. *Damn it all, I'm starting to like her.*

Then she put the Orion out of her thoughts. The convoy was due with the last of the refugees within the hour, and she had to find somewhere to put them. . . .

"You've got a message."

Quark sighed. He had gotten Treir settled temporarily in his brother Rom's old quarters. He'd been forced to bribe its current occupants, two Europani officials, with ten free holosuite hours, before returning to the delightfully overcrowded bar, only to have Frool announce what the blinking light on his companel already told him.

It was happy hour, and the place was near to bursting with Europani refugees. Apparently they preferred socializing, eating, and drinking to sulking in their assigned quarters, a philosophy Quark could easily get behind and happily exploited.

Ideally, of course, Quark would have brought Treir to his own quarters, but Gaila was there—and paying a princely sum for the privilege of rooming with his cousin, an amount that more than made up for the lost holosuite time. *But this'll do. And she'll melt before my charms before too long—and even if she doesn't, she'll definitely take the job. An Orion dabo girl! I may have to start charging admission.*

Quark's hand brushed against his lobe as he went to his private area behind the bar to take the message. *First Odo's gone from the station, replaced by the lovely Ro Laren, then I get to save her life, then I save Gaila's life, the station is full to bursting with Europani who are filling the tables in the bar, and now I have an Orion dabo girl. Life is good.*

The message was from Cardassia Prime. *Uh oh,* he thought, hoping it wasn't Deru.

Instead, it was Garak.

The always-smiling face of the former Obsidian Order agent smiled warmly at Quark from the viewscreen. *"Good day, Quark. I hope this communiqué finds you well."*

Oh, this is not good. Quark felt his lobes—which had been all tingly from the moment he'd entered Ro's office with the proposition for Treir—shrivel to the size of a human's.

"I just wanted you to know I recently spoke with Deep Space 9's new security officer, Lieutenant Ro. A delightful young woman. I can see the Promenade is in good hands. I hope you're treating her well—unless

I'm mistaken, she seems to have a soft spot for you. But then, I suppose no one is perfect.

"*The lieutenant was kind enough to suggest I look in on an acquaintance of yours from before the Cardassian withdrawal from Terok Nor—a gentleman named Deru. Perhaps you remember him from his days working in the military. Well, he's done quite well for himself in the private sector—made a sum of money that is, frankly, envious. Distressingly, though, he seems to have been involved in some, shall we say—illicit activities. Some kind of black-market dealings. A most unpleasant business for all concerned. Now he's fallen on hard times, the poor fellow. Most shocking of all, he's been saying the most slanderous things about you, Quark, suggesting you were somehow involved in the entire affair. You can rest assured, however, that I set him straight, explaining that Lieutenant Ro had vouched for you, and I had known you to be such an upstanding individual during our time together on the station.*

"*Such a pity about Mr. Deru, isn't it, Quark? Fortunes can change so quickly.*" Garak heaved a sigh, then said, "*Well, I must be going. A pity we couldn't chat directly, but affairs of state have kept me extremely busy of late. Perhaps at a later date we can catch up on old times—and new ones. Good-bye for now.*"

Garak had said it all in the most pleasant tone imaginable. He never lost his genial smile or his affable demeanor.

It was the most terrifying thing Quark had ever experienced.

23

THE DELTA QUADRANT

THE ALPHA TWISTED his blade into the prey's chest, then removed it. The Jem'Hadar's blood stained the broken sword end.

A most satisfying hunt, he thought as he rose from the prey's now-motionless form. *Now, however, it is time to see what that alarm is about.*

He went to the console. Sensors were working only intermittently, but he was soon able to determine a rather ugly truth: the power core was experiencing a malfunction. The tanker was likely to explode within the next fifteen minutes.

The alpha pounded the console with his fist. *To lose my ship was bad enough. Now I lose this one as well.*

Still, all was not lost. A quick check of the ship's

inventory—which took longer than it should have, with the console flickering in and out of power—showed that they had plenty of escape pods.

The deck seemed to disappear from under the alpha's feet as the tanker rocked to the side. The ship righted itself soon enough, but a quick check showed that the stabilizers were working at only forty percent of capacity.

It is time I took my leave, the alpha thought. He had had one disappointing hunt, but one great one with a foe he never thought he'd face. Ultimately, that was what mattered. The Jem'Hadar had been most worthy prey.

He was about to turn when a clattering sound drew his attention. The alpha spun to see the Jem'Hadar struggling to his feet, the Hirogen's rifle in hand.

The alpha smiled. *Truly this is worthy prey.*

Blood trickling out of his mouth, the Jem'Hadar spoke, every word sounding like an effort.

"Victory . . . is . . . life . . ."

Then he pulled the trigger.

It was a struggle for Taran'atar to make his limbs work. His right arm was completely useless, and his left arm was slow to respond as well. He felt a weakness in his chest, and his legs were by no means steady.

But the Hirogen was finally dead. Killed by his own weapon.

Oddly, the alien died with a smile on his face. Taran'atar did not understand how one could take joy in losing a battle.

Dropping the heavy rifle to the deck, he moved to the central console. While his body was gravely injured, his mind still functioned at peak efficiency. The Founders had made him well. It was the work of only a few minutes to figure out that the warp drive containment field was in danger of collapse. Within ten minutes, the tanker would explode.

Then he scanned the fifth planet. Readings were difficult, but he did detect a Bajoran life sign—however theta radiation on the planet was at fatal levels, and the life sign was very weak. It was only a matter of moments before Kira died.

Then the sensors went down. Taran'atar quickly manipulated the console and got them back online.

He no longer saw the life sign. And the theta radiation was increasing by the minute.

"No!" Taran'atar pounded futilely at the console. *It was my duty to die for her, not the other way around!*

I have failed my duty. I have failed the Founders.

A part of him was tempted to simply remain on the tanker and die when it exploded. But no, he still had a duty to perform. The same sensors that told him that Kira was gone also told him that the gateways were online—apparently ch'Thane's attempt to shut them down permanently had failed.

Taran'atar had to return to the Gamma Quadrant and inform Odo of his failure. For that matter, Kira's comrades on Deep Space 9—they too deserved to know how she died.

The ship rocked once again. *The stabilizers are failing. There are only minutes until the warp core breaches.*

The Hirogen had called up a schematic that showed the fastest route to the escape pods—no doubt intending to make use of one himself. Taran'atar ran in that direction, as fast as he could make his legs move.

24

EUROPA NOVA

"LIEUTENANT, SOMETHING'S COMING through the gateway."

Sam Bowers set down the birch beer he'd been drinking on the *Rio Grande*'s console and checked the runabout console. Ensign Roness's words were accurate—something was coming through. *About time something happened.* He'd enjoyed the relative calm after the chaos of the Europa Nova evacuation—for about twenty minutes. Then the restlessness kicked in. Roness hadn't actually said anything, but it was obvious from the looks she gave him that she was about ready to kill him.

She, of course, liked the quiet. Bowers hated it. He

had always been a man of action. That was why he went into tactical when he joined Starfleet.

"Looks like an escape pod," he said. "I think. It's just managing to squeak past the blockage created by the *Euphrates*. I don't recognize that configuration."

Roness said, "It doesn't match anything in the database. But I am reading a life sign." She looked up, a surprised expression on her face. "It's Jem'-Hadar."

"Taran'atar?"

Shrugging, she said, "That'd be my guess."

"Trying to get a transporter lock," he said, manipulating the controls. The theta radiation was still too intense, unfortunately. "Damn. Can we get a tractor beam?"

Roness nodded. "Yes, sir."

"Do it." Bowers then set a course for the next planet over.

"Tractor beam engaged. We have the pod."

"Good." Bowers took the *Rio Grande* forward. As soon as they were far enough from Europa Nova to engage the transporter, he did so.

Bowers had to admit that the sight on the runabout's small transporter platform was one that, in the past, he had enjoyed tremendously: a broken, bloody Jem'Hadar soldier. A part of him wanted to take pleasure in it now, but he forced that out of his head. *Taran'atar's on our side—hell, it was Odo who sent him. He's part of the team now.*

Intellectually, he knew that. It was convincing his gut—and his instincts, which had spent the last several years being trained to shoot Jem'Hadar on sight—that was the problem.

As he got up from his chair, grabbed a tricorder, and approached the unsteady form of the Jem'-Hadar—who collapsed to his knees as soon as he materialized—he asked, "What about Kira?"

"Colonel Kira . . . did not . . . survive," Taran'atar said.

Bowers felt like the temperature had lowered in the runabout. *Dammit, no, not another one,* he thought. First they lost Captain Sisko—and not even to the war, but to some ridiculous thing with those damn wormhole aliens—then they lost Commander Jast when those rogue Jem'Hadar attacked the station. To lose the colonel . . .

"I . . . must . . . return . . ." Taran'atar couldn't finish the sentence. Bowers could see why. The tricorder indicated that he'd suffered half a dozen internal injuries, not to mention the obvious stab wound to the chest. He needed Bashir's services posthaste.

"Set course for DS9, maximum warp," he shouted to Roness.

"Yes, sir." After a moment: "Course laid in."

"Engage."

It wasn't until after the runabout went into warp that Roness turned to Bowers. "What about Colonel Kira, sir?" Her tone implied that she wasn't entirely willing to take a Jem'Hadar's word for it that she was dead. *On the other hand,* he thought, *she did wait until after we went to warp to ask.*

"For now?" he said. "Hope to hell he's wrong."

25

THE DELTA QUADRANT
(FIFTEEN MINUTES EARLIER)

BLISTERS HAD NOW broken out on every millimeter of
Kira's skin. The tricorder told her that the level of ex-
posure was beyond what would be fatal to a Bajoran.
Her life could be measured in seconds.

There was no word from Taran'atar.

Breathing became harder with each second. Her vision started to cloud over.

Then, miraculously, the gateway came back online.
It once again went back and forth between Deep
Space 9 and the comforting glow of the Prophets.

Now the choice was easy. She was already dead. It was just left to her to take the final step.

Colonel Kira Nerys stepped into the gateway, determined to face what lay beyond . . .

TO BE CONTINUED IN . . .

STAR TREK: GATEWAYS, BOOK 7
WHAT LAY BEYOND

ACKNOWLEDGMENTS

Although it's just my name on the byline for this book, the number of people responsible for it coming to pass are legion—especially since this is both part of a crossover and part of an ongoing narrative. So I need to give them proper credit.

First of all, there's Pocket Books Editor Marco Palmieri, who has taken up the task of keeping the story of *Star Trek: Deep Space Nine* going beyond its magnificent seven-year television run. Marco's taking the unique opportunity to continue what has been, to my mind, *Star Trek*'s most compelling subfranchise, without any significant creative encumbrances, and he has done a superlative job. (And if you haven't, go out and read *Avatar* Books 1–2 by S.D. Perry and *Abyss* by David Weddle and Jeffrey Lang. Not because you need to read them to understand this book—you don't—but because they're damn fine books, more than worthy of the TV show from which they came.)

Secondly, there's Bob Greenberger and Pocket Editor John J. Ordover, who dreamed up the "Gateways" crossover, and the other authors—Susan Wright, Diane Carey, Bob, Christie Golden, and Peter David—who helped me bridge the gap between spiffy concept and compelling story. I think we succeeded admirably. (Thanks especially to Bob and Peter for their noble efforts in working with me to keep the *Next Generation*, *DS9*, and *New Frontier* books coordinated.)

Thirdly, I must thank the other nifty folks at Pocket Books and Simon & Schuster Interactive who keep *Star Trek* alive and well in book and disc form: Scott Shannon, Margaret Clark, John Perrella, Elizabeth Braswell, Kim Kindya, and most especially Jessica McGivney.

The creative minds of Gene Roddenberry—who created *Star Trek*—Michael Piller and Rick Berman—who got *Deep Space Nine* started—and Ira Steven Behr and his staff of loonies—who kept the show going—deserve the heartiest of thanks, as do the numerous actors who portrayed the characters seen within these pages, particularly Nana Visitor, Aron Eisenberg, Armin Shimerman, Alexander Siddig, Nicole deBoer, Michelle Forbes, Josh Pais, Penny Johnson, Andrew J. Robinson, and Marc Alaimo. Mention must also be made of Steve Gerber and Beth Woods, the scripters of the *Star Trek: The Next Generation* episode "Contagion," which gave us the Iconians (not to mention Captain Picard's fondness for archaeology and Earl Grey tea), and without which this crossover wouldn't exist.

Hearty thanks to the other members of "The Roness Nine": Jeannette, Michele, Andrew, Mike, Cathy, Maria, Tamra, and Charles, as well as Allan, Ann, and Judge Padilla, for alleviating what could've been a miserable jury duty experience. And hey, I got four chapters of this sucker written over the course of the five-week trial (I love laptops . . .).

As always, I have to give thanks and praise to the *Star Trek Encyclopedia* by Mike and Denise Okuda, with Debbie Mirek, and let me repeat my oft-stated mantra: nobody should write a *Star Trek* novel without this book and/or CD-ROM at hand. Other useful references include *Star Trek Chronology: The History of the Future,* also by the Okudas; the *Star Trek: The Next Generation Companion* and *Star Trek: Deep Space Nine Companion* CD-ROMs; the *Star Trek: Deep Space Nine Companion* book by Terry J. Erdmann, with Paula M. Block; *Star Trek: Deep Space Nine Technical Manual* by Herman Zimmerman, Rick Sternbach, and Doug Drexler; *Star Trek: The Next Generation Technical Manual* by Rick Sternbach and Michael Okuda; and the University of Michigan Student Chapter of the Health Physics Society's web site's FAQ on Radiation and Health Physics (www.umich.edu/~radinfo).

Not to ever be forgotten: CITH, the best writers group in the entire world, who, as ever, made my writing far better than it would've been otherwise; the Forebearance (The Mom, The Dad, The Party Vegetable, and The Tall Fuzzy One); the Malibu gang; the Geek Patrol (Marina, John, Hawk, and Andrea); the wonderful group of regular posters on the PsiPhi.org *Trek* novels bulletin board, as well as the good folks on the board at Simon & Schuster's web site, the

ACKNOWLEDGMENTS

"*Trek* Literature" section of the *Trek* BBS, Yahoo!'s *Star Trek* Books club, and PsiPhi.org's *DS9* and *NF* boards; the wonderful folks who run the Farpoint and Shore Leave conventions; and, of course, most important of all, the Official Editorial Goddesses, GraceAnne A. DeCandido and Terri Osborne.

ABOUT THE AUTHOR

KEITH R.A. DeCANDIDO has been watching *Star Trek* since before he was born (at least, according to his mom). After it provided him with so many years of enjoyment, he finally got to give some back with the 1999 publication of his *Star Trek: The Next Generation* comic book *Perchance to Dream*. His other *Star Trek* work includes the *Next Generation* novel *Diplomatic Implausibility* and the upcoming cross-series duology *The Brave & the Bold*. He also co-developed the *Star Trek: Starfleet Corps of Engineers* line of eBooks with John J. Ordover, and has written several S.C.E. eBooks, including *Fatal Error, Cold Fusion,* and (with David Mack) *Invincible* Books 1 & 2, with more on the way.

In addition to all this *Trekkin'*, Keith has written novels, short stories, and nonfiction books in the universes of *Buffy the Vampire Slayer, Doctor Who, Farscape,* the Hulk, *Magic: The Gathering,* the Silver Surfer, Spider-Man, *Xena,* the X-Men, and *Young Hercules.*

Keith lives in a lovely apartment in the Bronx with his girlfriend and two excessively goofy cats. Find out more than you could possibly want to know about Keith at his official web site at the easy-to-remember URL of DeCandido.net.

Look for STAR TREK fiction from Pocket Books

Star Trek®: The Original Series

Star Trek®: New Frontier

Star Trek®: Section 31

Rogue • Andy Mangels & Michael A. Martin
Shadow • Dean Wesley Smith & Kristine Kathryn Rusch
Cloak • S. D. Perry
Abyss • David Weddle & Jeffrey Lang

Star Trek®: Gateways

#1 • *One Small Step* • Susan Wright
#2 • *Chainmail* • Diane Carey
#3 • *Doors into Chaos* • Robert Greenberger
#4 • *Demons of Air and Darkness* • Keith R.A. DeCandido

Star Trek®: The Badlands

#1 • Susan Wright
#2 • Susan Wright

Star Trek®: Dark Passions

#1 • Susan Wright
#2 • Susan Wright

Star Trek® Omnibus Editions

Invasion! Omnibus • various
Day of Honor Omnibus • various
The Captain's Table Omnibus • various
Star Trek: Odyssey • William Shatner with Judith and Garfield Reeves-
   Stevens

Other Star Trek® Fiction

Legends of the Ferengi • Ira Steven Behr & Robert Hewitt Wolfe
Strange New Worlds, vols. I, II, III, and IV • Dean Wesley Smith, ed.
Adventures in Time and Space • Mary P. Taylor, ed.
Captain Proton: Defender of the Earth • D.W. "Prof" Smith
New Worlds, New Civilizations • Michael Jan Friedman
The Lives of Dax • Marco Palmieri, ed.
The Klingon Hamlet • Wil'yam Shex'pir
Enterprise Logs • Carol Greenburg, ed.